FEATHER LIGHT

Lorenz Font

The subtle layering of moods is one of Font's specialties and she uses it here, bringing whimsy into the bedroom and rage into a sanctuary without sacrificing the authenticity of the characters or the believability of the overall plot.

-Mavvy Vasquez, Author- The Truth Seekers

Books by Lorenz Font

The Gates Legacy

Hunted

Tormented

Ascension

Reckoning

Redemption – Coming soon

Indivisible Line

Feather Light

Pieces of Broken Time

The Prodian Journey Series

Rise of Alpha

FEATHER LIGHT

Lorenz Font

Talem
Publication

Second Edition

Copyright © Lorenz Font, 2016

Published by Talem Publication

Paperback ISBN- 978-0-9977823-4-9
E-book ISBN- 978-0-9977823-5-6

Cover Image - © Zurijeta | Shutterstock.com
Cover Artist - JC Clarke

Interior Design - Jennifer McGuire | JEMBookDesigns.com
Chapter Images - © Joingate | Depositphotos.com

http://www.lorenzfont.com

To Elise,
who will rise above every challenge that comes her way

CHAPTER ONE

"What do I always say on Mondays?" Parker called out as soon as he walked into his Los Angeles branch of Knead Me.

"Lie down and allow me to ease your troubles away," a chorus of masseuses, masseurs, and excited front office girls answered in unison.

Slaps of good-natured appreciation landed on his back, as Webster, his loyal assistant, pressed a half-filled, steaming, and lidded cup of Sumatra coffee into his palm.

"Three steps and the chair is to your left," she whispered in his ear. "Glad to see you bright and early, boss."

"Thanks. Happy to be back, Webbie. I missed this place." Parker set the cup on the conference table and sat on the chair she had directed him to. "Got another one for my baby bro?"

"Of course. Here's your decaf, Cork." The crisp sound of a cup exchanging hands followed.

"Thanks, Webbie," Cork answered from his left.

"Okay, folks, listen up." Parker raised a hand to silence the people in the room. Through his hazy eyesight, he saw a blur of figures taking their seats, and also heard the scratching of shoes on the carpet, signaling that everyone was settling down.

He took a quick sip of his coffee before he spoke. "Well, NYC is doing great. Thanks to our loyal customers and word of mouth, our New York branch has kicked off with a strong first month. I'm going to accept applications for transfers in the next five days. Anyone interested in trying out the cold, wet winter weather and hot as fuck summer, pardon my French, is welcome to give me their application, beginning today."

Laughter echoed throughout the room, letting Parker know everyone was in high spirits. Heck, he could practically smell their delight. Happy employees meant increased productivity, which, of course, would lead to satisfied clients. Bottom line—business had nowhere to go but up.

The southern California branch of Knead Me, his very first, had opened its doors three years ago, right when he'd been at the height of his confusion over this terrible disease. Then had come the San Francisco branch six months ago, which had been a huge hit, too. With the success of their expanded locations, Parker had hoped that he could find some free time. Boy, had he been mistaken. Although his major clientele were happy with his massage therapists' work, they still clamored for *him*, which left little to no time for himself. To continue to be successful, his diminishing sight, along with the desire for some much-needed downtime, would have to take a backseat to running the business.

Enter Cork Davis, his younger brother. Cork had quit his full-time job as a high school football coach to work for Knead Me. Single and still very much into himself, his brother helped in managing the entire operation, and had also acted as Parker's chauffeur and go-to guy. Cork had never divulged his reasons for leaving coaching to work for Parker, and he hadn't bothered asking. Sometimes family and work didn't go together, but in Parker and Cork's case, it worked just fine as long as they stayed out of each other's personal business.

"Webbie, I can sense your indecision, so I'll give you an all-expense paid vacation to Tahiti if you just promise me you'll stay here and keep my chair warm."

Webster's distinct melodious voice rose above the din of chuckles and giggles. "Aw, do I stink that much, boss?"

Parker could almost picture her pout. He flashed a broad smile in her direction.

"Fine, I'll stay. Just make sure I fly first class and my return ticket is open." Good-natured banter and light conversation had been the secret of their success as a unit.

"My dear Webster, curse your father for giving such a gorgeous woman an outdated name. If I didn't know you were a woman, I wouldn't even give you a second glance." He laughed.

"But you know I'm *very* female." More giggles exploded around him, as well as some throat clearing.

"And what's this about an open return? Are you going to leave me to fend for myself?"

"I'm happy here. I just have to rattle you from time to time so I can feel I'm still needed."

"You're always needed as far as I'm concerned, Webbie." Turning his attention to the group, he added, "Get your asses ready. Our ten o'clocks are going to pound our door in . . . five, four, three, two . . . one. Happy Monday to all! And please, knead their hearts out!"

"And knead we shall," Andy, another high-demand masseur, said from the door. Snorts and chortles followed him out as everyone spilled from the room.

Once the sound of the departing footsteps faded, Parker breathed a deep sigh and turned to Webster. "Who's my ten today?"

"New client. The name's Madame Baba. Does it ring a bell?"

"Hmm . . . no. But we'll find out soon enough, won't we?" He waggled his eyebrows in her direction and saw, through his dot-sized vision, her head fall back in laughter.

"I'm sure we will. I have room 101 set up for you. I also placed all the invoices on your desk at the two o'clock position. All they need is your John Hancock, and they're all set."

Efficient, quick-witted, and attractive, Webster had been a trouper from day one and a valuable asset to his staff, considering the pounding his schedule and his personal challenges posed for her. She had taken on the role of his personal assistant with a fresh outlook and one giggle at a time.

"Thanks. If you find an opening in my schedule this week, keep it open. I'm dying to go out and try the new, remodeled track at Road Runners."

Parker clicked his tongue, trying to remind himself to call Andrew, his running partner, before the day was over. He was adept in sighted-guide techniques and formulated ways to help Parker jog and run outside without the fear of falling and hurting himself.

"I'll make sure you get some running time, boss. If you're set, your client just walked in—raven hair, screaming figure . . . wait, beautiful, too." Webster grabbed the cup and handed it to him before she followed him to the door.

He had started counting his steps, so he knew Webster didn't expect a response from him. Multitasking in his head, he thought about the "beautiful" and "screaming figure" comments. He stopped and turned around. "You're joshing me, right?"

Her laughter answered for her, but before he could start counting again, she added, "Well, the humongous glasses are hiding most of her face. Hard to tell."

"You're still messing with me." He pulled her into a friendly hug before she stiffened.

"No more joshing. Hurry up. You don't want to keep a client who ordered a Monday Delight waiting, right?"

"Fine. Then stop distracting me." Parker turned around and resumed his descent to the first floor, where the majority of the massage rooms were located. The second floor was dedicated to holistic treatments, such as meditation and relaxation.

Counting had become necessary when his field of vision had deteriorated to dismal proportions. Parker's left eye recognized shapes, but in his advanced stage, his central vision had been affected. His right eye registered blurry objects. It had been a year since he had been declared legally blind—a politically correct term used to make affected individuals feel good about their new reality. Retinitis pigmentosa had now gotten the best of him. It was a degenerative disease without any known cure, so he was fucked.

For Parker Davis, his prognosis had ruled out the possibility of him ever driving a car. The disease had also ended his ability to read materials fully sighted people could, and most of all, it had terminated his visual appreciation of anything beautiful. On his good days, he saw specific shapes, but facial expressions and other small details were lost to him. Despite all that, he was never bitter. He was too busy to dwell on the things he couldn't do. He needed to concentrate on honing his remaining senses.

He reached room 101 and readied himself before knocking on the door. After his knock was answered with a soft and very feminine response, he walked in and smiled. "Good morning, Madame Baba."

Hers was such an odd name, but Parker knew better than to ask. These days, people seemed to run in weird circles. Maybe she was just looking for mystery and the added excitement of being on his table. He guessed he'd soon find out.

"Hello, Mr. Davis." The voice didn't live up to the image he had in his head, sounding more timid than his initial expectation.

Parker smiled at the tiny form sitting on the chair next to the massage table—tiny in the sense that his vision procured small images. "How about we dispense with the formalities? Call me Parker."

The ruffling sound of cloth was the only response. Parker suspected she had shrugged, but he wasn't sure, since little movements tended to escape his notice. Most people didn't realize the extent of his blindness, which, in a way, had been good for his ego. He still felt like a big part of the sighted world.

"Let's start you off with a full body massage, and then we'll move down the rest of the menu. There's a white robe for you on the table. I'll move over to the other room while you get ready for me. Strip down to whatever makes you feel comfortable and remove all jewelry, navel ring included, and lie face down. Say 'woo-rah' when you're done."

" 'Woo-rah'? "

Parker smiled. "Yes. It's my own unique way of knowing when my client is ready. So 'woo-rah' me when you are."

When he disappeared behind the curtain, he heard what sounded like plastic being folded and placed on the little table, which must have been her glasses or sunglasses. Parker pressed the first button on his left, and soft, ambient music filled the room. The light, though already set low, needed to be adjusted. He turned the knob down one notch before proceeding to wash his hands.

Parker strapped on his oil and lotion belt and heard Madame Baba's shy "woo-rah" a moment later. He returned to the room, using the flickering candle sitting in the corner of the room as his guide. Three steps to the left led him to the side of the massage table.

"Comfortable?" he asked, feeling the edge of the table until he found the cotton sheet folded at the end.

"Uh-huh." Madame Baba's voiced sounded remote, as if she didn't want to be bothered. That was understandable. Most clients wanted to be left alone, but Parker always found a way to draw them out and get more information on how to ease them.

With a gentle pat, he planted his palms on every pressure point, his way of marking the spots and orienting himself on the width of her body. Madame Baba had a long frame, judging from the length between her shoulder blades down to the base of her torso. She had a narrow waistline, soft skin, and baby-fine hair—and she was ticklish, made obvious by the way she jerked when he touched the small of her back.

The name didn't fit the owner of the body but instead evoked images of a frumpy matron, a deadly cougar, or an overly cajoling older woman. In his mind, he saw a young, inexperienced, waif-like little girl.

In a soft voice, he asked, "What do you find comforting, Madame Baba?"

Parker pulled out the oil bottle and squirted a generous amount of the warm liquid on one palm and then some on her back before replacing the container in its holster. Rubbing both palms together, he eased his hands onto her back and began working in rhythmic circles. She sighed, seeming content.

"I find long talks over an intimate dinner relaxing, rainy nights with a good book, and a nice person who's willing to listen . . ."

"Take a deep breath for me," Parker suggested. When she did, he increased the pressure, working on the knots in the back of her neck, her shoulders, and wherever else she needed release.

Kelly Storm had finally succumbed to her assistant's goading to get a massage. It was not just a regular massage, but a Monday Delight from none other than Parker Davis, the well-known massage therapist who could bring his clients to tears. Skeptical, Kelly had decided it was time to shut

Jessica up and secure an appointment at their LA location, which was closest to her home.

Since Parker had been out of town, she'd waited for a month until he had gotten back and a Monday slot had opened up. If Kelly had used her real name, getting an earlier appointment would have been guaranteed, but she preferred anonymity. She could do without a bunch of camera-flashing, question-hounding barracudas following her every move, so she'd decided to wait.

Kelly called for a cab to whisk her away from her Brentwood mansion under the veil of total secrecy. Most paparazzi camped outside her home would mistake her for Sima, her cleaning lady from the Middle East. Dressed in one of her many disguises, she walked into the Beverly Hills location wearing her black wig, a scarf to cover her head and mouth, and dark sunglasses.

This Parker guy better be good! Kelly shook her head as the perky receptionist led her to a well-lit hallway and into a cozy little room to wait. She took off her face covering as soon as the door closed. When Parker Davis walked in, her jaw literally dropped.

If she had done her homework ahead of time, she would have known the famed massage therapist was gorgeous beyond belief. Even in the darkened room with the glow of the candle illuminating his features, she could see his sparkling blue eyes and the strong set of his jaw, showcasing a full mouth that offered a wide and precocious smile. Serious muscles bulged from underneath his black cotton T-shirt, and his chestnut-colored hair was a glorious mop into which any woman would love to tangle her fingers. Kelly couldn't pull her gaze away from him.

Keeping her disguise in place, she answered Parker's questions with as few words as possible. Only when his hand touched her skin did she turn into a crumpled mess.

"What do you find comforting, Madame Baba?"

His question was nothing personal, but the quiet way he asked it compelled her to give him more details than she'd intended.

Parker's hands glided across her back, sending her to a place she hadn't been before. Firm yet prudent in every touch, he treated her body like fine china. Kelly felt delicate and precious. His sensual touches evoked desires within her that no other man had ever come close to doing. The way his hands probed every inch of her body pushed her to tears. She had read that with a good massage, toxins were released at a rapid rate, causing the body to feel tired or sore afterward. Every firm stroke of his fingers on her skin, along with his soothing voice, released a flood of tension that she'd been keeping bottled up inside.

Being on top wasn't always what it was cut out to be. She had become an overnight sensation after one blockbuster movie and since then had been hounded by the media every moment of her life. Kelly had no idea what the words *privacy* and *downtime* even meant anymore. Her every movement caused a stir, and every outing became excruciating instead of enjoyable. She wanted fame and fortune, but she also wanted a little time still to be herself—to be able to talk and not worry about repercussions, shop without photographers snapping her picture, or dine out with friends without someone asking her for an autograph or to pose for a picture with them.

A buried memory surfaced. One particularly crazed paparazzo had hounded her during one of the lowest points of her life. While they lowered her mother's coffin into the freshly excavated earth, the persistent photographer had squeezed through the tight bodies that surrounded Kelly, snapping several pictures with no regard for her right to mourn in private. Nothing had been the same for her after that incident. She'd begun to closet herself away from the public eye unless necessary, and she'd kept her circle tight. People seemed to forget that even though celebrities were considered public figures, it didn't mean every facet of their lives had to be displayed for everyone to see.

"If you could go out with a good friend, what would you talk about?" Parker asked, deepening his strokes. It felt as if he were digging into her soul, freeing her fears and allowing her to soar, even if only for a fraction of time.

Kelly listened to his even breathing, loving his tone's gentle caress and his unhurried rubdown.

"I want to share my innermost feelings without the fear of being judged. I want to be seen as me . . . simple but deep. There's more to me than what people see on the outside."

Parker moved to the head of the table, pumped more oil, and steamrolled his hands over her back in one long motion, like he was pushing out what had ailed her soul for a long time. With each thrust of his hands, she released a sob, and Kelly found herself crying like a small child.

He stayed quiet while her anxiety-filled sobs flooded out like an overflowing dam, keeping a steady rhythm until her tears were all cried out. His hands spoke for him, soothing her, clearing her muddled thoughts, and paving the way to a clearer perspective.

Parker handed her a tissue and kept going, adding different techniques geared to ease her troubles away. When it came to massaging her scalp, his thumbs and fingers worked in easy, wonderful strokes. His caresses released her coiled tension, allowing more positive reflective thoughts to move in.

By the end of the hour, Kelly knew Parker was the real deal. He wasn't just pleasing to the eye, but he was also able to get her to talk with his simple, thought-provoking questions. Now she understood why he was touted as magical—he worked magic. No wonder Jessica had sworn Kelly wouldn't regret showing up. Her friend had been right when she'd insisted the man known as Feather Light possessed the gift of touch—and could send anyone screaming for release.

CHAPTER TWO

Parker's day went by quickly. On his breaks between clients, he'd gone back to his office to attend to some paperwork that needed his signature and just to take a much-needed breather. Massage, though relaxing for the client, was a whole lot of work for him. He enjoyed making the process seem simple, but in reality, each session left him tired and quite hungry.

This particular session with Madame Baba had left him wondering. Her sadness came from deep within, somewhere he sensed no one had been allowed to see. She'd cried, not just for a much-needed release, but also for help. Parker shook his head, having no idea why he felt the need to protect the woman. He had to be losing his mind. After all, he couldn't see, let alone slay Madame Baba's dragons.

When the massage had ended, Parker could tell she was grateful by the way she'd taken his hand in hers and the sincerity in her voice when she thanked him. The sound of her footsteps had been distinctly lighter when she'd left. A happy new customer meant repeat visits and definite referrals, which was why his business had thrived. Almost all their clients left with a feeling of wellbeing, not only of their bodies but also of their minds.

He tapped the button on his watch and listened for the time. Cork would be waiting out front with the car. Parker hurried to review the notes he'd written for his appointment that afternoon: the exact words to be uttered, the costume, and where he would find her. He smiled after going over the plan and hit send. With precise movement, he crossed his office to the hallway, saying quick good-byes to the few people who were still around.

As usual, Cork was already waiting in the handicapped parking spot up front, a small perk Parker allowed himself to enjoy. Parking in LA was horrible to begin with, and walking several blocks without an aid would be a bit problematic for him. He still didn't believe he needed the aid of a white cane or a guide dog, although it was recommended by his doctor. Parker could still get by with his limited vision. All he needed was good lighting, and he could pretty much get around on his own. Also, Webster, Cork, and the two assistants he'd hired for the two other branches made sure he had everything he needed at his fingertips.

The smoggy air hit him as soon as he emerged from the air-conditioned building. As much as Parker hated the weather in LA, this was his home. Everything about the city was familiar, and he took comfort in that knowledge. Blindness was not an easy disease to deal with. He'd had to make some adjustments to his lifestyle and use adaptive measures to compensate for his lack of vision, but so far, he'd been coping rather well.

Parker saw the shape of a familiar car parked near the curb, exactly twelve steps from the building. He slid into the cool comfort of the front passenger seat. Soon after, they joined the already congested traffic as they made their way to the 405 Freeway.

"Hey, bro, can we drop by Gelson's first?" Parker reclined back in the seat and adjusted his sunglasses.

"Hot date tonight?" Cork's deep voice inquired. Parker's brother asked very few questions, but the one he *did* ask was one Parker wanted to avoid answering.

"Um . . . just hanging out." It was a nice, evasive answer—not giving away too much, but offering just enough without sounding trite.

"Fair enough."

Cork drove in silence, and Parker let the quiet relax him. His mind wandered back to his newest client, Madame Baba. There was something odd about the woman that he couldn't quite put his finger on. After a shy start where she'd given him three-word answers, she had broken down on his table and confessed her unhappiness. Parker had no idea what she did for a living, her status in life, or what her problems were, and he wasn't about to pry. If there was one important thing he had learned from this business, it was to let his clients do the talking.

He was the listener they needed or, better yet, the more affordable shrink. Parker often encountered clients who were willing to tell him their life story with very little encouragement. Most of them didn't come to sleep; they came so they could talk without having to deal with the stigma of seeing a head doctor. All Parker had to do was ask the right questions, and they'd take the cue.

Madame Baba had been the same. She'd babbled on and on about what others expected from her, and even though the circumstances she'd cited were vague, he'd begun to draw a mental picture of this intriguing woman in his mind. She had to be one of those rich women who had no idea what to do with their life—bored, unhappy, and lost.

"We're right in front of Gelson's. Do you want me to go in with you?" Cork broke into Parker's thoughts, and he opened his eyes. Open or not, it didn't do him any good. He chuckled at the thought.

Cork's shirt rustled against the leather seat, and Parker knew his brother had turned to look at him, probably wondering what the hell he was laughing at. "I'll be okay. I'll call you when I'm done."

He got out of the car with measured steps, using daylight as his guide to find the entrance of the grocery store. It helped that he'd been there more times than he could count. Everyone knew him, and there wouldn't be a problem locating the things he needed. Parker grabbed a basket by the front entrance and proceeded to his first stop, the dairy section. He chose a can of whipped cream and placed it in the basket before moving on to the fruit section, where he picked up some fresh strawberries and bananas.

Afterward, he went to the deli, where his preordered dinner was already waiting for him.

"Here you go. Pasta with sundried tomatoes and mushrooms, chicken strips, and last but not least—your favorite—Black Forest cake." Jerome handed him the plastic bag and patted him on the shoulder.

"Thanks, man. I owe you one." Parker saluted before turning away.

"Just schedule me for an hour in that Beverly Hills office of yours, and we'll call it even." He heard Jerome chuckle.

"No problem. Just call Webster, and she'll set you up. Thanks, bro."

After he'd paid for the items, Parker phoned Cork and waited out front. His brother was there within minutes.

"Looks like you bought a lot of stuff," Cork said.

Parker was certain his brother was eyeing the bags on his lap. "Just a few munchies," he replied, trying to sound nonchalant.

His mind was already in deep concentration by the time he turned the key in his front door. He smelled the citrus candles he knew were perched all over the living room.

"Jane, I'm home!"

"In here, George!" The sultry voice of Jane Jetson greeted him from the bedroom. He loved role-play and was glad she was a willing and able partner.

Parker placed the food on the kitchen counter and took the whipped cream with him.

"Are the children home from school?" he asked as he padded across the hallway and into the first door on his left. The scent of burning candles intensified when he entered his bedroom. The lights were off, just like he wanted. The blinds were drawn tight, and "Space Oddity" was already playing on the MP3 player.

"They're going on an after-school activity with the rest of the Orbit children."

"Come here, my space-age wife." Parker opened his arms after placing the can on the nightstand. A warm body slid into his. He skimmed his lips across the base of her neck before nibbling her earlobe. "Mmm . . . you smell like fresh cosmic flower."

She answered with a moan, and he smiled to himself.

He slid his hand to the small of her back and pulled her closer. The polyester fabric of her dress hugged her curves. Lowering his hand toward her ass, Parker then lifted her skirt and rubbed one of her tight cheeks, loving the feel of her bare skin on his palm. She rasped a moan and pressed her chest against his.

"Do you have anything to say?" He tilted her chin up so that he was looking straight into her eyes, or in the general vicinity. Allowing for the fact that he was a head taller than her, he calculated her head must be tilted about three inches for her to see his face.

"SSC." Her warm breath caressed him.

"Same here."

SSC—safe, sane, and consensual—a constant reminder they spoke to each other every time they got together. Parker picked her up and brought her to the bed. The feel of her bare leg made his shaft jerk as he laid her in the middle of the mattress.

He lifted her leg and placed it on the other side of his waist. "Remove my shirt," he said, his George impersonation lowering into a lazy drawl.

She sat up with pleasing obedience. Her warm fingers grazed his skin when she lifted the hem of his black T-shirt up and over his head. After throwing his shirt on the floor, she settled back and he straddled her.

"How was your day, dear?" Parker touched her face, feeling her emotions with his fingertips before reaching for the bun crowning her head. He felt for and removed the small ring of elastic holding her hair in place, allowing her blond mane to cascade loose. The scent of coconut shampoo wafted around him.

"Marvelous. I want your dick inside me," she said in a practiced voice with the exact words he wanted her to use. Parker twitched inside the confines of his jeans.

"Are you ready for me to taste you?" He leaned forward and trailed tiny kisses along her jawline.

She angled her head to give him more space to work with. "Yes, George. I'm ready."

That was all he needed to hear. He moved down and lifted her skirt. Parker closed his eyes and let his mind do the work for him. The stellar scent of her wetness drew him closer. "Give me the whipped cream."

He heard the snap of the cap being removed before the can was pressed into his outstretched hand. Inhaling deep, he let his other hand trace the contour of her inner thigh until it reached the juncture of her sweetness. She was bare, just the way he preferred. Parker spread her legs wide until her opening was facing him. He gave the can a vigorous shake and squirted a moderate amount of cream on top of her clitoris. A delightful moan erupted from her throat.

"Like that, Jane?" He couldn't wait to taste the puffy cream and the dessert underneath.

"Oh, George," she answered with yet another throaty moan.

Aching to taste the soft cream and licking his lips in anticipation, Parker inched his mouth closer. Sliding his tongue out, he touched the tip of the swirl. He circled the sweetness in a sensuous motion, tasting and swallowing until the whirly cream got smaller and smaller, until it disappeared. Another moan escaped her lips, and her fingers dug into his hair.

"I'm about to eat you."

He flicked his tongue once across her bud, and her hips bucked, her legs tightening around him like a vise. With the pressure of her hand on his head urging him on, he lapped the right side of her nub with his tongue. The purring response to his teasing was gratifying, so he moved to the other side of her clit while his hand slid underneath her ass. Parker pressed his face closer and let his teeth nibble away. She squirmed but stayed in place.

"Good Jane," he murmured and began brushing against her nub faster and faster. She gasped, and her fingers clawed at his scalp. Parker circled, lapped, and stroked her bud until her screams of ecstasy filled the room.

"Shout my name, now."

"Oh, George, George, George!" Her voice was raw with undisguised pleasure. His erection jerked, craving its own release.

With deliberate movements, Parker shoved himself up and slid off the bed —leaving her panting and aching for more. He pried off his shoes with his toes and pulled down his zipper. His steely shaft burst out of his pants and hung proudly in front of him. Shedding his jeans in one quick motion, he dove back onto the bed.

The breath coming out of her mouth in erratic beats was music to his ears and fueled the images in his mind's eye. He touched the tip of his dick to her sensitive clit and rubbed over and over again. She inched forward.

"Ah-ah," Parker said, stating his disappointment. She should have known better. She wasn't allowed to move or say anything until he said so.

"I'm sorry . . ."

As much as he wanted to let it slip, she knew how he wanted things done.

He slid off the bed, making sure she understood what was coming. Parker bent down, flashing his ass at her when he picked up his discarded jeans on the floor. He took the belt and looped it around one hand until a few inches were left hanging.

"I must do this, Jane. Turn around."

"Yes, George."

"Jane, what is your safe word?"

"Elroy." Her voice sounded strong, and he nodded.

"Use it if you need to."

Parker placed his hand on her face to feel her nod. Then he moved a hand to orient himself with her body. With one swing, he whacked one cheek. She pushed forward and stifled her cry.

"Good, Jane," he said and placed another one on the other cheek.

"Thank you, George."

"With every punishment, I intend to give you a reprieve." Parker gathered her body and positioned her to his liking until her back touched his chest. He ran his mouth along the nape of her neck, making sure her sobs were replaced by moans.

He kissed, licked, and nibbled on her earlobe while the other hand groped one of her plump breasts. Her body moved in rhythm to his while he ground his erection between her thighs. "Remove your dress and let me see you."

Let me see you. It was funny how he could use the word *see* so loosely. He helped her ease out of her costume and then threw the garment on the floor. Parker reached over to the nightstand and grabbed the small foil package she'd left for him. He tore the wrapper and sheathed himself.

"Relax."

She did so without a moment's hesitation, reclining her body against his. He ran his fingers to her opening, and wetness greeted his probing. He smiled, and his arousal peaked. Parker spread her thighs apart with one knee and angled her body until she was bent forward on all fours.

"You're wet, aren't you?"

"As wet as you make me." She drew haggard breaths.

"Good."

With one swift move, he guided his erection and penetrated her from behind. She froze just before her walls tightened around him. A burst of fire raged within him, and he pulled out to tease her. A tiny moan slipped from her lips in disappointment, and Parker pushed back in again. He reached a hand around her body and took hold of her breast.

In rapid succession, he pounded into her while rubbing his forefinger on her nipple, teasing the tip until it stood taut and hard. Her cries intensified. Thrusting harder, he was on the verge of release but would hold out until she came first. Parker shifted both hands to her waist and increased the pace. In just a few moments, her strangled cry of relief echoed, prompting him to follow. He pounded even harder until he exploded inside her.

She shuddered and collapsed onto the mattress, bringing him with her. Parker rested his body partially on hers, not wanting to crush her with his weight. "That was great, partner." He kissed her on the cheek.

By the movement of her jaw, he was certain she smiled. "As always." He loved the sound of satisfaction in her voice.

After they lay together for a long moment, Parker pushed away and rolled over on his back. He tapped his talking clock. "Eight PM," the mechanical tone announced.

"You hungry?" he asked.

"Famished."

"The food is on the counter. I'll meet you in the kitchen after I finish showering." He got up, and she slapped him playfully on his butt.

After they finished dinner, they talked for another half an hour about their common interests, such as hockey and music.

"The key is on your nightstand, six o'clock. I have to go and do my laundry. See you tomorrow at work, boss?" Webbie stood up and gave him a peck on the cheek.

"Not if I see you first." Parker smiled and popped a strawberry in his mouth.

Easy and no strings attached. That was his relationship with Webster. They understood each other, and they both wanted the same thing—a good lay with a person they trusted.

He heard the door ease shut while he cleared away the dishes. Another good day.

❧

Weeks later, Parker walked into his New York branch of Knead Me. Arianne greeted him with a hug, and then guided him straight to his office. He had yet to memorize the layout and positioning of furniture in his newest business.

"Coffee is at twelve o'clock. Your laptop is booted up and ready to go." Arianne's cheery personality and comforting presence added her to the long list of valuable people he couldn't live without.

"Thanks, Ari. Who's my first appointment?" Parker sat down and oriented himself with the objects on his desk. He activated JAWS, a screen reader program on his computer. The computerized voice announced ten e-mails.

"Your first is Mrs. Crawford."

"Ah."

He smiled, remembering the older lady all too well. Mrs. Crawford was a tiny woman in her late sixties with platinum blonde hair. She'd talked nonstop during their first hour-long session, and so far had been the only one to ask him questions instead of the other way around. Parker also remembered her telling him of an experience in one Asian massage parlor where the massage had been more like punishment instead of relaxation. She'd wanted a deep-tissue massage and had come out of the place with bruises, *and* she had ached all day.

"Your next one is Ms. Too Didley." He recognized the lightness in Arianne's voice, which meant she was on to something funny.

"You're kidding me?" Parker watched her blurry figure pirouette to the door.

"Nope. I'll take her to the room and come back to get you."

He shook his head and listened to the first e-mail, having no idea why Madame Baba crept into his mind. *Could it be?* Well, there was one way to find out. His fingers were itching to know.

CHAPTER THREE

Parker retraced his way back to his office to get a drink and catch a few minutes to relax. He had fifteen minutes before his next client. After an intense session with Mrs. Crawford, he needed a drink. Although he was hoping for a stiff one, drinking on the job wouldn't be a good example for his employees. Even so, Mrs. Crawford had used up his energy and tapped some of his reserves.

As he'd learned from Mrs. Crawford, she was filthy rich but had no heir. Her husband had died of cancer a few years back, and she was alone. Something was wrong with his favorite client.

She was a chirpy, older lady, who had come to their newly opened NYC branch and had demanded the best. Parker had stepped up to the plate and had given the woman what she'd asked for, and later she'd walked out looking satisfied and happy. Of course, he'd had no idea what the woman looked like, trusting what his staff had told him, but he'd heard the satisfaction in her voice.

Their sessions, for the most part, left him winded—not because the old lady demanded deep tissue massages—but because her constant chatter could bring even the most patient guy to tears. In fact, her usual request, a Hawaiian Lomi-Lomi massage that used long continuous strokes and a relaxing touch, was easy enough.

Parker would smile to himself when he ran his hands over her body and her wrinkled and loose skin would impede his movements. She'd chalk it up to old age, and he'd laugh every single time. Sure, he liked the old woman, but it didn't hurt that she was a generous tipper.

For some reason, today's session had been more difficult than usual. She'd been talkative in the beginning, but after a barrage of inquiries about his personal life, she'd turned quiet for a change.

Recalling the session with the old lady, Parker shook his head. Mrs. Crawford demanded too much from him with her unrelenting questions and nonstop babbling. Despite their business relationship, Parker could see a deeper connection with the woman.

"Parker, why aren't you married?" she had asked.

That was a question Parker hated. The woman was a straight shooter, and holding back her tongue was never her strong suit.

He took a deep breath. It was going to be a long hour.

"Because I'm too busy?"

"Or you haven't seen the woman of your dreams?"

That made him pause. Surely the woman knew that seeing would be difficult for him. He laughed. How difficult would it be to find the "right" woman?

"Mrs. Crawford, I'm not ready to settle down. I have a business to run and the world to conquer." Parker masked his discomfort by attempting a little joke, hoping his client would ease up on him.

"You're avoiding my question," she said.

"I guess I am." There was no point in hiding his uncertainty about what the future held for him.

Mrs. Crawford turned around and took his hands in her soft ones. "You're a good man, and these little meetings made me think that I should've had a son. Someone like you. Please pardon my directness. I just want you to be happy."

Parker couldn't answer. Maybe he should tell her to keep her opinions to herself, but the woman meant well. At the back of his mind, he knew she was right.

Bringing himself back to reality, he tried not to think of the prior session and what Mrs. Crawford had said.

Try as he might, he'd been unable to get her to say much. After several attempts, he'd given up and let the silence take over. Parker wasn't complaining. Well, maybe he was. As much as he tried to distance himself from his clients, there were still a few people who managed to get under his skin, either in a positive or a negative way.

With measured steps, he walked toward the little refrigerator and took out a bottle of water. Flopping onto his leather chair, he chugged the drink and closed his eyes, trying to clear his mind for the next scheduled client. What was her name again? Something Didley?

Trying and succeeding were two different things. Parker tried, but he didn't quite succeed in banishing his niggling suspicions.

Gulping down the rest of the water just in time for Arianne's reminder call, he pressed the intercom button on the phone. "Yes, Ari?"

"Ms. Too Didley just walked in. I'll set her up in room three, and then I'll come and get you."

"I think I can manage." After a moment's thought, he asked, "What does this Ms. Didley look like?"

He heard Arianne cup the receiver and then come back, her voice lower than usual. "Hard to tell. She has on big white sunglasses, but her face looked familiar. It's as if I've seen her somewhere before. She's wearing drab clothes, but her purse is to die for. Balenciaga, boss! Balenciaga!" she said through the phone line.

Parker rolled his eyes. Why did women always look at the purses?

"Get her situated, and I'll be there in three." He released the button and sighed before slinging the empty bottle in the direction of the wastebasket. With a swooshing sound, the bottle landed inside the receptacle, and he grinned with pride. It was amazing how the little things gave him pleasure.

He strode out of his office, walked down the hallway, and made a left, counting doors while his fingers felt the Braille numbers on the outside. Once he was standing in front of room three, Parker tapped the door and a familiar voice answered. Pushing the door open, he walked in and focused in the direction of the chair.

"Good morning, Ms. Didley. How are you today?"

"Okay." The response came from the opposite side of where he was facing. He turned toward the direction of the voice, a bit startled.

It took Parker several seconds to regain his composure. Not too many things could give him pause, but he didn't like being reminded of his inadequacies.

"I'm glad to hear that. So, what can I do for you on this great, humid day?" He plastered a smile on his face, hoping she wouldn't notice his momentary discomfort.

She moved toward the table, and he caught a whiff of her perfume—Hermes Perfume 24. Considering he relied on his other senses to compensate for his loss of sight, it wasn't surprising that he recognized the names of so many fragrances. His growing clientele in each of three major cities included a number of affluent athletes and people in the entertainment industry. Parker always asked them what scent they wore, and then committed their answers to memory.

"Swedish sounds good right now," she mumbled when she moved past him. Judging from her voice, she must have been several inches shorter than his five-eleven height. He heard shuffling of fabric and realized she'd sat down.

"Good choice. There's a robe at the foot of the table." Parker gestured toward the general area of the massage table. "Strip down to the level you're most comfortable with and put the robe on while I wait for you in the other room. Once you're ready, just say 'woo-rah' and we can—"

"Oh, I know the drill," she said.

Parker inclined his head and said nothing. Could his suspicion be true? *It has to be,* he thought.

"I'm sorry. I didn't mean to cut you off." There was a sad, if not apologetic, hint to her tone, and he took note of that fact.

"It's okay. Let me know when you're ready for me."

He smiled and turned to the small adjoining area divided by a heavy curtain. Parker pulled back the fabric and walked in while he pondered his suspicion. He was sure Ms. Didley was Madame Baba, even without the benefit of touching her. What was behind the name change? That was a lot of trouble for someone to go through. And why did she seem to be following him? He wasn't the only expert in Los Angeles.

Parker had built a solid reputation in the business and had been dubbed Feather Light for his efforts. It had started out as a joke. A famous singer had been interviewed by a local LA magazine, and one of the questions that had come up was how she'd managed to stay happy and focused despite her grueling schedule. She'd mentioned his name and had even gone so far as to describe the experience at his hands as orgasmic. Everything from that point on was history.

His popularity had skyrocketed after that glowing endorsement, which had enabled him to expand his business. But with every success came adversity. The challenge had come in the form of one tenacious reporter. He'd accused Parker of using methods that bordered on exploitative and improper. The article had gone on to state that his techniques were sexually charged, malicious, and disrespectful. Parker had shrugged it off and had continued to do what he believed was best for his clients and his business.

After washing his hands with warm water, he toweled off and strapped on his lotion and oil belt. Ms. Didley's "woo-rah" sounded, and he took a deep breath. He had no idea why she intrigued him, but everything about her made him ache to know more. His tactile sense told him enough about her physical aspects. If he could only get a chance to feel her face, then he'd have a better sense of the person.

Pushing the heavy curtain aside, Parker slipped back into the room to the soft, soothing sounds of cascading water and relaxing flute. The aroma of lilac floated around when he heard her adjust her body on the massage table.

"Before you start, I want to know what you can see and cannot see," she whispered. "You don't have to answer if you don't want to. I'm just curious because you don't seem blind to me. Your movement is so . . . so precise and tender. It's as if you're looking at me and know what I want and what pleases me."

Whoa! That was the most she'd ever said to him, not counting her monologue from their last meeting. He shrugged and laid his hand on her head, which she'd turned to the side. Gently, he started massaging her head, moving his way in a slow, rhythmic pattern down to her neck, then her shoulders and her back, until he reached the soles of her feet.

"I don't mind at all. I haven't always been blind. In fact, upon diagnosis, the disease gave me enough time to prepare. It wasn't an overnight change.

It took years for my vision to diminish. I won't go completely blind. I still recognize blurry shapes, but that's about all I can see at this point. I guess, in a way, I still move and act as if I can see. It makes people less uncomfortable in my presence." Parker shrugged. "Does my blindness bother you, Ms. Didley?"

Silence, and then she coughed. "No . . . not at all. In fact, and please pardon my forthrightness, it's liberating. It's like getting a fresh start."

Parker's brows furrowed. "Liberating? What do you mean by that?"

She pulled away. "Uh . . . nothing. Can we just move along?"

In response, Parker slid his hand to the base of her neck in light, easy strokes. She wanted to get personal, yet she held back when he prodded her to explain what she meant. That could mean she wasn't comfortable in her own skin. He moved his fingers behind her ears, rubbing and applying light pressure—another technique he used to feel someone's emotion by touch. Depending on one's mood, a heated face, temple, or neck could suggest discomfort or embarrassment. It could also mean the person was trying to hide something or a particular subject affected them. In Ms. Didley's case, he felt she was hiding something.

⁓

Kelly tried to keep her erratic heartbeat in check. She had said so much in such a little time, haranguing the man for information about his eyesight and then dismissing his question without explanation.

His sensual hands on her body didn't help at all. All she could think of was his fingers moving to places that hadn't been touched for a long, long time. Too long, actually. With fame came loneliness. Yes, there were friends and family, but Kelly needed intimacy. She wanted someone she could trust to share her bed at night. Famous actors had their own agenda, and the ones she'd associated with in the past had either wanted her as a red carpet accessory or just a one-night stand. They'd been too into themselves to understand or care about what she needed.

She'd had many massages, but none of the massage therapists had induced the response she had to Parker. Not only had he successfully punctured the barrier around her, making her break down and show her vulnerable side, the part of her she closed for everyone to see, but he had unearthed memories she'd rather forget.

Her mind flashed back to Matthew. The bastard. He had screwed with her head and made her afraid to trust men—and people in general. Exhausted, Kelly wanted nothing more than peace of mind and a chance to be herself again. But who was she nowadays? She shook off the reminders of her past mistakes and concentrated on Parker's hands on her body.

Parker Davis seemed content in his own skin. His blindness added to his aura because he acted so sure of himself. It didn't diminish his ability in her eyes. How could it even matter when he was one of the most gorgeous men she'd ever seen? Kelly worked in the entertainment industry, and she'd seen them all. Parker had the confidence of a man and the charisma of a boy. Add in the sculpted arms, the tapered waist, and the well-built physique . . . she was a goner from the first moment she'd laid eyes on him.

Kelly had gone home after the first session with him feeling like she could take on the world. Parker had the ability to listen and had made her feel good about herself. She'd worked ten days straight after that session and had even been able to endure the paparazzi hounding her. Without being aware of it, Parker had helped her in ways she couldn't explain. He'd lifted her spirits, and his gratifying touch had seemed to convey an unspoken sentiment. Could he feel her attraction to him?

He continued to trace his hands along her back—heaving, kneading, and taunting her into a relaxed state in which all she felt was pure bliss. How would it feel to have his arms around her? To hear him tell her how much he wanted her?

When he moved to massaging her scalp and the contours of her jawline and neck, Parker wasn't just touching her; he was looking at her. Kelly kept her eyes open and watched with guilty pleasure while his mouth twitched into a smile and his eyes closed.

"Ms. Didley?" His voice was a gentle whisper.

"Hmm . . ."

"What are you thinking at the moment?"

Parker moved over to her left leg. From her past experiences, most massage therapists started with the back, then the limbs, before graduating to the face. With Parker, he lingered on her face longer. She wasn't complaining. It gave her the chance to watch him, enough time to memorize his face with its slight bump on the bridge of his nose, sensual pink lips, and long lashes that framed his almost sightless blue eyes. *Talk about devouring someone with your eyes.* She feasted them on Parker like she had never done before, and it made her feel good.

"If there was anything you could have right now, what would it be?"

Kelly answered without giving the question much thought. "I guess I would want a man to tell me what to do." As soon as the words left her mouth, they sounded too honest, even to her own ears. What could he be thinking of her candor?

If she read his reactions correctly, Parker seemed to understand what she meant. She heard his breath hitch before he let out a long sigh.

"You sound like you need a break."

Her response was instinctive. Kelly curled her toes, and her center throbbed. She closed her eyes and let the warm sensation emanating from her girly bits engulf her senses. Those other people hadn't lied. This man could bring her, or anyone, to orgasm just by asking the right questions and saying the right things.

When the chime rang, signaling the end of the session, she groaned, unable to help herself. If it was possible to ask for an extension, she would've done it, but she realized his schedule was tight and he needed a break.

"If you're not doing anything tonight, would you care to join me in my hotel room for dinner? Maybe some drinks afterward?" she blurted out before she lost her nerve. "I know you're not from around here and you're just going back to your hotel room after the day is over. What could be better than two people getting to know each other over dinner?"

"Are you asking me out on a date, Ms. Didley?"

Kelly stiffened at the directness of his question but decided not to lie. "I find you fascinating, Mr. Davis."

Parker shifted on his feet, seeming to considering her statement. "Does your fascination have something to do with my blindness?"

"Not at all. I'm sure you know how attractive you are. You're charming, and it seems like you can carry on a decent conversation."

"You sound like you're in advertising." Parker smiled and shoved his hands in his pocket. "If we're to go out on a date, I would much prefer to take you dining at a nice restaurant with candlelight and soft music."

Stunned, Kelly tried to search for the right words to say. The last thing she needed was to be seen in New York City dining with her massage therapist. She preferred her privacy, and she wanted him alone with her, no interruptions, and everything else that came with that.

"If you don't mind, I'd rather stay in the hotel room. I promise you, the food will be superb, and the company will be excellent." She sounded desperate, but she didn't care. Parker was interesting, and she'd like to get to know him better. What harm could one dinner do, anyway?

He considered her for a moment. "Your offer is hard to refuse, so I will say yes. One condition, though. Please give me your real name."

Parker stared at Kelly like he was looking straight into her eyes. She felt a sliver of discomfort but shrugged it off. The man couldn't see, and she was being paranoid.

"It's Ann Sutton." She wasn't lying. Her real name was Kelly Ann Sutton. Storm was her mother's maiden name, which she used as her stage name because someone had once said it was catchy and easy to remember.

Parker reached out a hand in her direction and grinned. "It's nice to meet you, Ann Sutton."

She got up, not even bothering to cover her body, and clasped his hand. "Same here, Mr. Davis."

He held her hand a bit longer than necessary before he released it. "Call me Parker."

"Call me Ms. Didley." Kelly laughed.

Parker went back to his hotel room to get ready. He felt like a teenager going on his first date. Arianne had warned him, in a good-natured way, that she didn't trust the woman. *"Why would she use aliases if she isn't hiding something?"* Her tone had been full of suspicion ever since Parker had mentioned the date.

He wouldn't have said anything to Arianne if he'd had time to make the arrangements himself, but he had been booked solid for the entire day, leaving him with very little time to call a florist and arrange for his ride.

Parker barely had enough time to get back to his hotel to shower and get ready. Thank God for his fantastic dry cleaner. They sent back his outfits in the same bag they were delivered in, so the Braille label always guaranteed the right colors and combinations, eliminating the chance he'd end up wearing mismatched clothes.

After donning a dinner jacket over a black long-sleeved shirt and gray wool slacks, he worked on taming his hair. Parker should have gotten a haircut before he'd left LA, but his schedule had been too tight. He brushed back the wayward strands and applied gobs of gel until they felt right to him, worried about his appearance because she could see him. On the other hand, it wouldn't matter what Ann wore. She could be wearing raggedy clothes and have her hair all over the place, and he wouldn't even notice.

His car service was prompt and was waiting as soon as he emerged from the hotel. The flowers he'd ordered sat next to him, the scent tickling his nostrils. Ann was staying at the New York Palace, a favorite among celebrities. Parker wondered what she did for a living, because only the uber-rich could afford that famous hotel.

A concierge met him at the front of the hotel and whisked him to her suite. It felt odd, considering he thrived on control, to be dependent on other people at that particular moment.

Ann's request had thrown him off balance. Her simple idea of a date had disturbed his controlled and methodical life, and he had let it. Parker had no idea where the evening would take him, but the mystery behind the woman piqued his interest enough for him to take a look. He chuckled to himself.

"Here we are, sir," the man said when they reached the door of the suite. Parker shook the man's hand with a twenty dollar bill and collected himself before knocking.

There were muffled footsteps, and fabric brushed the surface of the door before it opened. "Hello, Parker." Ann's velvety voice was a soft caress.

He smiled at the sound. "These are for you." He offered her the bouquet of flowers Arianne had ordered for him.

"They're wonderful." Parker heard her sniff the flowers before she took his arm and guided him inside the room. "You look . . . amazing."

"Thank you. I wish I could say the same, but I'm sure you're gorgeous. If I'm going to base my call on your Hermes perfume, I'll say you smell ravishing." He grinned while they made their way into what he guessed was the sitting room. Ann ushered him to a plush sofa, and they sat next to each other. She released his arm once they were settled and comfortable.

"Dinner is arriving in ten minutes. Hold on. Let me call for them to bring a vase for these beautiful flowers." Parker heard the sound of her footsteps padding across the room and listened as she called in her request. Ann came back and sat next to him.

He decided to start the conversation with a safe topic. "What are we having?"

Her laugh was sexy, and he couldn't help but smile. "Are you hungry?"

Parker nodded. "Been a long day, and there's one Ms. Didley who took a lot out of me—energy-wise that is." He winked at her.

"Well, Ms. Didley's going to make sure you're well-fed and satisfied by the end of the night."

Okay. If he didn't know any better, he would swear that there was something sexual about the way she'd said that. "Really?" He raised an eyebrow.

"We're starting off with oysters in mignonette sauce. I ordered Cabernet steak with mushrooms for you and mahi-mahi with mango sauce for me. And for dessert, we're having chocolate truffle cake."

Parker coughed, unable to stop the surprise as soon as he realized everything she had ordered was an aphrodisiac. Mortified at his reaction, Parker was saved from further embarrassment by the knocking on the door.

He wasn't sure if he should feel flattered, because it was obvious the woman wanted him, or if he should start running. As much as he wanted her, his lifestyle wasn't for everyone, and he wasn't even thinking about his disability yet. Parker was thinking more along the lines of his sexual preferences.

It wasn't easy to come up to someone new and tell them he wanted a more controlled approach to sex. He wasn't tied to Webster by any means —they were mere sex partners who understood and trusted each other, and their shared preference worked out well for them.

Then Parker heard the sound of a cart being rolled into the middle of the room, judging by the echo of the wheels as their sound bounced off the walls. It was funny how blindness made him pay attention to details he had taken for granted in the past.

He couldn't hear what was being said before the person left. Ann spoke in hushed tones, which made it impossible for him to understand. Parker shrugged it off, but a sliver of suspicion began to creep in.

"Shall we?"

Parker got up and followed the direction of her voice. He looked down to catch any furniture in his way and made it to the makeshift dinner table without making a fool of himself.

"It smells good." He touched the edge of the table until he bumped into a chair. Feeling for the back of it, he pulled it out for her. Ann sat down, and he went around to his chair.

"Where do you want me to put your water and wine glass?"

Her attention to detail was touching, and he gave her a smile. "My one o'clock. Water on the left, and wine glass to the right." Parker listened to the sounds she made while she did what he'd told her. He fought the urge to compliment Ann on her obedience, something that came naturally to him.

"Thank you."

"You're welcome. Bon appétit." The sound of metal scraping against the china prompted him to pick up his own utensils.

They dug into the oysters first, and Parker's thoughts kept going back to the idea behind the food choice. "This is good."

"I knew you'd like it. You seem like an oyster man." Ann laughed but offered no explanation.

"What is an 'oyster man'?" he asked after he'd swallowed the first oyster.

"Someone who enjoys his *food*." Another innuendo.

Parker nearly choked and reached for his water. He must have drunk half of it, because Ann got up and refilled his glass. Wiping the beads of sweat from his forehead, he wanted to avoid the topic, but it seemed like he was being cornered.

"Yes, I do enjoy my food. There's a certain way I like to eat it, though."

He guessed she was trying to figure out what he meant when silence loomed between them. Instead of replying, Ann started clearing the appetizer plate and placed another one in front of him.

"Do you want me to cut the meat for you?" Her tone was laced with concern.

Parker shook his head. "Just tell me how big the steak is, and I can take it from there."

She leaned closer, enough for him to catch a whiff of her sweet scent. "Um . . . let's see. It's about the size of a CD."

"Thanks." He got to work, and after several minutes of biting and chewing, Parker leaned back in his chair and started a safe conversation.

"Tell me, Ms. Sutton, what do you do for a living?"

Ann didn't answer right away. He'd thought the topic was safe enough for two people trying to get to know each other, but he felt a subtle change in the room—some sort of tension he couldn't explain.

"I'm not doing anything at the moment," she said after a noticeable pause.

"Must be nice. I'm a slave to my work." He laughed.

"Let's just say I'm wealthy."

Parker had no idea what to say to that, so he went for whatever came to mind. "Even better. You're a rich bum. Tell me about your life as a bum, then."

There was another extended silence, which lasted longer than the first. "Nothing much to tell except I travel a lot. I have a sister in Chicago. That's where I grew up until I moved to Los Angeles several years ago. My parents are both dead. I'm twenty-six years old. That's about it."

"What's the color of your hair and your eyes?"

"I'm a natural redhead, and I have hazel eyes."

He inclined his head. "Light-skinned and freckles?"

"Well, I try to hit the tanning salon when I can." Ann laughed and took a sip of her wine. "And I have a gazillion freckles."

"I can just imagine."

"Tell me about yourself."

"I'm more of an open book, I guess, because of Knead Me's success. A lot of what is written about me is almost right. *Almost*." Parker chuckled before continuing. "I grew up in the San Fernando Valley, in Encino. I was into cross-country running before blindness got the best of me."

"Must be hard, I mean, you know . . . having to adjust to another lifestyle."

"As I said earlier, it didn't happen overnight, so I had time to make some adjustments. I still run on the track with a sighted guide. I learned some things before profound blindness took over. I took a crash course in Braille, I let the light guide me for directions, if I can, and I try not to hassle people if I can avoid it. Driving was the hardest thing to give up." He sighed.

"How do you get around? And how come you don't use one of those sticks?" There was no malice in her tone, just innocent curiosity, which was a breath of fresh air.

"My brother, Cork, came to work for me when I couldn't drive any longer. He lives a few miles from my place, and he handles the books. As for the white cane, I don't want it yet. I can still recognize shapes and distance. It's still good enough to get around. I try not to cross the street without company. Cork had inquired about a guide dog for me. The process takes some time, and I'm currently on the waiting list, if I ever want one."

"You seemed well-adjusted to your . . ." Ann paused.

Parker supplied the word she was searching for. "Disability?"

"I don't think that's the word I'm looking for. *Challenges* sounds better to me."

"In a way, I guess I am adjusted already. I have no choice. I have to live and make the most out of life, right?" Parker tried to look straight in the direction of her face, hoping his aim was right.

"Well, Parker, I'm happy for you. I wish everyone could be like you, happy with what they have in life." Ann drew in a sharp breath.

Her sigh raised another suspicion he couldn't ignore. "Are you happy with what you have?" he asked.

"Time for dessert." She got up and cleared the dinner plates, placing another dish in front of him.

He raised an eyebrow but decided not to press. Dinner was delicious, and the company, even more so. Parker couldn't remember the last time he had been out on an actual date and enjoyed himself since his business had taken off. He found it difficult not to give in to his curiosity about this interesting woman.

As the night progressed and the wine bottle emptied, they sat on the sofa, holding each other's hands. They skirted around the topic of sex, since Ann refused to talk more about herself.

Judging from her rapid breathing, Parker was certain of one fact and one fact alone—he desired her as much as she wanted him. But he wasn't about to say anything. Instead, he focused on rubbing her arm and trailing feather light touches along the back of her neck.

Ann moaned. "Parker . . . I think you have an idea how I feel about you." She got up and tugged on his arm.

He stood and pulled her close until their bodies touched. Inhaling her scent, he sighed. "I think I do . . . but . . . shit, how do I say this?"

"Tell me." Her voice was a husky whisper.

Parker shuddered. It was crazy, but he was about to tell a woman he hardly knew what he wanted. He had to if he wanted to give whatever they had a chance.

"I don't do regular sex, Ann," he said.

CHAPTER FOUR

In Parker's arms, Kelly felt inexplicably safe and desired because he asked questions instead of pushing her into bed like the others had done in the past. His genuine concern for her troubles made her feel special and was not the way most men would go about getting a chance to be with her. To most, Kelly was just a prize they want and not a real person to cherish. With the way she'd been throwing hints at Parker, others would have jumped her already. How could she ignore the fact that she was in awe of his control in her presence?

The emotional combination he stirred within her was enough reason to pursue the man even more. Kelly had been in relationships with men not involved in show business and with another one who had worked in the entertainment industry. None of them had been successful because they'd either had no idea what she'd wanted, even if she'd made herself clear, or they'd been too much into themselves to even notice her needs.

Kelly had long given up on finding someone with whom she could share herself in every sense of the word. Most men saw her as a beautiful face, an actress who fueled their erotic fantasy, or even an accessory to be used in advancing their career.

Such had been the case of her relationship with Matthew Campbell, a costar in one of her films. He was a budding actor, hungry for the spotlight, and she'd fallen for him and his manipulative ministrations, hard.

A few months after the success of their film and basking under the limelight, Kelly had found him in the arms of another woman, an actress with whom he'd been working. The tabloids and the media, though they'd taken Kelly's side, had gotten too involved in their "tell-all" quest to air Matthew's dirty laundry. Even if Kelly had been deemed the victim, most of their off-screen activities had been plastered all over for the whole world to see.

Kelly valued her privacy, or whatever was left of it. The media and her fans seemed to have forgotten that she still needed some time alone to regroup, to lick her wounds and feel the wind in her face without anyone clamoring to take her picture or chronicle her every movement. Contrary to what most people believed, public figures deserved a moment of peace, even if their fame placed them under scrutiny day in and day out.

Kelly shuddered at the warmth of Parker's touch, but his words left her feeling bereft. "What do you mean you don't do *normal* sex?"

Ideas began racing through her head. *For Christ's sake, please don't be gay! Just when I find a man close to perfect, there has to be an asterisk to what kind of sex he can do.*

Parker's eyes softened, and a tender expression crossed his face. He released her, and the sudden feeling of being lost strangled her. She wanted his arms around her. Kelly was proud of her independence and had always maintained she would never need someone to make her feel good about herself, but Parker was turning her into a woman who needed a man in her life. What had happened to her independent spirit?

He ran the back of his hand along the side of her face, as if he were reading her emotions. "I'm not gay, if that's what you're thinking."

"But . . . you said—"

To prove his point, Parker lowered his mouth to hers for a kiss she hadn't expected but immensely welcomed. His lips were soft, yet firm—just as she'd expected. Kelly couldn't afford to close her eyes. She wanted to look at him, to see his face up close, and feel his emotions transferring to her.

When his tongue sought hers, she responded with equal passion. She let him lead, loving the way his warmth spread all over her mouth. Kelly had been kissed before, but nothing or no one could come close to the excitement Parker evoked in her.

She burned with desire and pressed closer, feeling the hardness of his thigh muscles as they rubbed against her body. Her skin tingled with anticipation, wishing she could drag him to the bed right then and taste what he had to offer.

Feeling on the verge of losing control, Kelly pulled back. "I want to feel you inside me." Her breath came in strangled spurts. She watched his jaw clench, and he sighed.

Parker took her face, as if he wanted to *see* her reaction to what he was about to say. "Ann, I wish I could change myself, just for you, even for one night. But I'm afraid you wouldn't understand, even if I tried to tell you."

Not wanting to lose the magic of moment, Kelly stood on tiptoes and licked his mouth with her tongue. "I want you to *show* me what you mean."

He drew back, but his hands remained on her cheeks. "You have no idea what kind of loving I'm looking for . . . and besides, I'm not prepared. I didn't bring any protection." His breath was growing haggard, seeming very close to losing control. She could see the conflict in his face.

Kelly pulled him to the direction of the bed a little too forcefully because he almost stumbled. She steadied him and draped her arm around his waist. "I was a Girl Scout once. I've always kept one in case of emergency." Goodness, didn't she just sound so desperate? Thank God he couldn't see the horrified expression on her face.

"Ann, you have no idea what kind of person I am. You might not want me by the end of the night." Parker took hold of the back of her neck, albeit gently. She knew he was searching for uncertainty from her by way of touch.

"I would feel the same way I felt when I first saw you. Nothing would change it." Kelly led him to the bed. "Light on or off?"

Parker inclined his head, not knowing what to make of her. After a second, he gave his preference. "I need a little light, so I can see your silhouette."

Kelly's gaze traveled down to the tenting in his slacks. He was sporting a hard-on that was difficult to ignore. "Lights on, then."

"Don't take your clothes off until I say so."

Kelly stared at him in surprise and remembered what she had said earlier: she wanted a man to tell her what to do. She nodded her head. After a second, she realized he wouldn't know her answer unless she spoke. "Okay."

With a sweep of his hand, Parker enfolded her in his arms once more. "Let me taste you again." She obliged and closed her eyes this time.

God help me, Parker thought as his mouth descended on hers for another sweet kiss. Whatever happened between now and after, he would have to be careful with his actions, as well as his words. As much as he wanted to tell her what he was into, it wouldn't be easy. People just didn't come right out of the blue and explain their preferences, especially when it came to the nature of the kink involved.

Barring the negative ideas running through his mind, he swept Ann off her feet and placed her on the bed. The mattress dipped a little under her weight, which wasn't much to begin with. Parker couldn't deny the sweetness of her mouth, and he could imagine what the rest of her would taste like.

He hesitated for a moment, vacillating between taking her without explanation and giving her a glimpse of what being with him entailed. Emotion was a powerful thing, as well as the throbbing, living thing pulsating beneath his fly. This woman was short-circuiting his better judgment, yet he was going to stay, feeling the invisible magnet that was drawing him to her. Vanilla was foreign to him after years of sticking to his chosen sexual practice. The mere thought of going through the night without the control he thrived on gave him pause, despite the massive hard-on he was sporting. Her breathing and the thudding of her heart was all he focused on.

Ann tugged on his arm again, as if sensing his uncertainty. "It's not normal for me to ask men to sleep with me." There was an unmistakable twinge of disappointment in her tone.

Parker stood next to the bed, feeling the edge of the mattress and orienting himself to the position of the headboard. He trailed his fingers along the goose down pillows that cradled her head. Her hair was splayed over the fine material, and her chest heaved with every breath she took.

He settled next to her, touching the contours of her body before he straddled her. "I don't hesitate. Believe me, I *want to* take you, but there are few rules I want you to know first."

"Rules?" There was a slight tremor in her voice.

Parker nodded and focused on the round shape he believed was her face. He lowered himself close enough to get the feel of her body underneath him. "You don't ask what I'm doing. If you don't like it, you will give me a word you don't say very often."

"A word? What for?"

"Because I will make love to you the way I know how."

Another round of erratic breathing followed. "Um . . . what kind of word do you want me to use?"

"It's called a safeword. Anything out of the ordinary—something you don't normally use. It can even be a name." He let his lips graze along Ann's cheek, getting familiar with her scent. Parker felt her shudder, and she clasped her arms around his neck.

"Sapphire," she whispered in his ear. "Your eyes are the color of sapphire at night. They take on a different hue . . . I don't know how to explain it."

"Sapphire it is. Ann? If you feel uncomfortable with anything I ask you to do, let me know, and I'll stop."

She took his hands, which were exploring the curves of her body, and brought them to her face. "I will love every minute with you."

Man, that was all he needed to hear, and his cock hardened even more. Ignoring his body's immediate response to her declaration was impossible. "See what you're doing to me?" He took her hand and let her cup his erection. Her body trembled beneath him.

"You want me . . ." It wasn't a question. The sense of awe he heard in her voice struck him as odd, because she seemed like a desirable woman—at least from what his hands had told him.

"Wanting you was never the issue." Parker slid out of her grasp, leaving her reaching out for him. He stood at the side of the bed. "Take my clothes off while kissing me."

Starting her off with soft orders, so as not to frighten or scare her away, Parker reached for Ann's hand and brought her to her feet. Her hesitation lasted a few seconds before her eager hands went to work.

Ann tilted his face up until their noses touched. He felt her warm breath on his mouth before she kissed him. Plump and soft lips were always a plus. With a sensual caress, she sought entrance to his mouth, her tongue meandering, teasing with slow strokes of hot velvet that made him want her more while she started peeling off his jacket. A soft swish sounded when his coat landed on the floor. His shirt was next. With the release of each button, Ann's tongue intensified its assault on his mouth. She wanted to take charge, and Parker had to smile.

She pressed her pelvis against his as soon as the last button snapped open, revealing his body for her to see. Parker heard her appreciative moan when her mouth left his. He seized her face to keep her focused.

"I meant undressing me without breaking our kiss." Parker's voice sounded unsteady, despite the authority he tried to project. This woman was turning him into one hot mess. He felt his control slipping away. Her kisses made him want to forgo the foreplay and dive straight into her pussy.

"I wanted to see all of you."

Belligerence was one thing he hadn't encountered for a long time. Because she was unaware of his lifestyle and he hadn't explained the process to her, he was going to let that one go.

"If you want to see me up close, release my zipper now." Parker captured her mouth in one swift move, and Ann's back arched closer.

Parker felt her fingers tremble when she unbuckled his belt. He couldn't see her face, but her ragged breathing was enough for him to know how he affected her. Grunting against his mouth, Kelly pulled on his belt and tossed the leather away. It landed on the bed with a jingling sound. Next she worked on his zipper, tugging on the waistband of his pants with both hands until they dropped to his knees. After he stepped out of them, he pressed his erection against her belly.

A delightful groan tickled his senses. Her body swayed.

"Good girl," he whispered.

Before she could respond, he applied pressure on the small of her back with one hand and cleared the hair from her neck with the other. He let the tip of his tongue trace along her collarbone as he pushed her backward onto the bed and continued assaulting her soft skin.

"Pull my boxers down now," Parker breathed against her chest.

His dick was shouting for release. The confines of his boxers were stifling as his need continued to rise. He sprang free before the boxers even hit the floor.

"Parker . . . I want to tell you how you look to me."

He smiled and shook his head. "I want you to see what I'm going to do to you."

Parker got on his knees, bracing her body in between. He inched forward like a predator stalking its prey until his cock was close to her face. Bending forward, he let the blunt tip trail along her jawline. She moaned, and her fingernails scraped the sheets before she clutched at them.

"You like the feeling, my lovely Ann?"

"Oh yes . . . but you're teasing me."

He stopped her by pressing the tip to her lips. She gasped in surprise, and he took that opportunity to slide his erection into the warmth of her mouth.

"Remember to say *sapphire* when you want me to stop."

Ann's head moved back and forth with his cock still entrenched in her mouth. Her teeth rubbed against his sensitive skin, sending ripples of lust through him. Not wanting to get his high before she did, Parker pulled out even as her hands pressed against his ass in an effort to stop him.

"I didn't say *sapphire* yet."

Her petulant tone amazed him. Parker inclined his head and smiled in her direction. "You're an impatient woman, aren't you?"

Ann's throaty laughter filled the room. "I've never wanted a man as much as I want you."

"Your patience will be rewarded soon. Now, I want you to free yourself from this cashmere sweater and leave your bra on for me."

Her movements were as fast as lightning. The next thing he heard was the garment being tossed to the floor. Still on his knees, Parker moved back, his hands grazing Ann's satiny skin until they reached her tits.

He cupped her breasts until Ann squirmed in anticipation. They fit like they were made just for him. With his own lust mounting, he unhooked her bra, and her tits spilled out like waterfalls. Parker liberated her body from the lacy material and traced the roundness until his hands reached her rock-hard nipples. So full and firm. He let his thumbs circle the tips and squeezed. Ann moaned with pleasure, and her body arched forward, wanting more.

Parker pressed her back against the mattress. "I'm aching to hear you scream, baby." His mouth descended on one tip and sucked. He wanted her writhing against him, and she writhed. He sucked on her tits, his tongue flicking against the tips until her cries echoed in the room.

"Oh . . . Parker . . ." she cried over and over while her hips jolted up toward his. He squeezed her breasts together, licking the edges until his face was surrounded by her softness. Parker let one hand rub her naked torso, snaking under her skirt. He felt for the lacy thong and smiled to himself.

"Remove your skirt but leave that racy number for me."

The warmth emanating from her was a good sign. The sound of her body rubbing against the silky bed sheets when she removed her skirt was music to his ears.

"I'm . . ."

"Ready?" He supplied the word for her.

Ann didn't say anything, but from the slight movement of her body, he knew she'd nodded her head.

Parker beamed with satisfaction. "Woo-fuckin'-rah!"

"What's with that word, anyway?" She laughed, sounding breathless.

"I've had it playing in my head since I was a small child, so I decided to use it. It worked, even if people think I'm crazy or something." He gave her a winning smile before taking a deep breath. "Now, give me the belt."

The leather was pressed into his outstretched hand.

"What I'm going to do might push you to your limit. What is the word you're going to use if I push you too far?" He waited for Ann's answer.

"S-sapphire?"

"Just relax and let me take you where you wanted to be."

Parker took one of her wrists and lifted her arm over her head before placing the other next to it. He bound her wrists with the belt, making sure it wouldn't come undone, but was still loose enough to allow circulation.

Testing for slack and finding none, he kissed her to get her heart rate jumping again.

Abruptly ending their kiss, he heaved his body down until he came within inches of her moist center. Ann was radiating with readiness, and his shaft pulsated with excitement.

He pressed his hands against her waist and nuzzled against the skin of one of her thighs. Responding with a moan, she pressed her legs together, providing a welcoming cocoon. He continued to assault her senses with every lick of his tongue. Her moans came out as throaty sighs.

When her jerky movements ebbed, he sat back on his heels and traced his fingers over the lace of her tiny thong. Her stomach clenched when his hand rubbed her skin. Parker pulled the thong down, wishing he could see Ann in all her glory.

"I would give anything to see your pussy right now."

"I can describe my kitty for you . . ."

Expectation laced her tone, and it made him smile. Never, in his years of being blind, had anyone offered such sweet pleasure. Parker nodded and reached forward to touch her face. He wanted to feel her emotions as she spoke. She licked her lips.

"Well . . . it's cute, I think." Her mirth had a nervous tinge, and he joined in her laughter. "I like it shaved, leaving a landing strip, just for kicks." Ann's face grew hotter against his hand.

Another self-conscious laugh filled the room before she continued. Her voice fascinated him. Parker loved to hear her talk. There was a trace of huskiness in every lilt that was growing on him.

"I have a small labia minora hidden by plump labia majora." She giggled. "Do you want to touch my kitty so you know what I'm talking about?"

Brownie points for her for asking. Parker moved his fingers from her face, letting them drag along every inch of her skin, leaving trails of goose bumps in their wake, until they reach her pussy. He felt the smooth skin and touched the strip of hair in the center.

"Red hair?" He smiled.

"Uh-huh. Pink clit, and I'm wet now."

His cock throbbed at Ann's declaration. Without a word, he dove down to taste her. Tasting was always better than touching. Her body undulated, and a rippling shudder rocked her when his tongue brushed her tasty bud.

Ann hissed when he introduced a finger into her raging sex. He began pumping, creating friction against her wet wall. Her body gyrated with every thrust. Parker added another finger with increasing speed while her screams of ecstasy echoed as her release drew closer. Her thrashing intensified when she exploded around his fingers.

"Please . . . do it again. I want you inside me . . . please." Her strangled pleas stroked his ego. Parker straightened and inched forward.

"Where's the hazmat suit?" When she hesitated, he added, "Condom, darling, condom."

"It's in . . . my purse. There's . . . a . . . zipper inside." Ann was still catching her breath. "My purse is on top of the desk. If you get off the foot of the bed, it'll be to your right, at four o'clock."

Parker followed her directions, walking in calculated steps toward the desk. After he found the purse, he felt inside until he found the zipper, and then the foil. He tore the wrapper and unrolled the rubber before heading back to the bed.

"Are you still wet for me?" he asked.

"So very wet . . ."

He wanted his orders to sound more like a request but was unable to curb the urge to exercise his power. "Spread your legs for me."

Ann opened up for him. Parker slid in between her legs and propped himself up, supported by his hands on either side of her body. Slowly, he pushed his hips down until he was touching her sensitive skin. He teased her by aiming his tip to her opening. She bucked, eager to meet his aching erection.

"Please . . . don't make me wait any longer." The plea taunted his swelling pride.

In one swift move, he plunged his erection into her welcoming warmth. Her wetness allowed him to shift until her walls closed in on him. Parker gave a quick thrust, and she let out a smothered cry.

He silenced Ann with his mouth, kissing her with intense hunger and feeling very much in control now that he was inside her. Her bound hands wormed around his neck, and their bodies crashed together, adding more sparks to his lust receptors. Parker braced his body with his hands and began pounding into her with gusto.

Ann's arousal, mixed with his, created an incredible scent around them, and Parker quickened the pace when her legs twined around his waist and linked behind him. He stroked harder, soliciting moans of delight from her as he rode her. Her cries fueled his lust. Sweating and panting hard, Parker felt her ruptured release as her body shook underneath him. He reached his own peak in a matter of seconds, as if a bolt of lightning had exploded around him.

With a groan, he landed like a ragdoll on top of her. They stayed quiet for a long time before he found the strength to roll over. Man, *mind-numbing* couldn't even begin to describe his emotions at the moment. He felt her body tremble next to him, followed by a pinched sob.

"Ann, what's wrong? Why are you crying?" Parker bolted into an upright position and ran his fingers along her face. He felt the dampness on her cheeks.

"Woo-rah," her weak voice croaked.

CHAPTER FIVE

Really? After earth-shattering and heart-pounding sex, you're crying? Kelly silently scolded herself while she sought the warmth Parker's embrace provided. She snuggled closer, loving his scent and the rock-hard chest she nestled against. Burying her face, she tried to stifle her sobs but was powerless to stop the flood of tears once the gate was opened.

"Hey . . . did I hurt you in any way?"

Parker's eyes were gazing into hers. It made her ache to think he couldn't see her face. There was no way he would recognize her. She felt like a heel for subjecting him to unnecessary worry. If only she could put her trust in another man again.

"No . . ."

"Why the tears?"

His hands went to her face, no doubt to feel her emotions. In the few hours they'd been together, she'd discovered his gentle nature and wondered where he had been all her life.

"Just overwhelmed, I guess."

It wasn't a lie, but it wasn't the whole truth either. Still reeling from their amazing lovemaking, Kelly couldn't keep her tears at bay, because she hadn't felt this good in a long, long time. What must Parker be thinking? On both occasions they'd been together, she'd managed to blubber like a small child. How could she tell him that she'd been lying to him all along?

Well, maybe not a full-blown lie, but intentionally omitting the most important aspect of her identity constituted lying.

"Damn it! This is the part I hate." Parker's hands kept tracing the path of her tears to wipe them away. Although his mood had shifted, the hands on her face remained gentle and steady.

"Which part?" She looked up and found him staring at her forehead.

"I can't see your face. I can't make out your expression. I have to rely on what you tell me and what I can sense. It gets frustrating sometimes."

"Why?" Kelly propped up on her elbows to watch his expression.

"I don't think what I *see* is what I'm getting here." He plunged his fingers through his hair and sighed. "I know we don't know each other that well, but I feel some type of connection. Do you feel the same way?"

Kelly stiffened and looked away as an uncontrollable panic swept through her. Parker couldn't see her face nor read her reaction, and yet it seemed like he could. All of a sudden, she felt guilty because she had no plans to tell him who she was, and as he had said himself, they hardly knew each other. What made her think she could trust him? *You went to bed with the man. What he doesn't know about you is unimportant.*

"Ann?"

"Hmm . . ." Kelly slid out of bed and out of Parker's range. Perhaps if she wasn't close to him, she'd be able to think with a clear head and lessen the chance of him sensing her discomfort.

"Am I right?" She watched him angle his head to follow the sound of her footsteps. Kelly walked to the glass sliding door and slid it open, hoping to catch a whiff of fresh air and clear her mind. Instead, a wild gust of wind blew in, rustling the loose papers on the desk.

"Oh, crap." She ran after the flying papers and gathered them from the floor.

"Ann, why are you avoiding my question?" Parker asked, going down on his knees to help with the pick-up effort.

Kelly's gaze traveled down his naked body while he moved around, trying to gather some of the papers littered across the floor. Her eyes were glued to his form. His ass was perfect—each muscle contracting and relaxing with his every movement.

"I'm sorry, but I don't know what you're talking about." Kelly stood, holding a handful of stray papers she would have to put back together later.

Parker rose to his feet, dropping the stack of papers in his hands. His proud cock dangled before him. Even in its soft state, it was a sight to behold. She drew a deep breath, fighting the sudden excitement pulsating between her legs.

He strode to where Kelly was piling the mishmash of a script she'd been reading earlier.

"Don't play coy with me." He placed a hand on her arm. "Please, look at me."

Kelly had avoided many things in her life, and this brewing confrontation was something she could do without. With annoyance she didn't bother to hide, she turned around and faced him.

"For your information, I'm not playing coy. I don't know what you're referring to. If you think I'm hiding something, then you're right. We all have secrets, and this is personal. I have no intention of telling you what it is." Holding her tongue had never been her strong suit. She immediately regretted speaking her mind when a fleeting, wounded expression flashed across Parker's face.

"I apologize if you think I'm prying. I just want to get to know you better . . . but you know what? Forget it. It was nice spending a great evening with you, Ms. Sutton." Parker pivoted and walked toward the bed, picking up his clothes that were littered on the floor with his toes.

Stunned, Kelly just stood there as Parker dressed himself, finding each piece of his clothing without difficulty. Once he was done tying his shoelaces, he reached inside his pocket and speed-dialed a number. "Meet me at the front door."

Furious at herself for ruining a perfect night, Kelly crossed the room when Parker turned in her direction. "Parker, I didn't mean for it to come out the way it did. Please, forgive me." How could she explain herself without blowing her cover? Things had happened so fast, and even if Parker seemed the perfect guy, she wasn't about to bare her soul to him yet.

"I think you made your point loud and clear. You want to be left alone. You don't have anything to worry about as far as I'm concerned. Again, thanks for the . . . *lovely* . . . evening." Parker tilted his head before he walked out the door.

Dumbfounded, Kelly stumbled forward in her haste to follow him. How would he find his way to the elevator and down to the lobby? Before she could call out after him, she saw his hand skimming the wall for guidance, his gait rigid while he walked down the hallway.

She stopped herself from following. Offering help would insult him even further. Sadness swept over her when she closed the door and looked around the room. Parker's scent still lingered, and the makeshift dinner table remained, a reminder of a wonderful night that had ended in a disaster.

Parker had no idea who she was, since he couldn't see her face. Her name would be the only clue to give her secret away. Kelly tried pushing him out of her mind but only half-succeeded. She began picking up the rest of the papers on the floor. God, she had enough on her mind as it was. The last thing she needed was to tangle herself in another relationship that had zero possibility of working.

The media would be all over him, no doubt. Once they found out she was involved in any way with him, they'd dig up anything they could about him, and it wouldn't be pretty. His blindness would thrust him into an ugly limelight, which just might hurt him even more—not a place she wanted him to be.

And what made her think that, even if she and Parker had a connection, things would work out between them? She and Matthew had a connection, too, and where had it led them? Besides, she was done being on the tabloid's front cover. Her baby's death had been plastered in every single one without consideration for her privacy or even her grief.

Kelly opened her monogrammed LV trunk and yanked out a cream tank top and pink boxers before proceeding to the bathroom for a quick shower. Her skin still tingled from Parker's touch, and it was a shame she had to wash the remnants of their lovemaking from her body.

There was one thing she had been trying not to think of until that moment. As much as she'd enjoyed their moment together, the whole "wait for my orders, say the safeword" thing had scared her. "What the hell was that about?" she said aloud while she toweled off.

Walking toward the bathroom sink, Kelly wiped the steam off the mirror and caught a glimpse of her reflection. She hadn't lied to him about the color of her hair, her eyes, or her countless freckles. What she'd left out was her true identity. Not a good start if she wanted a relationship with him.

"But there won't be any relationship, considering the way things ended tonight!" she shot back and stomped out of the bathroom.

She glared at the clock and groaned. Two in the morning. Jessica would have a hissy fit when she saw the big bags underneath Kelly's eyes later. Powering on her laptop, she climbed into bed and settled in. Images of Parker kissing her and touching her in all right places began replaying in her mind. Remembering his stimulating hands on her body brought back another wave of desire she couldn't stop. She wasn't a prude by any measure, but Parker had awakened new and sensitive areas in her that she'd never known existed.

When the Google search engine popped up, she typed his name. Articles upon articles showed up with his picture, but one in particular caught her eye. The piece was an interview with a former lover, it seemed. The woman, whose face she recognized, had given an interview about what being in bed with Parker was like. She spoke about his dominance and how he wanted "control in the bedroom." This made Kelly pause and think about what she had with Parker. She had no idea what they'd just done or the name of the process he'd used. She keyed each term until several options came up. Clicking on one, she began reading. By the time she'd finished the article, her heart was racing and zooming along information highway overload. She read some more. An increasing sense of unease settled in the pit of her stomach. Kelly had no idea what she was reading, or if she could even trust the information on the Internet.

A small part of her had felt excited when he'd bound her hands, but in retrospect, it frightened her. She closed her eyes, feeling tired. Parker was a Dom of some sort, as the article suggested. And if she were with him, she'd be a *submissive*? Kelly wasn't sure she liked the word, but she couldn't shake off the thrill she'd experienced under his guidance either.

"I can't believe you overslept!" Jessica shrieked, lifting the pillow off Kelly's face.

"Go away," she mumbled and tried to pull the pillow back down. The sound of hushed voices came from the other side of the room, momentarily paralyzing her. Kelly bolted upright upon realizing she had company. She had forgotten about the Gucci photo shoot and the taping for the *David Letterman Show*.

"Oh dear!" She gasped when she saw the crews gawking at her and whispering among themselves. Some she'd already worked with in the past, but others were new faces. Kelly slid out of the bed and faced Jessica's fury.

Jessica Renoir was her assistant, gopher, confidante, and best friend. "You'd better have a good explanation for being late." Jessica pushed her to the bathroom amid the curious stares of the photographer and the makeup and lighting crews.

As soon as they were away from prying eyes, Jessica shoved Kelly's toothbrush into her hand. "Brush. It's all you have time for, considering how late it is." Her tone suggested she was irked, so Kelly complied without arguing. "I can see you had company last night . . .," her best friend observed with keen interest.

She finished brushing her teeth and splashed cold water on her face. Jessica yanked her back into the room, where the crew was already rearranging the furniture, leaving the sofa in one corner and adding some shimmery throw pillows and yards of orange taffeta-looking fabric in the surrounding area. A big, black canvas stood behind the sofa, and light fixtures were being assembled.

"Here's your first outfit, Ms. Storm."

A representative from Gucci lifted a garment bag before her. She took it while Jessica shooed her back to the privacy of the bathroom. Kelly hung the bag behind the door and pulled the zipper down. A white gown burst out of the confines, and she gasped. Fingering the fine material and the intricate embroidery around the bodice, Kelly removed the outfit and dressed in haste.

A hush fell over the room when she walked out. The men followed her movement with open admiration, their eyes fixed on the low-cut neckline that barely covered her breasts. The women were more guarded, but their expressions conveyed envy.

"Please, sit right here." Fiona, a makeup artist Kelly had worked with a couple of times in the past, gestured to the space she'd set up next to the bed.

Jessica followed and pulled a chair next to her as Fiona began applying the basics to Kelly's face. "We have less than two hours before the limousine arrives for your taping," Jessica said while consulting her Blackberry. "I will ask my questions later. For now, just pray Fiona can do magic on those horrible bags of yours."

Fiona giggled, and Jessica continued reciting her schedule for the day. Kelly tuned them out after they began chattering and closed her eyes. The next two hours were as excruciating as getting her teeth pulled—changing outfits, posing for a millionth time, and being under the hot lights as if she were a piece of cooking meat.

As soon as the photo shoot was over and everyone had left, she changed into a simple black sheath and high-heeled shoes. She left her hair the way Fiona had arranged it. The makeup artist and the hair expert at the studio would change them anyway. Kelly grabbed her purse, slipped on her dark glasses, and followed Jessica out the door.

"You ready?" Jessica asked once they stepped off the lobby elevator. The plush carpeting muffled their footsteps while they headed to the front door. A doorman dipped his head and held the glass door open for them.

She took a deep breath and plastered on a winning smile. "I guess."

Hundreds of lights flashed when she emerged to make her way to the waiting limousine. Despite the rope cordoning them off at a safe distance, several bolder shutterbugs got closer. One of them was Rigor James, an annoying man who was dead set on making Kelly's life a living hell. They'd had several run-ins in the past, with Rigor pushing her to her limits. The last one had been the most upsetting yet, ignoring the unspoken boundary between privacy and what the rest of the world was entitled to see. Rigor had taken snapshots of Kelly on a private getaway on a friend's yacht off the coast of Marseille that was meant to get her head together after her very public breakup with Matthew. The picture had been snapped when she had been crying her eyes out to Jessica.

"Kelly Storm, I'm watching you," he shouted above the clamor of snapping sounds and questions raining down on her. Kelly shot him a disparaging look while the man pointed to his eyes.

She hated threats and disliked the man with a passion, but she didn't have enough credible evidence to convince the court to grant her a restraining order.

"Rigor, why don't you shove your camera up your ass and beat it?" Jessica shouted, pushing Kelly inside the waiting limousine.

"Thanks." Kelly gave her friend a grateful smile and massaged her throbbing temple once the car started moving.

"Don't mention it." Jessica regarded her with obvious curiosity before she pushed the button to raise the divider between them and the driver. "What did you do last night?"

Here we go . . . "I invited Parker for dinner." What was the point of lying to Jessica? Kelly's friend possessed Superman's x-ray vision and Daredevil's radar sense. There was no hiding anything from her for very long.

Jessica's eyebrows shot up so high they almost disappeared into her hairline. "And?"

Kelly turned her face to the window to watch the throng of people trekking the city. She loved the cosmopolitan buzz of the Big Apple, but lately her fondness for the place had been replaced by a phobia of rushing fans and crazy paparazzi. "He spent the night." She didn't meet her friend's inquiring gaze and wasn't surprised when Jessica snorted.

"I could tell. Your bed looked like it had been hit by a cyclone." Jessica's tone turned somber. "What, may I ask, made you to go to bed with a stranger? I mean, you've seen the guy twice, and you know he's . . ."

Kelly whipped her head around in amazement. "Blind?"

Jessica seemed contrite, and Kelly felt bad for snapping at her.

"I'm sorry. I didn't mean to shout. I'm confused, Jess."

Jessica reached out and patted her on the knee. "It's okay. That was a bit callous of me. I just feel like he'd be another piece of baggage you don't need in your life right now, after the fiasco with Matthew." Her face clouded in anger.

"Parker is wonderful. He's independent and very capable. There is nothing the man can't do. His blindness is just another test he's going to overcome." Kelly had no idea why she was singing the praises of the man who'd evoked both happiness and terror within her at the same time.

Jessica gaped at her. Her green eyes sparkled with undisguised mischief. "If I didn't know you better, I'd say you're falling for this guy. What gives? What sets him apart? Why so sudden?"

Kelly shook her head. Who knew what she found most attractive? Was it Parker's body or his erotic lovemaking? "How do I explain instant attraction? I don't know. He's easy to talk to . . ."

"I guess this question is in order, then. Does he know who you are?" Jessica had always been the nagging conscience she'd refused to listen to and yet couldn't ignore.

Kelly shook her head. "I told him my name was Ann Sutton, and on the two occasions I visited his office, I was in heavy disguise."

"And you think you're being fair?" Jessica spoke without waiting for an answer. "What's more deceitful than that? The man is blind, and you masquerading under different names and costumes won't make it better. I sure hope you know what you're doing, Kels."

Kelly had no answer to offer. She gazed out the window and stayed silent.

It had been several weeks since Parker last saw Ann, and he felt like he was ready to scream. He had walked out of her hotel room like a pouting teenager whose parents had refused to let him borrow their car. Now, he felt like an ass and had no idea how to rectify his actions.

He'd tried to call the number she'd supplied in her record, but his call had gone straight to voicemail. With his aversion to leaving messages, he'd hung up and stewed for days. Now Parker was back in Los Angeles, and he had no other choice but to continue with his life pre-Ann. His perspective had undergone a slight shift, along with his plans. It seemed like he wanted Ann in his life. There was a burning deep inside him to get to know her more. He had no idea how she felt about him, except for her confessed fascination with him. Whatever it meant, he hoped it was enough to build on.

"You're being foolish, Parker." He threw his hands up in frustration and jammed them through his hair. A squeaking sound alerted him that he wasn't alone. He turned to the direction of the door. "Who's there?"

Her scent wafted around him before she answered. "It's me, boss," Webster answered, and the soft click of the door closing sounded. "Since when did you become foolish?"

"There you are." He smiled in her direction and motioned for her to take a seat. "I've been hoping to talk to you but haven't found the time."

"Sure, I'd love to talk, but before we do, you have Peggy Reese up in room two in five minutes. What's up, boss?"

He listened while she took the chair opposite his desk and sat down. The rustling of her clothes indicated she was comfortable. Parker leaned forward, resting his elbows on a bunch of papers sitting on his desk. He made a mental note of the room number.

"Okay, room two, Reese." He punched the talking clock to get the time. Four minutes. "I wanted to let you know that I'm releasing you from our . . . contract." Silence greeted him. Parker reached for Webster's hand. "Say something."

CHAPTER

SIX

"Webbie? What's wrong?"

Parker rose from his chair, walked around the desk, and sat on the side right in front of her.

"Um . . . you're letting me go?" Her voice was a mere squeak.

As far as he could remember, their contract had been pretty straightforward. Though nothing had been put into actual writing, their verbal agreement had been clear. Crystal. Should anyone decide to step away for any reason, no questions would be asked. With the lighting in the room, Parker tried to read her expression through the haze but couldn't.

"Yes . . ."

Another painful silence stretched before them. He got antsy. It never occurred to him that it would be difficult to break their contract. Webbie had been a good sport about their whole arrangement from the beginning, agreeing to keep their pact until either one of them found someone else. And though he had not known Ann that long, there was no mistaking he was drawn to her. Her sweet voice, laced with a pain he felt he understood, gave him an inexplicable connection to her and a desire to see more of her. He found himself wanting to peel back the layers one by one until he discovered the real woman behind the mystery.

"Care to explain?"

He jerked at Webster's clipped tone. "But . . . I thought we didn't need to give an explanation."

"Maybe *you* don't need an explanation, but I do," she said. "What am I going to do now?" There was a hint of sadness in her voice that made Parker feel like a heel.

"Webbie, I'm sorry. I know I'm about to leave you without a partner, but I don't feel it'll be fair to you if I'm going to pursue another woman."

"Why are you going after a woman you don't even know? And what makes you think she'll want you the way you want her? You're taking a big blind step here. Excuse the pun, but you aren't seeing things clearly enough."

He couldn't detect humor in her tone or a clear indication that she was offended with his sudden rescinding of their arrangement.

"That may be the case, but I'm willing to take a chance. I don't want to keep using you when it's obvious my interest lies elsewhere. Who knows? This might be a good time for you to find a suitable guy. You've been out of the dating circuit for some time now."

Webster fell silent, seeming to consider what he'd said. "I'm good as it is right now, and besides, I only switched since you won't let me dominate this arrangement." She gave a nervous laugh.

"Well, good luck on finding a man who will let you take charge. But as I was saying, I really hope you find someone you can have a long and meaningful relationship with. I really wish you the best, partner."

Parker tried to lighten things up and sound more upbeat, not wanting to show that he was wound up so tight inside. He couldn't believe he was going to put himself out there. Dating was one thing, but pursuing a woman in his present situation seemed to be a big hurdle.

"It's your call, boss. But know this—once I move on, there's no getting me back."

He rubbed his neck and sighed. Why was she making it difficult for him? Parker thought they'd made things perfectly clear. On impulse, he reached forward, hoping to feel her emotions, but then pulled back.

"May I?"

Her head bobbed up and down. Reaching forward, his deft fingers followed the lines of her lips. The crease on either side of her mouth was pulled downward. He felt a stab of guilt he couldn't explain.

Beneath his fingertips, Webster's mouth twitched upward, and her laughter filled the room. "Gotcha, boss!"

Parker tightened the grip on her face, not to hurt her but to make sure he understood her. He traced her laugh lines to the sound of her mirth echoing around him. After another moment, he let go, rose to his feet, and shoved his hands in his jean pockets.

Stunned, he glared in her direction. "You're such a jackass!"

Webster continued to laugh, oblivious to his growing irritation. He listened to her annoying cackle while he began forming a plan on how to get back at her. Strangling her with her favorite hot pink cuffs would be a good place to start.

"You . . . *ha ha ha* . . . thought I was going to give you a hard time, huh?" she asked once she'd contained her laughter.

"You're an idiot. Watch out, Webster. Payback's a bitch!"

Webster walked to the door, still laughing at him. "It's that Baba chick, isn't it?" She laughed and closed the door behind her without waiting for an answer.

"Yeah, yeah," he muttered, indignant.

Left alone in his office, he thought about how it had all started between him and Webster. It had been a good run for them. They'd been friends for some time, even before he had succumbed to the disease. Their sexual preferences had brought them together by necessity. An agreement had been put into place that respected their quests to find their own partners, while still enjoying their own brand of play.

In the beginning, he hadn't been sure if she was picking up on the signals he'd been sending her. It had been a silly gut feeling on his part that led him to see if his hunch was correct. One night, after a stressful day at the office, Webster had offered to help with the mountains of paperwork he had to go through. He'd ordered pizza and taken out a bottle wine to start the de-stressing process. One thing had led to another—the alcohol had reduced their inhibitions—and they'd started talking about kink. Looking back at it now, he'd almost fallen off his chair when he discovered they had the same desires in the bedroom.

It hadn't taken long for Parker to realize he needed to be in complete control during their role-play. Webster seemed to understand his insecurity without requiring a long and embarrassing explanation. It wasn't easy to admit he was afraid of losing control of everything in his life due to his blindness. He may not have been able to control things when interacting with people outside of the bedroom, but when they entered his domain, it was all about who was in charge.

Parker kept his rage at being the unlucky gene lottery winner under a tight lid. He'd made a silent vow never to show weakness. So far, he'd been successful, except for that one day a reporter had insinuated that he was bordering on being sexually inappropriate with his clients.

He'd gone home frustrated and had gotten carried away with the paddle during one of their role-plays. Although Webster had been a good sport about it, she'd caught a glimpse of the monster he tried so hard to hide. After that, he'd made a conscious effort to rein in his temper and had promised himself never to lose control again.

According to his talking watch, his next appointment would be waiting for him. As he made his way to the massage room, Parker was left with a niggling doubt. Pursuing a relationship with a woman he knew nothing about could very well be suicide on his part. He tried to push his fears away. No one knew how insecure he was since his blindness had taken over his life. Parker put up a façade, poised and self-assured, in hopes of masking the terror he felt inside. He projected an image of a man with confidence, even if deep down he often struggled with doubts. After Rebecca, his girlfriend of two years, had left at the onset of his disease, he'd taken care not to let himself be vulnerable again. A man could only handle so much rejection, and he'd had his fair share of pain.

He'd maintained a relationship with Webster, thinking he could handle the sexual experience without needing the emotional ties that went with it. Then Ann had come along. What was it about her that made him set aside his fears without giving it a second thought? The question had been rolling around in his head for several days. Was it the vulnerability he sensed in her? Or the fact that she seemed just as lost as he was? Wasn't there a saying that 'misery loves company'? If that were true, then he'd met the woman he'd been looking for.

Kelly woke with a start, disoriented and hearing the echo of her scream. She sat up, still shivering from the nightmare and drenched in sweat, her face wet from crying. Sweeping her gaze over the unfamiliar surroundings, she remembered where she was—her hotel room in Milan. Her heart rate began to slow to its normal pace while she struggled to regulate her breathing.

The nightmare still lingered. She covered her face with her hands and sobbed. The memories were as vivid as if she were watching herself on a big screen—every single detail in full color and slow motion, so clear and heartbreaking.

It had been a gloomy, fall morning. The gray clouds had hung oppressively in the sky, intensifying the somber emotions that surrounded her. Her dress was of simple lace, as befitted the occasion. Her sister, Debbie, and her husband, Joe, Jessica, and several of her closest friends were gathered around the burial site.

Everything around her was white—everyone's clothes and even the tiny roses she'd requested. White, the color of purity, was fitting for a chaste soul, and that was how she wanted to remember her child. When they lowered the coffin into the ground, her cries grew louder and more intense, as if her heart were being torn in two and then shredded to pieces.

Even though it had been a year, she still hadn't gotten over her loss. That all-too-familiar feeling of guilt and heartbreak forced its way back into her soul, making her relive the past year. Matthew had been filming out of town when she'd received the good news. They had decided to start a family even before getting married. Although they'd been together for two years, just like every other relationship, they had their own set of challenges, but they were in love—or so she'd thought. Starting a family hadn't been in the forefront of their plans, since their individual careers demanded so much of their time, but the idea hadn't been an unwelcome one. Belonging to a small family that consisted of her parents and her sister, Kelly had always dreamed of having a big brood of her own, so when she'd found out she was carrying a child, she'd taken the first flight out of LA to the hotel in New Mexico where Matthew had been staying while filming a western movie.

Armed with a bottle of apple cider for their celebratory drink, she'd decided to surprise him with the exciting news. They had on occasion surprised each other in the past, so it wasn't something she hadn't done before. What she hadn't expected was to catch him in bed with another woman.

As much as she would have loved to stay with him, rumors had been flying about his philandering ways throughout their relationship. The gossip, in her opinion, had been unfounded in the beginning, so she'd chosen to ignore the earlier signs until she'd seen him humping a woman with her own two eyes.

Matthew never found out about her pregnancy. No one knew about her condition except Jessica, her sister Debbie, and Dave, her publicist. With their urging and support, she'd taken a hiatus, leaving everyone to speculate that the breakup was the main reason for her disappearance. She'd wanted a peaceful pregnancy and a chance to recover way from public scrutiny.

Turning on the light, she glanced at the clock on her nightstand. It was always the same dream that plagued her. As upsetting as it was, sometimes it comforted her. In that short moment, she felt real.

Kelly had been in her eighth month of pregnancy when she'd noticed that the baby hadn't moved for some time. The tumbling and kicking had disappeared. After conferring with her doctor, she went in for a quick checkup. Nothing had prepared her for the shocking news that followed.

Everything had happened so fast. She was whisked into the emergency room when the ultrasound failed to register a heartbeat, and labor was induced, only to deliver a stillborn baby. Kelly had cradled her dead child in her arms before she was taken away.

A lump formed in Kelly's throat while errant tears trickled down her cheeks. She brushed them away. She'd only had a few minutes to hold her daughter—a few measly minutes, and then a lifetime of misery. What had she done wrong? The question still haunted her even after a year.

However, life as she'd known it had changed. Gone was the trusting Kelly; she vowed never to get involved with anyone, keeping herself out of reach. But why did it seem like her resolve was about to break? What was it about Parker that drew her to him and made her want to try her luck with a man again?

Shaking the jarring dream away, she wiped her tears and began her morning preparations for another long day of promotions and photo shoots.

Kelly chose a crisp, dark brown blazer over faded jeans, along with some complementary jewelry, and she was ready to go. She was meeting Damiano, the Gucci representative, in the hotel lobby. They made it a point to get together over a cup of coffee every time Kelly was in town and always before any business was conducted. As a result, they'd grown very close over the last few months.

He smiled and opened his arms wide for her. *"Buongiorno, mia bella ragazza!"*

Kelly rushed into his welcoming embrace and felt the warmth she wished was Parker's. She held on a moment longer than necessary.

"Good morning, darling." She pulled back and took an appraising look at his crisp beige suit. *"Il tuo vestito è stupendo."*

Damiano laughed and pulled her to the lobby exit. "Your Italian is getting better, sweet cakes. Thank you. My baby boy chose it for me." He rolled his eyes.

"He chose very well." Kelly looped her arm through his. They emerged from the lobby to find a sea of paparazzi and fans waiting for them. She groaned inwardly. Taking a deep breath, she plastered on a dazzling smile and waved.

"I love you, Kelly!"

"Hearts Afire will be your Oscar ticket."

"I can't wait for your new film. Kelly! We love you."

She kept waving and acknowledging their praise and encouragement. Pictures were taken, blinding flashes snapped in her eyes, but Kelly continued smiling until she reached the open passenger door. Then she heard it.

"Got over Matthew yet? Isn't his wife pregnant? How do you feel about it?"

The pap smiled with forced sweetness, as if he were just asking some innocent, ordinary question.

Kelly shrugged and waved him away without answering.

Once they were in the privacy of the car, Damiano patted her hand. "Don't worry about those, um . . . how do you Americans say it again?

Assholes?" He laughed at his own joke, and Kelly joined in.

"Yes, that's what most of them are." She took a deep breath, intent on forgetting what she'd just heard. She and Matthew were through. *More power to him!*

"Oh, darling! You're the media's sweetheart, and the public adores you. Don't let a few idiots ruin your day."

"*Grazie, tesoro.* Now, let's grab a latte and some *dolci* before the torture begins."

The week dragged on at a lumbering pace for Parker. Too many times, his mind wandered to Ann. Would he ever see her again? Without a valid phone number or any other verified information, he had no means of contacting her. Waiting would be the key, and patience wasn't a virtue he had an abundance of these days. He was like a junkie who needed a quick hit. She was suddenly the air he needed to breathe. Her presence was intoxicating, and he longed to hear her voice.

How had she managed to crawl under his skin and dismantle his guarded self-control? In his mind's eye, Ann was vulnerable and lost. If he based his opinion on their two meetings when she'd ended up in tears, he'd say she was carrying some heavy emotional burdens. What a pair they made. His lack of vision placed him at a physical disadvantage, but this was one aspect he refused to give in to. Parker planned to make the most of what he had in life, and that included getting to know the woman whose gentleness had rocked his world.

After the last client of the day had left, Parker returned to his office and pulled out his cell phone. He listened to the voice announce three text messages. Two were from his mother inviting him and Cork to drop by for a barbecue that weekend. Another was from an unknown number. Parker felt a shot of excitement as he listened.

Parker, this is Ann. I'm so sorry for how it ended the last time we were together.

That was the extent of the message, and it gave nothing away. Not how she felt—besides feeling bad about how their night had ended—or where she was or how he could find her. With the unknown number, he was back to where he'd been before—lost without answers and feeling sick to his stomach. How could he have let someone he hardly knew walk into his life and crack the rigid walls he'd built around himself?

Groaning, Parker pressed a speed dial code and waited. "Cork, it's Friday night. Got any plans?"

It came as a surprise when his brother said his schedule was clear that afternoon. Like clockwork, Cork stayed with Parker from the morning until he was driven home from work, and he would work with the city league children afterward.

At their prearranged time, Parker met up with his coworkers at the bar they all frequented, which was one block away from his massage parlor. The loud voices of the guys suggested they were already having happy hour.

"Parker, over here," Andy hollered from end of the bar.

From what little he could recognize from their blurry shapes, Cork was seated next to the bar with Andy and Mark, his two other massage therapists. It hadn't been planned when all the masseuses they hired had been deemed "the hottest males with magical hands." From Webbie's vivid descriptions, Andy, dark-haired and tall, and Mark, a buff blonde with a quick wit, were good-looking and full of hot masculine pride. He smiled at the colorful picture Webbie had painted and took her word for it.

The place was already teeming with activity, the usual after-work patrons wanting to jumpstart the weekend. Friday nights were crowded and busy, but the bar owner had always given Parker and his buddies a special seat whenever they swung by.

They bumped fists and slapped hands before he took a seat between Andy and Cork. The music overhead drowned out any possibility of quiet conversation, so he had to shout above the noise.

"Cork, Mom called. She wants us to come by on Sunday afternoon for a barbecue. Are you available?" he yelled.

Cork appeared to shrug, but Parker waited for a verbal response. His brother remained unfazed by his impairment, which made him feel better. He didn't tiptoe around Parker like others sometimes did. Cork never cleared the path for him but instead forced Parker to depend on himself to find the pitfalls or sense danger. His younger brother had made his transition from the sighted world to his new reality a bit more bearable by treating him the same way, and Parker was thankful for that.

"I'm . . . going out that day. Maybe I should call Mom to see if she'd mind switching the barbecue to tomorrow." His brother had always been awkward, saying very little and admitting even less.

Andy chuckled from Parker's right. "If I didn't know any better, I'd think your baby bro has a date."

"Is that right, Corky?" he teased, using the nickname he'd christened his brother with when they were younger—a name Cork hated.

Cork shrugged again, and the sound of his glass scraped the surface of the table. He chugged his usual Sam Adams beer until it was gone. Parker didn't prod, and the conversation moved to safer ground, at least as far as Cork was concerned.

The LA team was playing for the Stanley Cup, and the bar was more crowded than usual. Parker listened to the play-by-play from the announcer to follow the game. Time flew for them, and by the time they made their way out of the bar, it was close to eleven.

"Talk about happy hour," Mark mumbled while they walked to the parking lot adjacent to their building.

Parker walked a step behind the guys, as was his usual practice when he hung out with them. This had more to do with safety than anything else. Since he didn't use a walking stick or a guide dog, this helped him gauge the surface of the pavement, the dips and bumps.

He heard the jingling of keys from his companions when they got closer to their parking spot. They stopped next to what seemed to be a dark stretch limousine that was blocking their cars.

"What's up?" Parker asked, squinting to see as much as he could in the darkness.

"There's a limousine blocking our cars," Andy said. "Let me see what's going on. For Christ's sake, there are a hundred spots available now. Why would the idiot double park?"

Parker put a hand on his employee's shoulder to stop him. "Let me find out what's up." *Why are they assuming something is wrong?*

Andy didn't object, so he felt his way around the vehicle until he reached the driver's window. He tapped on the glass twice, and the window rolled down in an instant.

The person on the driver's side spoke before he had a chance to ask. "Sir, Ms. Ann Sutton sent me here to pick you up. She's flying in as we speak, and I am to take you to meet her for dinner and drinks."

"Ann sent you?"

His heart spiked, and he felt heat rushing to his face. The tone of the man who'd spoken sounded professional enough, so when Parker heard the click of the handle, he stepped aside to allow the door to open.

"Yes, sir. Here's my business card. It has the address and phone number of the company who employs me. I was told to give you one and another one to your brother, so he knows who is to be held accountable if there is any doubt with regards to your safety. I'm also instructed to drive you home right after."

A card was pressed into his palm. Parker smirked at the thought that flashed through his mind. *What good will a card do me if I can't read it?* He took the business cards to avoid further explanation and walked around the car to where Cork and the guys were waiting for him, most likely curious as to what was going on.

"Cork, go ahead. I have a ride home." He didn't bother giving one of the cards to his brother.

"Who's that guy? What's going on?" Cork asked.

Parker hated hearing the concern in his brother's voice. He was a capable, grown man, but still he felt compelled to put his worry to rest. Putting an arm around Cork's shoulder, he tried to reassure him.

"It's all good, Corky. I got this. I'll call if anything comes up. Call Mom if you want to reschedule the barbecue. I'll need a ride, so let me know if plans are changing." Cork hesitated, but Parker didn't give him a chance to speak. He turned to Andy and Mark. "See you on Monday, guys. Drive safe." After they exchanged slaps and fist bumps, he slid into the backseat of the limo.

Parker stayed quiet during the first few minutes of the ride. He had no idea where they were headed. They weren't going very fast, and judging by the stop-and-go traffic, he figured they were taking the surface streets. If he had to guess, he'd say they were moving away from Beverly Hills, based on how long they had been traveling.

The drone of the limousine's engine lulled him while he pondered the questions in his head. He was still unable to grasp the rationale behind Ann's peculiar approach. Why couldn't she just call him and ask like a normal person? What was behind the thick veil of mystery? After a few frustrated moments, Parker gave up trying to figure it out. He had more questions than answers.

"So where are you supposed to take me?" he asked, trailing his fingers along the plush leather seats.

"To a cottage in Santa Monica, sir."

"Have you been driving Ms. Sutton a lot?" Sneaky question, but he'd take any information he could get.

"No, sir. I have no idea who Ms. Sutton is. My boss is the one who takes the calls, and I'm just given the directions."

The straightforward answer led him nowhere. Parker decided to sit back and just enjoy the jazz music coming from the speakers instead of grilling the driver for information. After a few more minutes, the car came to a stop. He tapped his watch for the time—close to midnight.

The passenger door opened, and Parker slid out of the car. The scent of salty air was strong, and in the distance, he heard the lapping waves. They had to be less than a quarter mile away from the beach, if his estimation was correct. The night seemed clear, the wind docile. He sniffed a couple of times while he tried to recover his equilibrium.

"Follow me this way, sir."

They walked slowly while he followed the hazy form before him to a graveled path lit with candles.

"Two steps up," the driver directed.

When they got to the door, the man pressed a key into Parker's palm and closed his fingers around it.

"Here's the key to the door. I will be waiting for you in the car, however long it takes." After giving him what Parker guessed was a salute, the driver left, leaving him standing alone in front of the quaint, wooden door.

So much secrecy surrounded this Ann Sutton. Now Parker's interest was more than piqued. After feeling for the keyhole, he inserted the key and hesitantly pushed open the door. The house held a floral scent, and a soft glow filled his vision everywhere he turned. Candles lined the floor. After closing the front door, he followed the lit trail with slow and careful steps.

"Hello?"

"I'm in here, Parker." Ann's voice came from the direction where he guessed the candles would lead him. He tapped what he thought was a bedroom door before opening.

"Ann?"

"Are you hungry?"

Warm hands circled his waist from behind. Operating on instinct, he turned around and placed his hands on her shoulders to get his bearings. She'd startled him, but he wasn't about to let her know how he despised being caught off guard. Parker felt her bare skin, and he stepped back. *Is she naked already?* A shudder spread through his body and pulsated down to his cock at the picture he drew in his mind. He groaned. Just as quick, he was sporting a massive woody that would have put a baseball bat to shame.

"Yes," he answered before running a hand along her face and touching her lips. "Actually, I'm starved."

CHAPTER SEVEN

"Starved?" Kelly asked, using her most seductive voice while she linked her hands behind his neck to pull him down for a kiss.

Parker nodded. He grasped her waist with both hands and lifted her. She wrapped her legs around him, and they ended up on the bed without breaking the kiss.

"What am I eating?" Parker drawled after they surfaced for air.

"Something delectable and mouthwatering, but before I feed you, I want to tell you something." She watched his brows crease into a frown.

"What is it?"

"I feel bad about how our night ended in New York. I didn't mean to sound curt—there are things I'm not ready to talk about."

Parker seemed to consider her words before he nodded. "I feel bad about the way it ended, too. I hope we can get over my little temper tantrum." He picked up her hand and kissed it.

This was going all wrong. Parker had done nothing to offend her. Kelly, on the other hand, had been unwilling to answer his simple questions. They were the type of questions that wouldn't bother a regular person. Someone who wasn't hiding something.

"I'm hoping for the same thing—that's why I wanted to make it up to you. How about you shower while I get things ready? You smell like you've had enough to drink." Kelly nibbled on Parker's lip before pulling at his arm until he stood. He let her tug him to the bathroom. "Here's the shower." She guided his hand to the glass door. "The towel is right here, and the sink is directly opposite. There's a robe hanging on the door for you. Is ten minutes enough?"

Parker turned and licked his lips. A devilish grin revealed the crinkles in the corners of his eyes. "I can finish in three."

"I'll be ready in *ten*. You know where the bed is."

Kelly stood on tiptoe and kissed him again before stepping back. Parker moaned, reaching for her when she closed the door behind her. She tied her hair into a quick bun on top of her head and heard the sound of running water before she padded down the candlelit hallway to the kitchen.

She loved this cottage. It had been one of those purchases made on a whim, a beachfront property she'd snagged with her first earnings from acting. This had been her home when she'd started her trek up Hollywood's who's-who list. By the time she'd moved into her Brentwood estate, the property had doubled in value, so she'd decided to keep it. *It sure comes in handy now*, Kelly thought, smiling to herself.

Opening the Sub-Zero refrigerator, she pulled out the items she'd had one of the girls buy for her and placed them all on the tray. Kelly picked up some napkins from the counter and hurried back to the room. *Seven minutes left.* Her heart pounded to the beat of her movements while she climbed on the spindle bed and placed the tray next to her. Before she got to work, she made sure that a condom and the cuff keys were lying on top of the nightstand so it would be easy for Parker to access them. Then Kelly placed the metal cuffs she'd purchased just for the occasion by her side. A thrill raced through her body at the sight of them.

It was amazing how much she'd learned about Parker from that one article. Though she hated the fact that one of his ex-girlfriends had decided to take a shot at five minutes of fame, she'd found out enough about his humor in the bedroom and his penchant for role-play. Kelly had to admit curiosity had won out, and she was game to play for Parker. This man's approach to life, head-on and with no regret, reminded her of the person she'd once been.

Kelly glanced at the digital clock. *Four minutes left.* She had to hurry. Methodically, she arranged Parker's meal on her body. She worked for the next three minutes until she heard the shower turn off. Lying down, she closed her eyes and took several calming breaths. She wanted to do this for him and had been planning it even before she left New York.

At last, she watched him walk out of the bathroom, a trail of steam following in his wake. The faint glow of the candles cast an erotic shadow on his face. Parker walked with measured steps to the bed, his muscles rippling as he moved, his cock hanging with pride before him.

"Ann?"

Parker stopped at the side of the bed and tilted his head up when he caught the scent of the meal she had waiting for him.

"Your food is ready, my dear Emperor."

He inclined his head as if he was digesting what she had said. "Ann? Are you messing with me?" he asked in disbelief.

"My Tenno, your feast awaits you. If you would be kind enough to step forward and take this from me, I'm at your service, and I will walk you through your meal as we go along." She jiggled the cuffs for him to hear.

Parker looked up and hesitated. "Are you aware of what you're doing?"

"Yes. You can tell me if it's up to par—baby steps. If you're okay with that, then I'm all yours."

Though she still had a few reservations about the whole process, Kelly wanted to get to know him more, and that was enough reason to try it. At this point, she would climb Mount Kilimanjaro if he asked her to; she hoped he wouldn't find her efforts silly and awkward.

Taking a step forward, he closed his hands over hers and felt the metal cuffs she was holding. "You're going all out on me here, my sweet little Ann. Now tell me, what is your safeword?"

"Shogun." She made sure he heard her, despite the distraction of her heartbeat as it pounded against her chest. "There are spindles on either side of the bed. You can start with my right hand."

While Parker felt his way through the process, she grabbed the can resting next to her, shook it, and spread a generous amount on her chest.

"Mmm, is that what I think it is?" Parker's head whipped around to follow the sound.

"You'll find out soon enough." She presented her other arm to him. He held her wrist before clasping the cuff with a click. Once her hands were fastened and secured, Kelly spread her legs even wider, loving the softness of the silk sheets against her skin. "You're to start at the foot of the bed. Stay in the center, between my legs."

As Parker trailed his fingers along the side of the bed for guidance, her excitement grew and her center throbbed. When he reached the foot of the bed, she began her planned seduction.

"The chopsticks are between my legs if you care to use them, my dear Emperor." Parker climbed onto the bed, running his fingers over her feet and feeling his way up. He tossed the chopsticks on the floor and waited for her. "Picture my thighs as sushi boats. On the left one, you'll find two Hamachi sashimi laid out like fallen dominoes. Next to it is a dab of wasabi and ginger. On my belly, you'll find a tuna roll. On my right thigh, there are Toro sashimi with wasabi and ginger. Up top is a cucumber roll. Dessert will follow when you're done."

"You're full of surprises, my Empress. I don't think I can keep up with you." His eyes gleamed with enthusiasm. Kelly shuddered as soon as Parker lowered his mouth to skim along her left leg. She strained to raise her head so she could watch him. Taking his sweet time, Parker's seduction began with his tongue moving in a slow, languorous pattern across her thigh, creating ripples of goose chills wherever he touched her. He picked up each sashimi with teasing precision. After his first swallow, he licked the surface where the food had rested. Kelly's responding groans drew a wicked smile from him. He worked his way up, tasting, chewing, and enjoying her offerings. Before he moved to her other thigh, Parker grazed his lips across her nub, teasing and causing her to quiver.

She moaned, feeling the rapid pulsing in her core and imagining him between her legs. Staying still was proving to be difficult because Parker made sure his tongue elicited a visceral response.

By the time he'd finished eating from her right thigh, she was exploding in orgasmic bliss and could barely think straight. All she felt was his tongue caressing and playing with her. Kelly screamed in agonizing joy when he sucked at her clit and lapped at her folds.

"You're going to kill me, your Imperial Highness!"

"No . . . I'm eating you alive." Parker looked up and licked his lips, seducing her even more. "I'm ready for dessert."

"Would you like a drink of water? Or perhaps *saké?*"

Parker shook his head. "I want something sweet."

"Taste your way up."

Still basking from her orgasm, Kelly crossed her legs, savoring the pleasurable tugging in the pit of her stomach. Who would have thought Mr. Davis had so many tricks up his sleeve? Parker straddled her and skimmed his lips over her nether region, grazing her belly button with his tongue before trailing upward and licking the whipped cream from her skin. When he arrived at her breasts, he sniffed long and hard.

"Strawberries. How did you know I liked them?"

"I didn't. It was a lucky guess."

"You did well, Ann. After I eat, I will show you how I properly thank a woman."

Parker's promise sent her reeling with anticipation. Had she done well? The whole idea had scared her in the beginning. Jessica had called her a fool, but Kelly had never wanted a man like she wanted him. He was potent, a therapeutic drug she couldn't do without, and she was powerless to stay away. She had such wicked dreams about him, and no matter how much she tried to deny her attraction, her body wasn't listening.

Parker curled his lips into a knowing smile just before he began nipping at the rich cream covering her breast. With his hands, he traced her curves and rubbed her heated skin. He circled, trailing his tongue slowly along her chest, climbing up to her jaw to get to her mouth, offering the sweetness to her. With eagerness, Kelly accepted his offering with her tongue before sinking back into the mattress. He continued his assault on her breast until all but one slice of strawberry was left. Picking up the fruit with his teeth, he presented it to her, and she took it eagerly.

He straightened and touched her face. "Who do I have to thank for the lovely dinner?"

"Matsuhisa of Beverly Hills."

"Now it's my turn to give *you* pleasure."

"But you have given me pleasure."

"Give me the key to the cuffs, and not a word from you. All you have to remember is your safeword."

"It's on top of the nightstand, next to the condom." She watched while he retrieved the key. "Can I ask a question?"

"Sure."

"What do you expect from me at this moment?"

Parker smiled, seeming to understand her hesitation. "I expect you to do what I say so that I can do my thing. It's important for me to know that you're enjoying yourself within the boundaries of our exploits here. I'll lead, and you'll follow."

"Okay," she said.

"And remember, no questions. You only speak if you're uncomfortable with my commands. This is all about us having fun together."

It sounded like a promise.

After Parker released her binding, he gave her wrists a brief massage, kissing the spot where the cuffs had held her. Kelly wanted to burst into tears. His gentleness was so overwhelming, but the last time she'd cried had ended in disaster, so she reined in her emotions.

He slid out of bed and scooped her up as if she weighed nothing. Kelly wound her arms around his neck.

"Where are you taking me?" she asked.

"I don't want you to speak until I say you can."

Kelly remembered what he'd said. So she clamped her mouth shut and let him take her to the heaven he'd promised.

Parker carried her with confidence toward the bathroom and kicked the door open with his foot, depositing her on the bathroom counter while he felt his way back to the shower. He turned on the nozzle and tested the water until he was satisfied with the temperature.

"Come here," he commanded, reaching for her hand.

Kelly jumped down from the counter and almost skipped to him, unable to contain her excitement. Thank God he couldn't see her or else he might think her girlish. Placing her hand in his, she let him lead her inside the shower. Parker grinned when she wrapped her arms around his waist while they enjoyed the warm spray of water overhead. The mist swirling around them was a deliberate invitation, but she had to wait for him to tell her what he wanted.

He drew her closer to him as the invigorating water caressed their skin. Parker filled his hand with liquid bath gel and began lathering her chest, his hands working their magic until he reached her legs, where he took great care rubbing her feet, one at a time. Then he began rinsing her, lingering between her thighs and leaving her helpless, whimpering, and wanting more.

He straightened, his body rubbing against hers. "Your skin feels like velvet. I could touch you forever," he murmured.

Seeming satisfied with the rinse job, he pushed her against the tiles and caressed the contours of her body as his mouth closed in.

The only thing Kelly could do to keep from screaming was to run her fingers through his hair, clutching with impatience. All she wanted was him inside her. He continued to stroke her nub and toyed with her taut breasts, igniting the desire in her veins.

Afterward, Parker lifted her until their faces were touching. She hitched her legs around his waist and thrilled at the feel of her body pressed against his. It was enough to shatter her waning self-control.

"I'm dying to make love to you," he said, followed by a soft sigh.

She wanted to answer, but remembered his order. He nibbled on her earlobe, eliciting another long shudder from her. He trailed tender, little kisses along her neck. Kelly arched backward to accommodate him while he explored and ground her body against his, slow and deliberate. This earned her a rumble deep from within his chest. His guttural voice was enough to unravel her.

"You want me to take you now?" Parker asked, as if reading her mind.

Kelly grabbed his hair in response and willed him to focus his mouth on hers. They kissed with hunger and impatience, with his erection punching her skin, tight and hard. She ached to touch him. Instead, she buried her fingers in his wet hair. Water cascaded around them while their kiss grew more intense. When they pulled apart, he set her back on her feet and turned off the water.

"Come with me." Parker took her hand, and they stepped out of the shower. Still dripping wet, he led her over to the toilet and lowered the lid. "Sit on me."

Kelly no longer had any inhibitions. She gingerly sat on top of him, allowing his weapon to enter her. And then she jumped.

"We're not protected."

Parker groaned in frustration. "You have ten seconds to get it before this rocket takes off."

Kelly sprinted back to the bedroom, her boobs bouncing around and water trickling to the floor as she went. She returned within the allotted ten seconds, ripping the foil and pressing it into his hand.

"Good girl. Now arm the missile." Parker smiled in a mischievous way and handed the condom back to her.

"Yes, sir."

She worked with fevered speed, gripping his erection and securing the rubber in one fluid motion. His groan made her smile.

"Sit on me," he ordered.

This time, he held her by the waist with her back resting against his stomach. Parker guided his cock to her entrance, and then held back while her walls adjusted to the intrusion. She hissed, feeling pain intermingled with pleasure. When he filled her, he moved her hips in a grinding motion, making sure she felt him inside her. Kelly moaned and dug her fingers into his thighs.

"Go ahead. You can touch me."

The order was what she'd been waiting for. Raring to go, she bent forward and slid her hands down to the base of his penis to stroke his balls. He shivered with undisguised satisfaction and rained kisses on the back of her neck, pushing her closer to the edge. As if he knew she was close to reaching her peak, he gripped her waist tighter and pumped harder. The exquisite sound they created together was a lovely music she'd never forget. Their bodies pounded as one in rhythmic synchronicity—in tune with each other.

"Scream for me, Ann. Come!" It was as if her body was already trained to respond to his command; she clenched, her walls tightened, and she burst into ecstasy with a scream. Parker kept pounding into her for several moments before he grunted and convulsed as his release gushed out, his fingers digging into her skin. Kelly kept twisting and moving her hips in circles until he relaxed and wrapped his arms around her.

"Sweet . . ." he murmured.

Kelly rested her back against his chest, and they stayed that way for some time before either one of them gathered the strength to move.

"Thank you, Parker." Satisfied, she closed her eyes.

After they'd cleaned up, they went back to bed, content to hold each other. Kelly rested her head on his chest, loving the feel of his strong arms around her.

"How did you know?" he asked several minutes later.

She propped her chin on Parker's chest. "I had no idea, at first, but I kept thinking about it the entire time we were together that night. After you left, my curiosity won, and I scoured the Internet for answers. I read a particular article from one of your ex . . . um . . . a past girlfriend."

His jaw muscles clenched. "And how do you feel about it?"

Parker traced his fingers along her back, and she arched her body in response to his gentle touch, feeling the heat rising in her once more.

"I'm not sure. It's different. I don't know that much about it, but I want to be with you, so I'm willing to give it a try if you're willing to show me. I had no idea how my body would respond. It was amazing. Was it too silly, Parker? Were you disappointed?" Kelly thumbed his nipple until he moaned.

"Don't tease me. I don't tire easily." He smiled, and then turned to watch her, his eyes moving, searching. "It's not for everyone, this *lifestyle*, but there's no need to doubt yourself. It shows your daring personality and need to please. I find that endearing, and I'm touched by your effort. I'll let you be who you are, because no two couples practice this way of life the same way. We'll learn from each other and find 'our style' together."

Kelly couldn't answer. He was talking as if he wanted her for the long haul. Although she'd enjoyed every minute of it, she still wondered if she had what it took to be the designated follower. She wanted to be, if it meant being with him, but she was still unsure.

"Am I going to see you again?" Parker asked.

"I can't make promises, but I'll call you when I'm in town. You have my number, so anytime you want to talk to me, just leave me a voicemail, and I'll call you back as soon as I can."

His expression soured for a moment before he smiled again. "I guess I'll just have to wait for your call, then."

She leaned forward and captured his mouth with hers.

"I promise I'll call."

Parker fell asleep right after, but rest didn't come so quickly for her. While she lay beside him, she couldn't help feeling guilty for hiding her identity from him. There was no doubt the man fascinated her. He'd been gentle, despite the control he'd exhibited in the bedroom, but there was something about his tender touch and unspoken sentiments that made her want to know more. It made Kelly wonder if it were possible to trust another man again.

As strange as it seemed, her vow to stay away from any type of relationship had been disregarded after their first night together. With her chaotic life, she needed order, and in Parker's arms, she felt secure and peaceful. When she was with him, she forgot the misery of being alone, of being lost and afraid. Granted, this was only their third meeting, but Parker, in his own way, had given her a glimpse of how life could still be normal and safe. Celebrity life gave her all the glitter and wealth any woman could ever ask for, but it also placed her up on a lofty pedestal where she felt the need to hide her misery and tears. The cameras only saw her smile, not her true feelings; those she kept hidden from judgment.

She'd be a hypocrite if she denied that she enjoyed her celebrity status, but the glitz and glamour came at a price. Existing under a microscope left a lot to be desired. All Kelly longed for now was a moment of peace from time to time. It wasn't too much to ask. This night with Parker had been heaven, but how long could it last? The very minute the media found out about him, he'd be under that microscope with her, guarding his every move and watching every word that came out of his mouth. Would he still want to be with her after discovering what she had to offer? Would he choose another woman over her just like Matthew had?

Kelly snuggled closer to Parker, fearing the time when he'd tell her that he couldn't handle being with her. Closing her eyes, she wished for the courage to let him in and reveal her true identity. She hoped he would still look at her the same way after realizing his quiet life would soon be over.

❧

Sleep came fast, but within a few hours, Parker woke up with the urge for release, his dreams of Ann fueling the fire once again. Still wrapped around her like a blanket, he trailed his fingers along her body. Ann mumbled incoherent words while his hands explored every glorious arc of her body. She was perfect—too perfect.

He wasn't one to subject himself to crippling doubts, but the woman lying next to him raised some questions that he couldn't ignore. What was she doing with a man like him when she could have anyone she wanted? Even without the benefit of sight, she felt beautiful to him. Her curves said as much, and her ample breasts told him the same thing. Her skin felt like expensive velvet beneath his fingers, and her scent was to die for. Was he just a novelty for her? Someone she wanted at the moment and would later grow tired of, just like Rebecca had? He gritted his teeth at the thought. God, his questions would kill him.

Parker had never been a pussy, but this woman was making him less confident than usual. He wanted her—there was no doubt about it. But what he wanted was to know how she felt about *him,* the man, and not the persona that the press portrayed or the stigma associated with his blindness.

"Parker?" Ann mumbled, soundly sleepy.

"Yeah?" He traced his fingertips along her face without knowing what he was searching for.

"What are you thinking?"

He dithered, unsure of how to answer. "I'm just thinking about how I can see you more often. I don't think this 'once every two weeks or so' is going to work for me."

"I'm sorry, but my schedule is a little tight. Would a phone call every day work?"

Parker sighed. Since when had he turned into a Needy Nancy? "I'll take what I can get."

"Can I ask you one favor?" Ann lifted her face closer, and he could almost see its contours.

"Sure."

"Can you make love to me again?"

He smiled and felt the jackhammer in him come alive. "You don't even have to ask twice."

CHAPTER EIGHT

When Parker awoke, he had no idea of the time. The room was bathed in light as far as he could see. If his guess was correct, sunlight was streaming in through the glass doors that led straight to the beach. The steady sound of lapping waves and crying seagulls was a nice change from the usual sound of kids riding their bikes in his neighborhood. His three-bedroom townhouse sat in a convenient but busy enclave. Its proximity to the supermarket, dry-cleaners, theater, and bank made it easy for him to live independently.

Parker had no idea where his clothes were—they could be anywhere in the room. He should get up to check his phone for messages, and maybe check the time, too. By the intensity of the light coming from the windows, it had to be around ten or eleven. His stomach growled, establishing the fact that his guess was most likely accurate. He tried to move, but Ann's body was draped across him.

And what do you know? His hand was cupping her breast, staking ownership. Parker smiled, enjoying the feel of her against him and the way their bodies melded together as if it was the most natural thing in the world. He could get used to waking up next to her every morning.

Ann raked her hand across his chest, and then moved it toward his dick, her fingers caressing his skin. She inched closer, igniting the sleeping flame within him. "Are you awake?" Traces of sleep colored her tone.

"Yes, you?" Shifting to face her, he slipped an arm underneath her head to cradle her closer.

"Um . . . hmm . . ."

"Got plans today?"

"Yeah . . . I'm planning on going horseback riding," she answered with a hint of mischief in her voice.

"Sounds like fun."

Parker lifted her chin and focused on her face, trying to gauge her mood. Last night had been great, even though he knew very little about the woman next to him, except for a few tidbits of information she had shared. He was literally groping in the dark, trying to learn some things about her.

"Yep . . . in fact, I'm going to start now." Ann sat up and climbed on top of him, straddling his waist, her red hair covering her face. "Giddyap horsey." She slapped his thigh.

Parker chuckled and grabbed her waist. "You're full of energy—you keep going and going and going." He pulled her down until she was lying horizontal on top of him. His shaft twitched, awakened. "Can you feel that, sweetheart?" Her teasing had made him harder. He pressed his erection to her center, and her body bucked rodeo-style.

"Oh yeah," she answered as she gyrated, her moist hub rubbing and leaving kisses on his sensitive skin.

"You're going to kill me."

Ann continued moving, eliciting roguish pleasures in him. It took a tremendous amount of self-control to rein in the raging inferno she'd started. With their faces close enough to touch, he could almost see her, see that she was gazing down at him as she continued to "ride" him.

"I would love to pleasure you again, but we need to eat." He kissed her, slipping his tongue into her mouth and lapping hers several times. When she responded with a moan, Parker touched his forehead to hers. "Let's do something else, like talk and try to learn more about each other. As much as I enjoy making love to you, there are other things I look for in a relationship." He laughed. "I know it's a bit odd—most people think men have insatiable sexual appetites, right?

"Uh-huh."

"I'm afraid I'm losing ground here. I don't want you to think I'm some sort of perverted control freak. The bedroom is the only place I intend to practice more power over you. It's what I need so I can feel like I still have a say in my own life."

Parker felt her stiffen.

"And you think that you'll find gratification by controlling me in the bedroom?" Ann's voice held a hint of defiance.

He held her face and gazed in the general direction of her eyes. "Don't misunderstand me. I'm just talking about the bedroom. Out there, it's a different story. I can't do much if we're out there, because there will always be a certain degree of dependence in my life, no matter how much I want to believe otherwise."

She grazed her mouth against his lips and relaxed a little. "It's going to be a work in progress," she whispered.

"I appreciate your efforts—trying to please me with that appetizing setup last night—but it left out the most important aspect of this lifestyle that I want to remain intact."

"Is control that important to you?"

Parker sat up and leaned against the headboard, urging her to move up and rest her head on his chest. He trailed his fingers along her back before he spoke.

"It's all I have. Imagine losing control of everything around you. The bedroom is a place where I can still have the command that was taken from me. I don't expect you to fully understand my situation, but I'm just afraid that if I let it go on, I'm going to feel trapped because I didn't say something earlier."

She straightened and sat on her heels. "Are you getting rid of me already?"

The hurt in her voice stroked his ego. He smiled and shook his head. "I just want to make things clear on how I want to go about this . . . relationship. I know I said last night that I wanted us to find our 'style' together, but that doesn't mean I'm ready to relinquish domination in the bedroom. You still have to follow my lead and do what I ask of you within your comfort zone." Parker knew he sounded selfish for putting his need before hers, but this was important to him.

Ann paused. He could guess she was considering what he'd said.

"To be quite honest, I feel the same way you do: like I'm trapped, and my life is slipping from my grasp. But unlike you, I don't have the need to control. Instead, I want a little quiet time, like what we're having right now."

"Why would you feel trapped?"

She sighed. "It's a very long story. I promise I'll tell you all about it when the time is right. For now, let's just enjoy each other."

Parker nodded in understanding and was relieved to hear she would soon entrust him with her secrets. He took her hand. "Since we've decided to just enjoy ourselves, let's go to this little hole-in-the-wall favorite of mine. Their breakfast quesadillas are to die for."

Ann faltered. "Um . . . I don't feel like dressing up. Why don't I whip up something for us? My sister says I make one of the best mushroom and Swiss cheese omelets there is. We can eat on the veranda and maybe take a walk on the beach."

Parker recognized the signs of evasion. The first thing that came to mind was that she was embarrassed to be seen with a blind man. The thought made his stomach churn with disappointment. Was that one of the secrets that she was hiding from him? He chastised himself, remembering that Ann had promised to share everything with him as soon as she was ready. For now, he was going to take her sage advice and just enjoy the company.

"Sounds good to me." He slapped her butt and eased her off him. "Now tell me—where the heck are my clothes?" When she moved away, he planted his feet on the cold hardwood floor. Parker heard her footsteps as she made her way to the bathroom and returned with his clothes.

"There's a new toothbrush on the vanity for you," she said before closing the bathroom door. "I'll be in the kitchen. Just holler if you need help finding your way around," she added before her footsteps faded away.

"Thanks." Parker felt for his phone in his jeans pocket and activated the time. Then he listened to the voice-over announce eight text messages, five missed calls from Cork, and three from his father. "Oh shit," he muttered. He pressed the speed dial and slipped into his jeans while he waited. Parker heard movement in the bathroom and figured Ann was getting her morning ritual underway.

Cork answered on the third ring. "Dude, did you even make it home?"

"Good morning, baby bro. What's with the inquisition? Last I checked, I was born two years, seven months, and several hours ahead of you. That makes you unqualified to give me the third degree."

His brother ignored his teasing. "Mom's worried about you, and Dad's called several times wanting me to report you as missing when you didn't answer my calls or texts."

Parker rolled his eyes. His parents had been as solid as Cork had been when his blindness had unleashed its fury. But regardless, they still treated him like he was a child. His mother, Dorothy, had often requested that he inform them of his activities, not because they wanted to meddle but more for their own peace of mind. Their constant worrying about his safety was unnecessary, even if he refused to use a guide dog or even a walking stick.

"Um . . . I lost track of time."

"I was calling to tell you that, since you 'lost track of time,' Mom canceled the barbecue. She wants us to meet her and Dad for dinner tonight. They want to celebrate. It sounds like they have some good news. I'll pick you up at seven." Cork wasn't going to be deterred by any feeble excuses.

Parker groaned. He wanted to stay with Ann, but there was no getting out of this dinner with his parents. "Fine, I'll see you then."

After they hung up, Parker made his way to the bathroom and brushed his teeth. Feeling a bit out of his element in an unfamiliar house, he sighed before venturing outside the bedroom. It should be simple. All he had to do was to use the walls to feel his way around. Of course, most things were easier said than done. As soon as he took the first steps out of Ann's bedroom, he tripped over something on the floor. There was no way to stop the fall. All he could do was protect his head with one arm and try to break his fall with the other. He landed on the floor with a loud thud.

Parker heard footsteps running in his direction. "Oh my, are you okay?" Ann rushed to his side. He felt around, reaching blindly until his fingers closed over the culprit—something small and smooth that felt like glass.

"Oh, Parker, I'm so sorry. I forgot about the candleholders. Let me get the rest of these out of your way."

He gritted his teeth and tried to calm down. Then he pushed himself up using the wall as a guide.

"Are you okay?" Ann held his arm, leading him forward.

It's just my pride that's hurt, he wanted to say. "I'm fine. Don't worry. It's not your fault. It's hard to blind-proof a house." Parker tried to lighten his statement, but it still came out sounding stiff. "Just walk ahead and I'll follow you."

Ann hesitated before starting out. "It will take about ten feet to reach the kitchen, which is to your left. You'll pass the dining room on your right. I'm going to turn on the lights so you can at least see the doorway and the two big vases on either side of it."

He was grateful for her clear instructions, and it touched him when she didn't stick around and hover over him. That would have been mortifying. He took a moment to compose himself before starting off down the hallway again. It wasn't every day he made a fool of himself in front of people. This one stung more because it magnified his problem. Taking a deep breath, Parker began to count and walk in the direction of the whisking sound until he was standing next to Ann.

"Can I help?" he offered, trying to put the incident behind him. His male pride had not only taken a beating, but he'd also embarrassed the hell out of himself in front of the woman he wanted to impress. *Way to go, Parker!*

She kept beating the eggs but stood on tiptoe to reach his mouth with a kiss. "Sure. Can you make coffee?"

"Tell me where to find things." He smiled in her direction, loving the way she made him feel needed.

"To your right, about six steps, you'll stand face-to-face with the cupboard. On the second shelf, you'll find the coffee filters. The coffee is in the freezer. Starbucks okay with you? The fridge is behind you, by the way."

"Oh, yeah. Where's the coffee maker?"

"Right here." Ann took his hand and guided it along the counter until he felt the coffee maker.

Once the coffee was set up, Parker sat on the barstool and listened to Ann's movements, following her outline while she started the omelet. "So this is where you live?" he asked, hoping to get a good conversation going

—anything to find out more about her.

"Yeah. I have another house, but I like it here. I love living close to the water and the fact that it's private." She sounded wistful, and he wanted to hold her in his arms, to ease whatever ailed her.

"Private?"

Because of his blindness, he depended on people to describe certain places to him. In this instance, he had no idea what she was talking about.

"The whole one-mile stretch is private, so only the owners and their guests are allowed to enter the estate. There's a security gate at the entrance to keep out unwanted guests." There was a hint of triumph in the way she explained the area, another addition to his growing list of questions about the mystery surrounding Ann.

"I take it you like your privacy?" The aroma of the eggs cooking wafted around them, and he followed the inviting scent with his nose.

"Who doesn't like privacy?"

Parker thought of what else he could ask her. "What do you do when you're home? Do you have any hobbies?

"Oh, I like to read and watch old movies. And when I find the time, I enjoy a leisurely run and long walks. Anyway, I don't have anything planned for the rest of the day. I was hoping we could rent a movie after taking a walk on the beach."

Parker chuckled at her invitation. It was always a welcome change when people forgot about his vision impairment. "I'd love to . . . oh crap!" He smacked his forehead, remembering the dinner with his family.

"What's going on?"

"Christ. I was just talking to my brother. My parents arranged for the four of us to have dinner tonight." Groaning, he wished he could cancel but knew his mother would be disappointed if he did.

"Time with family's always important. Why don't you give me your address, and I'll come by your place tomorrow? That is, if you want me to."

Before he had a chance to answer, Parker heard the doors open, and salty air breezed in.

"Join me out here on the veranda. I'm about thirteen steps from where you are. Just watch out for the little bump on the floor by the door."

Parker smiled at her attention to detail and was grateful that she hadn't coddled him or made him feel like a total freak.

"Thanks." He followed the tantalizing sound of the ocean and was surprised by the feel of the wind in his face.

"I have a run scheduled with a friend of mine at the track in the morning. Any time after lunch is fine with me. I'll text my address to you right now."

He settled into one of the cushioned patio chairs and inhaled the fresh air. After a long indulgent moment, Parking pulled out his cell phone and started texting the information to Ann via the voice-over application.

"Can you imagine if you didn't have the technology we have now? Coffee cup is next to your plate. Right side."

Parker looked up and smiled. "I would be living in the dark ages, no doubt about it. I guess, in a way, the timing is better."

It wasn't a joke. He and Cork had talked about the what-ifs, if his disease had struck maybe ten years earlier. There would have been no screen reader to aid him in using the computer and no voice-over to stay connected through texting.

"How do you know so much about locating techniques?"

"Let's just say I was curious." Ann took his hand and placed it on her face. "I read a few articles after I met you."

Touched at her effort, this gave him the opening he needed to ask her an important question. *How does it feel to make love with a blind man?* But he couldn't bring himself to put it in those exact words. Parker tamped down his insecurity and took a deep breath. "Does it bother you that I can't see you?"

There was no hint of hesitation when Ann answered. "Not one bit. And contrary to what others might think, I believe you can see better than most people. You're more aware of those around you and in tune with their feelings. Does that answer your question?"

Not all of it. "Yeah."

He would've preferred she elaborate on how she felt about him and, to be more specific, his blindness, but that could push her away. Parker wasn't ready for that, so he nodded his head and concentrated on her movements.

"Your fork is at nine o'clock. The omelet is plump, the size of a burrito. How would you like your coffee?"

"Just black. Thanks." He placed his phone in his pocket and picked up the fork. "Oh, is there any ketchup?"

"Here you go."

Parker lifted the lid and felt around his plate for a spot to squirt the ketchup. He gave the bottle a shake and pumped some out. There was a sucking sound before the thick stuff splattered all over his face, and he assumed, on his shirt and the table. Ann laughed and moved closer.

"Look at you. You're a mess." She pressed a napkin into his hand. "Let me get the stuff off of your face first.

Instead of wiping his face with a napkin, Ann kissed every inch of it, dabbing her lips on every spot where the ketchup had landed. His heart rate soared at the erotic act, and he dragged her across his lap.

"If you don't stop what you're doing, I doubt we'll be able to even touch our breakfast." Parker's voice came out raspy, arousal lacing every syllable.

Ann laughed and pressed her mouth to his, teasing and probing. She wound her arms around his neck and molded her body closer. Parker more than obliged, liking the idea of this woman being unable to keep her hands off him.

After their long and lingering kiss, they paused to gulp some air. "Woman, you have to eat. You're using too much energy, and you need to replenish it." Parker stood up and carried her in his arms, depositing her into a chair. He kissed her once more. "Eat."

The conversation during the meal was light and easygoing. Parker learned a few more things about Ann, which enabled him to draw a mental picture of the mysterious woman who had him feeling like a teenager again.

"My sister's children are simply adorable. They refuse to go to bed until Auntie Ann reads them a bedtime story."

"How old are they?" Parker inquired, enjoying the lilt in her voice when she spoke about her sister and her kids.

"Little Sean is two, but he talks like he's seven, and Hilary is six going on twenty-one." She laughed.

He could tell Ann adored children by how animatedly she recounted her last vacation at her sister's house.

"You're all by yourself here in LA?"

Parker rested his hand on top of hers. He had no idea how it felt to be away from family. Theirs was a tight unit, and he couldn't imagine either he or Cork moving away.

"Yeah. My sister and her family live in Chicago. I try to visit them around the holidays if I can get away. They try to come here, too, but having kids and flying is never easy. Good thing my best friend, Jessica, lives close by." Ann pulled her hand away and started clearing the dishes from the table. "Maybe I should introduce the two of you one of these days. She's adorable but outspoken—sometimes too outspoken."

He followed her to the kitchen. "I would love to meet a friend of yours," he said as he settled next to her, listening to the sound of the running water while she scraped the scraps into the sink. "I would love to meet every person who means a lot to you."

Parker sensed her quick withdrawal at his words. "One of these days," she murmured.

"Are you still up to walking on the beach? I have a few hours to spare before I have to leave." He traced a finger along the back of her neck and was rewarded with a moan. She turned off the faucet and faced him.

"I'd like for you to stay the night if it's possible, but I know you have that dinner tonight. The walk will have to do for now." Ann kissed him. "But I need to rinse your shirt before we do. You smell like food, and I'm afraid I'll eat you if we don't get that off."

"I can forgo walking on the beach." Parker laughed and slapped her in a playful manner on the butt. "I don't mind a nibble or two." He winked in her direction.

"You're just as crazy as I am, Parker."

She led him back to the bedroom where another round of sparks lit up. This time, Ann obeyed his orders with fervor, letting him lead them both to another sensual and explosive experience.

Kelly reveled in the aftermath of Parker's lovemaking, adoring every minute of being in his arms. She remembered the kisses that had sent her reeling with lust, the likes of which she'd never felt before. Every persuasive touch awakened newfound sensations in her body.

"When I touch you here, do you like it?" Parker peered at her, slinking a finger along the juncture of her legs.

"I can't explain it, but I do. You've always touched me in the places that give me the most pleasure. It's funny you mentioned it, because I was just thinking about that." Kelly rubbed his relaxed penis, toying with the tip, circling, and arousing.

"I don't intend to just touch your body, Ann. I want to touch your heart, too." Parker pulled his finger away, leaving her throbbing with want, and tipped her face closer to him.

Kelly faltered. Her hand paused mid-rub on his scrotum. In all her life, no man had ever expressed such a deep desire for her. Parker had been creeping his way into her guarded emotions—emotions she had repressed out of fear of getting hurt again. She looked up at him, her eyes moistening; she wasn't ready to get this involved this fast. What she'd thought to be a benign sexual release, a guilty pleasure, was now beginning to tear at her resolve. Parker's commanding strength, along with his gentleness, was sweeping her off her feet. If she wasn't careful, this could end as dreadfully as her previous relationships, only for a much different reason.

"Ann?"

"Hmm . . ."

"I don't expect you to feel the same way about me. I know it's too soon. Believe me, this is the last thing I was looking for, but there are situations in life we just can't control." Parker raked his fingers through his hair, looking vulnerable, almost shy. "I'm just asking you to give me a chance to be with you more often so I can get to know you better."

Kelly stared at him, unable to speak, and brushed a shaky hand across his face. He leaned toward her touch. "I want what you want, but I don't know if I have what it takes . . . to fully give myself."

Parker wrapped his arm around her, letting her head rest on his chest. "All I'm asking is for us to take baby steps. Let's just see what each day brings. Are you okay with that?" He kissed her hair with such tenderness.

You might not want a woman who can't get over her past. "I think so."

Kelly's stomach churned from the conflicting emotions within her. She wanted so much to believe him, yet an inner voice warned her of the pitfalls of being in a relationship, especially for someone famous like her.

They lingered for another hour until Parker had to leave for his dinner appointment with his family. Kelly couldn't even walk him to the car without the fear of being recognized by the limousine driver, so she kissed him good-bye at the door.

After stashing the rest of the dishes in the dishwasher, she set out for her much-needed walk. She took the beach access straight from her property, wearing shorts and a tank top, with her hair up in a loose ponytail.

This had always been her refuge, a place where she could think and be herself without fear of being watched. Kelly stopped and picked up a tiny rock that caught her attention. Wiping the sand away, she slid it into her pocket to be added later to her growing collection.

She thought of Parker while she walked back to her house. The man still had no idea who she was, and her warning bells told her she should confess soon. Would it matter to him if he found out the truth? Only he could answer that question. When she got home, she took a long, luxurious bath and pondered her personal dilemma.

Her life was under intense scrutiny, and that was something she had no control over. Now she had a man who wanted to control yet another aspect of her life, and in the one place she'd thought she was free to express herself. Kelly wanted to deny what he'd asked of her, but if she were honest with herself, she'd have to admit the man also filled a void in her heart. As strange as it sounded, the more time she spent with him, the more she realized she couldn't live without him. She wanted Parker as he was and let him lead her into what promised to be an amazing relationship.

Since she had the afternoon all to herself, Kelly lounged on the veranda and read over a script her agent, Connor, had asked her to review. Recently, she had accepted roles based on her willingness to get away, to forget. Out-of-town filming was more to her liking, but with Parker worming his way into her heart, filming in South Africa had lost its initial appeal. After an hour or so of reading, she gave up on the script and decided to call Jessica and meet up for dinner. Kelly drove up to Chateau Marmont in her Range Rover, not even bothering with disguising herself. She was much too happy to even care.

When the valet opened her door, she pasted on a smile and braced herself. Flash after flash snapped in her eyes, and rounds of questions, both hurtful and inane, came her way. She shielded her eyes from the blinding lights and hurried into the lobby.

Jessica waved at her from where she was already lounging with a drink, looking chic in a white cotton tunic and body-hugging jeans. "They'll seat us in fifteen minutes. I took the liberty of ordering you a glass of wine. Cab, as you prefer."

They hugged and sat down. The famous landmark hotel was humming with activity, which was to be expected from a place where entertainment celebrities and famous athletes hung out.

"Thank you. It's a little rough out there." Kelly glanced one more time at the flood of paparazzi with their long lenses, trying to peek through the glass doors to get a picture of anyone they could capitalize on.

Jessica scowled, her usual reaction to Kelly's plight. "Some stupid one asked the same question again?"

Kelly nodded and took a big sip of wine. "It'll never end. They'll never let me forget. It hurts, you know. I just wish I'd never met Matthew and lost . . ." She took a gulp this time, wishing she could forget the past, along with its ugliness and sorrows.

"Hey, now. No need to think of the past. We're here so we can catch up." Jessica reached out and touched her hand. "Tell me, what have you been up to since you came back from Milan?"

Being the new face of Gucci, Kelly had been attending advertising campaigns and one soiree after another to promote their newest line of handbags—a welcome distraction for her. Moreover, the traveling, though exhausting, had kept her from thinking about her loss.

"Well, I sent a limo to pick up Parker, and we spent the night together." She giggled like a silly school girl, feeling the blush rising up to her cheeks.

Jessica almost choked on her wine and glared at her. "And you still haven't told the poor man who you are?"

Her smile faded. "No . . . but I will. I just haven't found the right time." Kelly paused, unsure why she wanted to keep this little detail to herself.

Jessica narrowed her eyes, a surefire way to keep her talking. "Kelly? What else are you holding back?"

"To be honest, it feels like you're reading my mind." Kelly took another sip and dabbed a napkin on her lips. "It's refreshing to have someone attracted to me without knowing who I am. I can be myself and not worry that he is taking advantage of me."

Her best friend let out a sigh. "How many times do I have to tell you this isn't a game for Parker? You think you're being yourself by concealing your true identity? Don't you think you're carrying this attraction or . . . or this game of yours a little too far?"

Groaning, she leaned forward and nudged Jessica. "It's not a game. Granted, it started out as a mere attraction, but I'm not playing now. I think I'm falling . . ."

"You're falling for him, aren't you?"

All Kelly could do was nod.

"You're going at this all wrong." Jessica shook her head.

"As crazy as it sounds, I want him for all the right reasons."

"Which are?" Jessica prodded, raising her eyebrows.

"He's smart, independent, amazing, and he sees me as a real person."

"You sound like you're in advertising," she said dryly.

Kelly laughed. "He said the same thing."

Her friend turned somber. "I just worry about you. You seem to like the guy, but you're not being fair to him by withholding a very important detail."

Kelly knew she was cornered. "Can you, for just one moment, not be my conscience? Yes, I've thought about the stuff you said, but I'm not sure I can trust him yet."

"I know you have trust issues given what happened between you and that good-for-nothing leech. But you're making things worse by stalling. Just don't hurt the man. He seems nice." Jessica fished for something inside her purse and shoved a magazine on the table.

Kelly stared at it. Parker was on the cover of *Health and Fitness*, and his smile, as always, made her feel warm inside. "Where did you get this?" she asked.

"Believe it or not, when I recognized the gleam in your eyes, I made it a point to find out more about the man." Jessica gave her a knowing look.

It was no use pretending in front of her friend. "And what did you find out about him?"

"I read some articles about him. He is fascinating, low-key, and well loved by his employees, as well as his clients. If you break his heart, I think a lot of people will be upset and will be coming after you with pitchforks. Many of his admirers are women, young and old, and well-known celebrities who are protective of him. I'm sure you know the rest of what I'm trying to say here."

Kelly took one last gulp of her wine before answering. "You make me sound like the Wicked Witch of the West."

She was spared Jessica's snarky response when the seating hostess announced their table was ready.

They were digging into their shared steamed artichoke and swapping entertainment gossip when someone caught Kelly's eye. Parker walked into the restaurant, escorting an older but regal woman. Following them were two well-dressed gentlemen—the younger one looked like he could be Parker's twin. They walked past her table to get to theirs. The younger one caught her looking and held her gaze for a brief moment.

She turned around, heart hammering against her chest. "Oh, no."

Jessica leaned forward to whisper. "What's wrong?"

"Parker's here with his family."

CHAPTER NINE

"It smells good in here," Parker said when he pulled the chair out for his mother. He took the seat opposite from her as his father, a tall, dashing man in his early sixties, sat down next to his wife.

Cork settled in next to him. "It must be that woman's perfume, the one who's staring at you, Park."

"What woman?"

It sounded like Cork was turning around to look at something. "Um . . . oh shit! Are you freakin' kidding me?"

"Cork, watch your language! You're never too old for me to wash your mouth out with soap." The soft reprimand came from their mother, Dorothy.

"I'm sorry, Mom." Cork chuckled, and then jabbed Parker on the arm. "Dude, if I'm not mistaken, the woman who was staring at you when we walked in is none other than Kelly Storm." The starstruck awe in Cork's voice wasn't hard to miss.

There was a collective rustling between the three, and Parker was almost positive they had all turned around to look at the woman Cork had mistaken for the famous actress.

"Kelly Storm, the actress?" He had no idea which direction to look, so he kept his eyes on his mother's face. "Dude, if you're just pulling my leg, you'd better quit, or I'm going to kick your ass." Parker grabbed his brother by the neck and ruffled his hair, which Cork hated. The guy had always been meticulous about his hair.

"Okay, enough of the teasing, boys. I'm not going to sit here and listen to you children cursing or threatening to kick each other's behind." That was their mothers "no nonsense" voice, the one that meant they'd better watch their words or else a pinch to the ear would follow.

Tyler Davis laid a hand on his wife's shoulder and squeezed. "It's okay, dear. Let the boys have their fun."

She shook her head, smiling. "To think we tried to set a good example. Just listen to how they talk and horse around in a formal restaurant." Dorothy clucked her tongue as she always did. "Why don't we check out the menu?"

"Wait, I think you should go to her table and introduce yourself, Parker." Cork sounded amused, and Parker couldn't help but chuckle.

"It might be a look-alike. How sure are you that it's her?"

"One hundred percent! See? She's glancing this way again." Cork's enthusiasm was becoming annoying.

"If you're so interested, why don't *you* approach her?"

Parker didn't bother checking the menu. He had scanned it earlier and already knew what he wanted to order.

"I'm not interested, and anyway, she only has eyes for you. She keeps glancing this way. If you want to know, we passed her table on the way here. Let's see, about seven tables down, so maybe about ten big steps."

Parker had no intention of making a fool out of himself in front of a famous actress and whomever else might be watching. Regardless, he was still a tad bit curious why a famous person like her would be checking him out. It must have something to do with his business. Many celebrities were curious about his services, and he'd encountered a few who'd wanted to meet him in person.

If he remembered right, Kelly was quite a stunning woman. She was beautiful, with a beguiling smile, fiery red hair, and a "to die for" figure. In his opinion, she was on the thin side, but she was a definite regular in every man's fantasy, including his. The woman was gorgeous. He'd seen some of her movies, and her acting wasn't half-bad. It was unfortunate that Matthew moron had screwed her over. There was no way he would be looking at another woman if he had a Kelly Storm in his life. It didn't hurt that she was rumored to have a kind heart, too. He'd heard she'd set up a foundation for hungry kids in Africa. Now who in their right mind would let a gem like her go?

"Dude, give it a rest." Parker turned to address his father, who seemed to be in good spirits. "Dad, why don't we order a bottle of Dom? Sounds like you and mom have some exciting news."

"Dom?" Cork sputtered.

Parker turned to his brother. "What's wrong with you?"

"Nothing . . . you said something funny." He cleared his throat. "Just forget about it."

Tyler laughed. "Sure, son, and yes, there is a bit of good news. I'll make the announcement when our bottle gets here."

Parker sought out his mother's hand. "Are you guys having a baby?" he teased and felt, rather than saw, his mother's piercing gaze. "Okay, okay, so you're not having a baby. Then what are you guys up to?"

Cork nudged him in the ribs. "See? You should have gone over there and introduced yourself. Now she's leaving!"

Parker shook his head, getting a bit irritated by his brother's persistence. "I'm sure she came here to dine in peace. No one should be pestered while they're trying to have a cozy dinner. And would you please stop gawking? You're giving pigs a bad name."

His father howled with laughter, and even his mother joined in. He sensed Cork's embarrassment when he heard his brother clear his throat.

"Fine. You just lost one great opportunity to add another well-known celeb to your client list. I was just looking out for your business."

"I think I'll live, Corky. Don't worry about it. Why don't you check the menu so we can order?" Parker elbowed his brother. "Changing the subject, why do you sound so happy all of a sudden? You haven't been this peppy since what's-her-name."

Parker guessed that his mother was rolling her eyes at the mention of Cork's last girlfriend. Dorothy used her as an example of the type of girl she hoped her son would never marry. The woman had treated his brother as if he lacked the ability to think for himself, oftentimes telling him what to do.

Cork punched him in the arm. "Shut up. Why don't you tell Mom and Dad where you've been?" Cork had a cunning way of shifting the attention away from him and onto others, a skill Parker had yet to master.

Tyler jumped into the conversation. "Where were you last night, anyway?"

Parker raised an eyebrow in his father's direction. "Just out with a friend," he answered, being vague. He wasn't sure if he was ready to talk about Ann yet, at least not with his family.

"Would this friend be the same one who had you picked up by a limousine?" Dorothy chimed in, and by the lilt in her voice, she wasn't going to accept any evasive answers. Parker believed his mother had some sort of seventh sense, if there even *was* such a thing. He'd given up a long time ago trying to keep things from her. She'd always find a way to get information out of him.

"You're such a blabbermouth, aren't you?" He ruffled his brother's hair again to annoy him and hoped their mother wouldn't prod anymore.

The arrival of their champagne halted their teasing. When each of them was holding their flutes, Tyler cleared his throat. "Your mom and I bought a house in Hawaii, on Maui. We're both retiring in three months, so we're planning on spending half the year there and shuttle back and forth if necessary," Tyler said with pride, kissing his wife before they toasted.

"That's wonderful! I know it is something you've both talked about for years, though I never thought you'd actually do it." Cork stood and gave his parents a hug.

Parker shook his father's hand, and then was pulled into a bear hug by his parents.

"I want you and your brother to visit us. And watch out for Corky. You know he could get lost without his mommy and daddy," his mother whispered in his ear.

Parker smiled and lifted a hand to Dorothy's face, seeking the smile he knew was there. "I want you and Dad to enjoy yourselves. Don't worry about Corky-boy. I'll keep him in line." And here he had been thinking his parents would worry about him, yet they were more concerned about his younger brother. How could he not adore these two people, who were adamant in their refusal to let his disability get the best of him?

"You know I'll be expecting a daily phone call." Dorothy touched his face the same way, tracing her soft hand over his cheek.

He nodded and kissed her on the forehead. "I will call, Mom."

"Are you guys talking about me again?" Cork asked.

She sat down and turned to her youngest son. "I'm just telling your brother to make sure you eat your veggies," Dorothy teased, taking Cork's hands in hers.

After the congratulatory greetings subsided and questions about their upcoming move were answered, their meals arrived and halted their conversation. Parker dug into his salmon and thought about his time with Ann, relishing the memory of the feel of her body against his and the sound of her laughter.

He shook his head in astonishment at the dawning realization that he could be falling in love with her. The signs were all there and already beginning to engrave themselves into his psyche. He could no longer deny it, but he'd keep it from her as long as he needed to. A declaration of his love might scare her away, if her agitation on previous occasions was any indication. Just when he thought the questions about Ann had been forgotten, his mother spoke as if she'd read his mind.

"What's the big secret? Who's the girl?" Dorothy asked. "Parker, don't you dare keep secrets from me."

Groaning, he let out a frustrated sigh. "She's a client." Parker kept his answer short, hoping she would be satisfied. He forked another big bite of salmon into his mouth.

"And?" she prodded.

Cork leaned closer and snickered. "This is going to be interesting. C'mon brother, do tell. Don't leave us groping in the dark."

"Watch your words, Cork," their mother warned.

"Aw, c'mon. Park knows I don't mean anything by it."

"Mom, it's okay. I like people not tiptoeing around me. I guess that's what I like about *this* girl. She's not in any way turned off by me or my inability to see her. She's beautiful—"

Cork cut him off. "How can you tell?"

"I'm not *completely* blind, you know. I can see the shape of her face. Maybe not the finer details, but I've felt her face, and she's amazing."

What had started off as a reluctance to divulge any information about his newfound attraction had turned into a full-blown confession. He could sense the interest surging around him in waves.

"I hope she's beautiful on the inside, too. I think that's more important." Parker's father gave his opinion, which was always insightful. Tyler was a man of few words but rich in wisdom.

"That's what I'm hoping to discover soon. We've just gone out a couple of times. She can be a little jumpy, but maybe that's because we're still in the early stages of getting to know each other. I'm not going to lie, I like the girl already, but I'm trying to slow things down. I don't want to scare her off." Parker chuckled.

The table was quiet, and he could feel everyone's eyes on him. He squirmed a little, wishing he could see their expressions or at least hear what they were thinking. "Um, hello! What's with the silence?" he asked.

"Wow, dude, are you kidding me? Are you falling for this girl already? Who is she? Which one? I've seen some pretty amazing women go in and out of your massage rooms, but I've never noticed anyone you might be interested in."

Parker inclined his head and frowned. "What are you using as a standard?" Cork probably thought he knew him so well, basing his judgment on his past relationships.

"I know your tastes, bro. You like redheads, and I haven't seen any of those coming out of your office."

Cork's words gave him pause. Hadn't he seen Ann? Maybe he hadn't, considering she'd been to their LA office once and the other time had been in New York, when his brother hadn't been there with him.

"I'm sure you'll meet her one of these days."

"Don't forget to bring her to meet us before we leave for Hawaii," his mother said.

Dorothy's voice was too chirpy. Was it his imagination, or did she sound like she was ready to marry him off? Parker was only twenty-eight years old. He had no intention of giving up his single life yet. It wouldn't be easy to find someone willing to share a lifetime with a man who had limitations. Not that he spent any sleepless nights worrying about that, but the thought had crept into his mind a few times. Well, as his mother often said, *que será será.*

"We'll see, Mom. We'll see."

"Can you slow down a little? What's the rush?" Jessica tugged on her arm as she handed her parking ticket to the valet. They'd exited the restaurant in haste, leaving their meal untouched.

Flashes snapped around them, adding to Kelly's extreme nervousness. She spotted Rigor in the herd of photographers with a smirk on his face. He took shot after shot, and when their gazes locked, he pointed to his eyes and waggled his eyebrows.

Jessica followed her gaze, saw the tail end of Rigor's antics, and bristled. "Don't mind that idiot. He's just out to irritate you. Don't show any sign that he's affecting you."

"I just want to get out of here. Meet me at the cottage, and we'll order pizza. I'm sorry if I ruined your dinner."

"Don't worry, hon. Pizza is something I've avoided for a long time, but I want one right now. I'll follow you to your place."

They got into their respective cars amid a flurry of snapping pictures and questions from the paps. Kelly breathed a sigh of relief as soon as she settled in and the doors were locked. She pressed the gas pedal and sped away. Her heart didn't stop thudding until she was close to home.

Of all the places in LA, Parker and his family had to dine at the same restaurant as she. What were the odds of that happening? The city was massive, so bumping into him had never even crossed her mind. To get her mind off the narrow escape, Kelly called in the pizza order while she drove. Traffic was light, and they reached her place in less than a half an hour.

They pulled into her driveway at the same time, and then walked toward the front door. Neither spoke as they entered the silent living room. Kelly turned on a single lamp and opened the doors leading out to the veranda. They flopped down on the rattan chairs and propped their feet up.

"I knew he was gorgeous, but I didn't expect perfection. The man should be an actor or a model. That face is amazing," Jessica gushed.

"Stop it. I don't want to talk about him. I feel bad about walking out of there without saying anything, but I didn't know what to do." Kelly covered her face with her hands, feeling dejected and ashamed.

"Talk or don't talk? You want to me to stop talking, and yet you're blubbering like an idiot. I think you need to grow up, girl. You've had it bad the last couple of years. I know it still hurts after losing . . . you know. But you have to get over it and move on. Not everyone is out to take advantage of you. You've learned from your mistake—now you have to live a little and allow yourself trust someone again."

"The more I talk about it, the more miserable I get. I know I shouldn't be leading Parker on this way. It isn't fair. But I want him to want me without the added burden of knowing who I really am." She trembled under the weight of her present predicament. Lying hadn't been part of her plan, nor was leaving him clueless about her celebrity status. Would it matter to him?

Jessica got up and walked around the table until she was standing behind Kelly and stroked her hair. "Who exactly are you? And don't you think you are selling Parker short? From what little you've told me and what I've read, I don't think he has a judgmental bone in his body."

Kelly looked up with tears in her eyes. "I'm screwed, I know, and the worst thing is, I think I really am falling for him. God, I'm so happy when I'm with him but miserable because of the lies. We both know how it'll end up if the paps find out about him. They'll swarm him. And the media will chew him up and spit him out. I don't want him to go through that because of me," she sobbed.

Jessica pulled a tissue out of her purse. "Here, don't go smearing that mascara all over your beautiful face." Her best friend dabbed at the black streaks running from the side of her eyes. "I want you to think about this. You don't have to say anything, just listen. Let Parker decide what he can handle and what he can't. Don't just assume that he'd be miserable being with you because you're famous. If you give him the ammunition of truth, he'll be able to face whatever else comes his way. There's nothing good that will come out of a relationship based on lies. If anyone should know this, it should be you."

The tears continued to flow while Kelly digested her friend's advice. If she wanted to be with Parker beyond just a string of covert meetings, she had to come clean and confess her little white lie. Soon.

"I'll try."

"Good girl. You won't regret telling him the truth. And I quote, 'the truth shall set you free.' " Jessica giggled and gave Kelly a hug just as the doorbell rang. "Must be our dinner."

"I'll get it." Kelly attempted to get up, but Jessica stopped her.

"I've got it."

Jessica hurried to the front door with her wallet in hand. Reacting on sudden impulse, Kelly reached for her cell phone and called Parker. He answered on the third ring.

"Ann?"

"Hi. Did I catch you at a bad time?"

"We're about to leave the restaurant. What's going on? Are you catching a cold?" He sounded worried, and that warmed her heart.

She was forced to breathe through her mouth because her nose was clogged from crying. "I'm fine. It's the breeze. It's getting nippy out here on the patio."

"Better go inside or get a blanket and cover yourself.

Kelly shifted gears. "Can I come over around four tomorrow? Should I bring dinner?"

"Four is good, but don't bring dinner. It's about time you tried my roasted chicken."

"You can cook, too?" She smiled at the image of Parker getting busy in the kitchen. "What else can you do, Mr. Davis?"

"Of course I can cook. You're talking to a Cordon Bleu dropout." He chuckled, and despite her misery, she joined in his laughter. "I can make sweet love, too," he added, his voice a husky whisper.

"That I already knew, but I would love another sample." Her heart pounded in erratic beats as she pictured Parker's *very* male body on top of hers. She licked her lips at the perfect vision. "Okay, I'll bring the wine, then. See you tomorrow."

"Oh, and Ann?"

"Yes?"

"I miss you. I haven't been able to think of anything but you all evening."

Her heart skipped and she clutched the phone in a tight grip. "I miss you, too. Good-night, Parker."

"Night, my lady."

"So are you talking to your hunksicle?" Jessica snuck up behind her.

Kelly laughed at Jessica's nickname for her sizzling hot masseuse, blushing at the same time. "Yeah. I'm going to his place tomorrow."

"Ah . . . and you're going to do what? Hell, why did I even ask? Don't answer that. Just make sure you get enough sleep for the press junket on Monday."

"I'll get plenty of sleep, don't worry." Of course, that was a lie. They would sleep but after several hours of fun. The thought of what they would be doing made her blush even more.

Her cell announced an incoming text message. She glanced at the display, which showed Parker's name, and smiled.

Wait for my text with instructions tomorrow. Sleep well, my lady.

Not only was she blushing, but now she was grinning like a total idiot.

Jessica gave her a look of disbelief before rolling her eyes. "Let's pig out."

Parker placed his arm around the top of the driver seat. "Don't think for one minute I'm letting that slip of yours in the restaurant go."

"What are you talking about?" Cork's voice cracked, sounding defensive.

He raised an eyebrow. If Cork and his parents were allowed to grill him about his relationship with Ann, he'd be damned if he was going easy on his brother.

"Spill, dude. I know you've been seeing someone." He smirked in Cork's direction.

"What happened to respecting each other's privacy?"

"You flushed it down the toilet when you instigated the nonstop questions back at the restaurant." Parker changed tactics. "I know you, little brother. You always get evasive when you're seeing someone. So quit avoiding the question, because I'm not going to let this one go."

Cork snorted and accelerated. "Damn it. I don't sing like a girl."

"Sure you do!" Parker chuckled. "I'm *still* having nightmares from your stories about Suzanne, Rosemary, and Trish. Wait . . . there's Mindy and Donna, too."

"You're such an ass."

Parker could tell his brother was on the verge of blurting his secret. He crossed his arms in satisfaction. "So, who's the new girl?"

"It's Webster."

Parker couldn't help but laugh. *Man, I thought I worked fast. The woman didn't waste any time.* He almost blurted it out but caught himself in time. "Webbie? Our little Webbie . . . Webbie?"

"*My* Webbie." Cork sounded like a dog obsessed with guarding his bone.

He coughed. "Um, congrats, bro. She's a good woman." *Isn't this awkward?*

"I'm well aware that you two have a history, and I'm good with it. But that's all in the past, so let's just keep it that way."

To put his brother's worries to rest, he nodded. "I agree. Let's keep it that way."

If there was one thing he was sure of, it was that his brother and Webster were perfect for each other.

CHAPTER TEN

Light was about to break when Andrew, Parker's running buddy, honked the horn outside his townhouse. They always left at six thirty in the morning to beat the weekend rush at the track. They got to Road Runner within minutes amid a light drizzle of rain. Parker loved the feel of the little drops misting his face as he looked up to the sky. The weather was perfect, and the track would be even better—not muddy, but damp enough to get rid of the dust. They parked their water bottles and towels on a bench and started their pre-run warm-ups.

Parker attached the leash to his wrist and secured it with Velcro. This was his connection to his running buddy. Andrew would issue nonverbal cues by tugging on the leash should they need to stop, if a pothole was in his path, or if they were about to overtake another runner.

They had perfected the process and had been running together every week for almost a year. Andrew had been a close friend in high school who'd pursued a career in sports medicine and athletic training. When he'd found out about Parker's impending blindness, he'd offered to use a technique that would give him the freedom to run outside. On days when their schedules didn't coincide, Parker would use his personal treadmill in his small home gym.

"What have you been up to?" Parker asked.

"Well, I got an offer from a minor league program for a position as an assistant trainer. I haven't accepted it yet, but they offered to let me try it out for a month to see if it's the perfect fit."

"That's amazing! What are you waiting for? Isn't it a dream of yours to work for an athletic program and travel at the same time?"

When they stepped on the pavement of the track, Andrew gave their leash a little tug, his signal to get ready. Parker nodded, and they started off the first leg of their run with a jog.

"I'm going to try it first, and then decide later. If I accept the position, you might be without a running partner." Andrew tugged once after they'd covered half the track and increased their speed to a full run.

"Don't worry about me. I can post something on craigslist for a running partner. Do what you have to do, Drew. I'll be fine."

He gave Drew a smile of encouragement, and then they stopped talking so Parker could concentrate on the silent prompts. Parker had loved running for as long as he could remember. It was one of the things he'd hated to give up once the blindness had taken over. If it hadn't been for Andrew's insistence that he try running with a partner, he would still be using his treadmill and missing all the fun of being outdoors.

After fifteen laps around the track, they called it a day. Webster was due to pick him up in thirty minutes to take him grocery shopping and run a few errands before he had to start cooking and getting ready for Ann.

Ah, Ann. He could almost smell her and taste her in his mind.

As usual, Webster arrived on time. "So what's the hurry?" She unlocked the front passenger door of her sedan, and Parker slid in.

"I need your eyes to help me choose outfits and some other stuff for tonight. And I wanted you to take me grocery shopping, too." It had always been difficult for him to ask for favors, but with Webster, it was different. Maybe it was because they understood each other's needs without having to explain.

"Big date, huh?" she asked while they cruised along the main thoroughfare of Sepulveda Boulevard.

Parker nodded. "Let's hit the grocer first. I'm anxious to get back in time to cook and shower." He drummed his fingers on the window. Anxiety and excitement had been eating away at him since he'd woken up. The run had done very little to ease the building tension within him.

"It's that Baba chick, isn't it? Gosh, Parker, do you even know the woman? I mean, she gave us a phony name. How can you fall for her?"

He detected skepticism in her voice that was unusual for her. His head shot up in defiance. "Her name's Ann Sutton, if you want to know, and I think I know her well enough."

Parker heard her pound on the steering wheel. Webster had always been supportive of his every decision, so it surprised him to see her so distrustful of Ann. They spent the rest of the drive in stubborn silence. When they arrived at the strip mall, she looped her arm in with his, and he knew what had happened in the car was forgotten.

"You know, boss, I'm happy if you are, but I can't help being a little protective of you. Women are just as bad as men when it comes to getting what they want, using whatever method they can. I'm just looking out for you, and I don't think I'll ever stop, even if you get married." She wrapped an arm around his waist as they walked past the shops along the busy street.

"Whoa! Stop right there. No one's getting married. I just happen to be dating. Nothing serious, got it?" Parker pulled her head toward him and gave her a friendly kiss on her hair.

"Fine . . . but you can't stop me from doing what I want."

He could almost imagine her pouting, and he grinned. "Fine. Do what you want—just don't scare her away."

Grocery shopping was easy with Webster describing every detail for him. The shop had everything he was looking for, so they were in and out in less time than he'd anticipated. After the initial stress of not keeping to his schedule, Parker began to relax, and the rest of his errands became more enjoyable.

Webster maintained a steady flow of chatter while pushing the cart. She kept him entertained with work gossip as they walked up and down the supermarket aisles. While he was away visiting the other branches, his eyes and ears at work had always been Cork and Webster, unless Cork came along to keep him company.

When they reached his townhouse, Webster stayed to help with the setup. She wrote down some instructions that he dictated while he prepared for dinner. She even offered to arrange the gloriosa lilies he'd ordered from the florist earlier. From Webster's description, he could almost picture the flowers in his mind. They had the fragile, exotic appearance of crushed red velvet, and while they were not true lilies—growing on a vine rather than from a bulb—they still represented the same sweetness and elegance as their authentic counterparts. Just perfect for what he had in mind.

At a quarter past three, Webster gave him a quick hug, wished him luck and left, assuring him that everything was perfect. With the chicken cooking in the roaster, he sent Ann a text and hurried to take a shower.

Taking meticulous care with his appearance, which was laughable since he couldn't even see himself in the mirror, he tried to fix his hair as best as he could, pushing the strays back into place that always managed to break free from the gobs of gel he used to tame them. He dressed and chuckled, remembering Webster's exact words. *"You look like an idiot, but a good looking idiot, and very forgivable."*

His alarm sounded, informing him the chicken was done. Parker hurried out of his bedroom to his small kitchen. Not bothering with the lights, he proceeded to set the table and checked the mashed potatoes. He pressed his watch for the time. Five minutes. He took one stem from the vase and walked back to his room to wait.

Kelly found a parking place right away when she spied a car leaving a spot close to Parker's home address. She read his text several times and wondered what he meant by it. Texting back, she promised to do as he'd asked. She found the key to his unit underneath the doormat and, with the bottle of red wine in one hand, let herself inside the house.

The scent of vanilla candles mixed with home cooking greeted her. The entire room was dark except for the candles scattered everywhere, giving the place that homey feel she'd always craved. Happiness bubbled within her when she opened the first door to her left—the powder room.

Inside, she found the things he'd mentioned in his text. On the vanity, an envelope awaited her, lying next to a little glass pendant engraved with her initial and tied to a black cord. She gasped with pleasure at the thoughtful gift. Kelly caught sight of herself in the mirror. She looked happy, judging by the pink in her cheeks and the sparkle in her eyes, and she was.

Picking up the first note, Kelly read it. Smiling, she unzipped the garment bag hanging behind the door. Inside was a purple outfit made of rich velvet, the bodice accented with muted golden brocade and damask. *Beautiful*, she thought. It was just like the ones she'd used in one of her movies, *Hearts Afire*, a period film set in the fourteenth century. She pulled it off the hanger, pressed the gown against her body, and closed her eyes.

Parker was so full of surprises. She dressed and checked her appearance in the mirror. Her breasts looked enormous because of the tight waistline that pushed her bosom up and out. Kelly gasped at the sight of her enhanced boobs. With care, she pulled her hair up into a loose chignon and used the hair accessories provided in the small velvet pouch that accompanied the dress.

She found the next note, read the rest of Parker's instructions, and silently applauded him for his attention to detail and meticulous planning. So far, his surprises had been exciting and well-thought-out. Kelly reread the note and memorized her lines. Leaving her things behind, she sauntered barefoot out of the bathroom toward the room he'd instructed her to enter, which was the last one in the long hallway, on the left.

Kelly knocked and waited for an answer.

"Come in, my fair lady," Parker answered.

When she entered, he was standing by the window with his back to her. City lights twinkled from beyond the glass panes. The entire room would have been dark if not for the light glowing from an oil lamp on his nightstand. Parker turned around, and bending at the waist, he offered her a red lily.

"Good even. I trust thou hast deemed the provisions I left for thee acceptable?"

Walking closer, Kelly devoured Parker with her eyes, taking in every single detail—his sculpted blond hair and the black knight surcoat he wore over matching leggings and boots.

He straightened just as she reached for the flower. His smile projected just the right amount of flirting—enough to send her reeling with excitement. "My lord, the flower is most beauteous. Such pleasure doth give."

Parker took one step and circled an arm around her waist, pulling her close. "I wish to behold thy beauty up close." He grazed his lips across her temple before sliding to the side of her cheek and then capturing her mouth.

"Thou art dapper, my lord. Make haste and show thine lady . . ." she paused, unable to remember the lines he had her memorized, then added, "how a lord loves his woman." Kelly smiled, unable to believe the words coming out of her mouth. He was making her ache already in the places she wanted him to be.

Parker licked his lips while he traced her curves, his fingers moving in sensual, rhythmic strokes—caressing every inch of available skin until he reached her face. He moved a fingertip around her parted lips, smiling in the process. "And thou art a vision of loveliness."

"I am thy humble servant. Do what thou must." Heat raced through her veins, making her shudder with anticipation.

"Follow me."

He took her hand and led her out of the bedroom across the hallway to another room. When he opened the spare bedroom, a burst of flowery scent surrounded her. The room was as dark as the other one, illuminated by two candles, one on top of the bureau and another atop the window sill. A massage table, imposing, sat in the center of the room.

Not knowing what to expect, but loving the mystery, her heart did a little flip. He took her by the waist and hoisted her up onto the table. "Stay here."

Parker opened the closet to reveal shelves full of sex toys that she had seen in shops. But instead of picking toys she thought he'd use, he opened a small, personal refrigerator. He pulled out two chilled shot glasses, grabbed the bottle resting on top of the fridge, and then moved in her direction, a mischievous smile on his face.

"This is Everclear. We're just having a shot, just to smooth the rough edges. You're not driving home tonight. You're spending the night with me, in my arms, fucking me until the wee hours of the morning. What say you, my lovely maiden?" Parker resumed the role-play after explaining his intentions.

She'd heard Everclear was the strongest alcoholic drink there was. Kelly nodded, and then remembered she had to say something. "I am at thy mercy." She took both shot glasses, allowing him to pour their drinks. He placed the bottle on the table, next to the votive, and took one of the glasses from her.

"To my fair lady."

Parker raised his glass to her, and she did the same. They pulled the shot down at the same time. The liquid blazed down her throat and smoldered in her system. Parker let out a whoop and blew out through his mouth. Taking the glass from her, he sat them both down on the small table. He nudged her legs apart, letting them dangle, and then leaned in between them to pull her forward.

"I will lead, and you follow," he whispered in her ear.

"Aye."

Kelly linked her hands behind his neck when his mouth sought hers, plastering her body against his. One minute she felt normal, the next she felt like a ball of lust ready to explode.

They kissed until she could no longer breathe and was forced to pull back a little to gulp some air. Parker sank to his knees, lifting her skirt to reveal the chastity belt he'd asked her to wear. He traced his fingers along the leather belt, hovering at the area of her pussy.

"What is your safeword, my lady?"

"Huzzah," she answered without hesitation.

"SSC?"

"Google is very helpful. SSC." The tingling effect from the alcohol began working its magic.

He glanced up at her and smiled. "Lie down on the table now."

Like an obedient girl, she scooted and lay down. Parker produced a small pillow and placed it underneath her head. Kelly looked up at him, noticing the little smile twitching at the corner of his mouth. She wondered if she should speak in plain English, since he had reverted a couple of times, but she remembered his instruction for the role-play. "I am at thy mercy, my lord."

"Before the feasting begins, understand that I will do what I want with you. You can moan and touch me, but you cannot come until I give the permission. What say you?"

"Thy will is mine to uphold."

A smile of satisfaction spread across his face. "The chastity belt is a bit of an oxymoron, because keeping you chaste is not my intention. I will take you. I want it there because it tells me you are mine."

"I pray thou taketh me. I belong to thee." She wanted him, there was no doubt about it, but not coming was going to be tricky.

Parker pressed a button on the music player in the corner, filling the room with the strains of a saxophone instrumental. He returned to the foot of the table, and with both hands, he reached for the hem of her dress and pulled it over her head. It fell to the floor, forgotten.

Seeming like he was inspecting a piece of meat, Parker walked around the table, trailing his fingers along her leg, up her thigh, the curve of her hips and waist, until he reached her tits. Using his index finger, he began stroking her nipple, circling, tracing, and awaiting the inevitable hardening of the tips. Goosebumps rose when her body responded to his feather light touch.

A wishful moan escaped her lips. She shuddered while he played with her nipples, pinching each one. Then he climbed on top of her, securing her legs within his own. Her mound became his playground. He licked it, his warm breath caressing her folds and making her cry out in want.

Kelly pushed her mound up to meet his mouth and keep the fire burning in her already-heated core. She wished his tongue would alleviate the pain in her kitty, but the more he taunted and probed, the more he made her throb with need.

"My lord, I want thee within," she whispered.

"Thou will have me, my lady. Patience is a virtue thou lacketh. I will teach thee fortitude and endurance." Parker dove down to her tits again. This time, he sucked long and hard at her nipples, making her breasts swell.

The sound of her strangled breathing and the banging of her heart against her ribs made it impossible to think. He cupped her tits and lasciviously stroked her swollen mounds with his tongue. Kelly groaned while she attempted to deny her own orgasm, panting, straining, and yelping with the effort to stop the inevitable.

"My lord . . . thy actions make it impossible for me to fulfill . . . thy request," she cried as the throbbing between her legs increased.

Parker raised his head. The glow of the candlelight reflected the wicked gleam in his eyes. "Thou shalt be steadfast in thy efforts, my lady." Again, he flicked his tongue across each nipple with renewed enthusiasm.

Kelly was forced to resort to grunting in an attempt to keep from climaxing. No matter how unladylike she sounded, it worked, stopping her from reaching the peak and buying her more time. Parker continued his teasing while he traveled down to her stomach. She was overheating as his firm tongue flitted along her skin, and she twisted her body to meet his mouth—to feel his caress.

It would only take a matter of seconds before she exploded. Her orgasm was coming closer, and her mind begged for release as the last of her self-control slipped away. She clawed at his muscled arms and wrapped her legs tight around his torso.

She threw in the towel. "Huzzah! Huzzah! Huzzah!"

The moment Parker lifted his head in response to her weakened cry, her release came hard and sweet. Kelly gasped in bliss as her core unclenched with satisfaction. She tried to focus on his unreadable expression and felt an overwhelming embarrassment for being weak.

"Alas, I failed thee."

Parker shook his head and shifted his body so that their faces were almost touching. "Thou didn't fail me. Thou hast done what I asked of thee. You used your safety net to alert me of your discomfort. No punishment will be given when such action is necessary. I applaud you for being obedient but also for expressing your true feelings." He kissed the tip of her nose.

"Would my lord give me another chance?" She cupped his face in her palms, loving every minute of being with such a wonderful man.

"We have all night, my lady. But for now, I must feed you." Parker eased his body off hers and climbed down from the table. She took his offer of a hand and let him help her sit up. "Dress and come to the kitchen."

Kelly jumped off the table after he left and hurried to get dressed. Parker was in the process of lighting several candles when she walked into the dining room. He flashed a gracious smile and pulled out a chair for her.

"Sit, my lady."

"Verily, I'm pleased with thy hospitality." She took her seat. Seeming like they were off the role-playing, Kelly began to relax but decided it was best to ask first. "Permission to speak freely, my lord?"

"Of course." Parker's eyes were focused on her.

"Is there anything I can do to help?

Parker shook his head. "Serving you is such a pleasure."

He went to the kitchen and returned with a platter of roasted chicken garnished with rosemary, parsley, and orange wedges, surrounded by fries. Her stomach growled, and she looked at Parker in embarrassment. Even though he couldn't see her face, he let out a hearty laugh. He returned to the kitchen once more and came back with two wine glasses.

"Can you do me a favor and open the bottle of wine you brought?"

"Of course." Glad to have something to do, she hurried and retrieved the bottle from the bathroom and found Parker cutting the chicken with remarkable ease.

"Corkscrew is in the first drawer."

Parker pointed to the kitchen's center island. She uncorked the bottle and poured for both of them.

"We are eating with these." He wiggled his fingers in her direction. At that same moment, they both headed to the sink to wash their hands.

Dinner was delicious. Kelly decided after they'd enjoyed his home-cooked meal, that nothing Parker did should surprise her anymore. There seemed to be nothing the man wasn't good at. They engaged in relaxed conversation, focusing on each other's pleasure. They touched as they ate and fed each other.

"You're not only a master in the bedroom but also an excellent cook," Kelly said, then licked each of her fingers. It was liberating to be doing something unconventional for a change.

"I still have room for dessert." Parker cleared the plates from the table. Kelly stared in surprise. She had no idea what was on his mind.

He strode from the kitchen with a determined look on his face. Without a word, he pulled her to her feet and lifted her onto the table. He seized her mouth while snaking his hands underneath her skirt to release her belt. As soon as the lock disengaged, he pulled his leggings down without breaking their kiss.

Savoring the taste of his mouth on hers, she linked her legs behind him when he pressed his erection against her clit. A wave of uncontrollable desire spread through her, making her ache and throb. He continued to tease her before he speared his hard lance into her opening. Kelly groaned at the delicious intrusion. When he filled her, Parker began pumping at an enchanting pace, creating friction while his shaft pushed her into a maddening frenzy.

He watched her with hungered passion when his thrusts grew more urgent. The veins in his arms bulged as he held her. "I'm going to come," he whispered in a ragged voice.

"Come . . . come." She dug her fingers in his shoulders, urging him on.

Parker let out a feral cry as his body convulsed. Kelly savored the feel of his wonderful release within her, and then peaked herself a moment later. He kept grinding long after she'd collapsed against his hard body. They held each other for a long time, enjoying each other's embrace before Parker abruptly pulled away.

"Damn it! I forgot to wear a condom."

Kelly hadn't realized they had been unprotected until he'd mentioned it. "Oh, my. It slipped my mind, too." Her stomach lurched, and she was afraid to even think of the possibility. She tried to count the days in her mind, but it was difficult to do because of the irregularity of her menstrual cycle.

"We got carried away . . . I mean, *I* got carried away. I apologize for my carelessness." Parker was staring into her eyes, searching.

She felt a mixture of apprehension and delight, and she wasn't sure whether to laugh or cry at the absurdity of their situation. Regardless, this night with Parker had been fabulous, and she wasn't going to allow the uncertainty to dampen her high.

Kelly smiled up at him. "Don't worry about it."

"Is there a possibility that you could . . . um . . . get pregnant?" He cupped her face and pulled her closer to him.

"Let's cross that bridge once we get there."

What was the point of worrying about it when she had no idea what to expect? Prudence had given way to carelessness, and there was no one to blame for her own mistake. She'd known better. But for now, Kelly refused to dwell on the situation and would worry about it when the time came—if it ever.

Parker drew a long sigh of relief. She wasn't sure if she should feel happy or insulted.

"Will you tell me if you are? Heck, just let me know either way." Parker looked at her, filled with expectation.

Kelly nodded, and then remembered once again that she had to say something. "I promise I will."

One thing was for certain—she was going to tell Parker about her lies first thing in the morning. But for now, she just wanted to enjoy the evening with him and not ruin the mood.

"I have something for you," she said, changing the subject. Kelly pressed the item into his palm.

Parker jiggled the square, flat case. "What is it?"

"I wanted to get you a card, but since you couldn't read it, I decided to record my sentiments so you could listen to them." She felt silly for acting on a whim.

He grinned and pulled her onto his lap. Kelly rested her head against his chest and savored the perfect moment.

"Thank you. This is the sweetest and most thoughtful gift anyone's ever given me." He closed his eyes and trailed his finger around her lips. "I haven't told you this before—and you have to understand it isn't easy for me to talk about my blindness—but I want you to know that I feel so lucky to have met you. I never thought a guy like me could ever find a woman who would accept me just the way I am."

"Oh, Parker. You have so much to offer, and you have given me far more than I deserve. I don't care that you can't see me, because I know you feel me and you know what's in my heart."

"What's in your heart, Ann? Tell me."

He kissed her with so much affection that she was moved to tears. She sighed, wanting to tell him how she'd fallen for him. Kelly brushed the wisp of hair from his eyes while she searched for the right words to say.

"I want you like I've never wanted another man. You've touched my heart and made me ache to love again."

His kiss was long and intense and filled with promise.

"I intend to keep that ache burning until you fall in love with me. I'll be the happiest man alive when that day comes."

Kelly shuddered at the weight of his words. The day was already upon her, but she couldn't quite speak the truth, not until she was certain Parker felt the same way about the real her.

After they shared the cleanup duty, they retreated back to his bedroom. This time, she managed to rein in her excitement. Pleased with her obedience, Parker took her to new heights, worshiping her and making her feel loved and desired. He controlled the tempo of their lovemaking, but he gave her room to enjoy every lingering sensation along the way.

Exhausted but content, they ended their marathon well past midnight. When she succumbed to sleep, Parker's arms were tightly wrapped around her, and the issue of their unprotected romp had already been forgotten. The last thing she remembered was listening to the soft cadence of their hearts beating in perfect rhythm.

A sharp ring jolted her awake. Kelly glanced around, not quite remembering where she was. A strong arm tightened around her waist, a reminder of what happiness meant. She snuggled closer, locking her legs around his, but the phone rang again.

She jumped when she realized it was her phone causing the noise. She had no intention of answering it until she saw the name flashing from the caller ID. Jessica wouldn't call unless it was important, and besides, it was way too early for her press junket, which wouldn't start until late in the afternoon.

"Jessica, what's wrong?" she whispered.

"You better get your ass back to your house. I'll meet you there." The urgency in Jessica's voice was enough to sound the warning bells inside Kelly's head. She was wide-awake now.

She shot up, despite Parker's steely arms around her.

"Ann, go back to sleep," he murmured.

"It's an important call, sweetie. Hold on." Kelly cupped the receiver and hissed at her friend. "What's going on?"

"You might want to wait until you get home to ask."

"Tell me now."

"Your face is on the front of a tabloid. It looks like the exclusive work of your most hated paparazzo." It took several moments for the words to sink in. "I don't want you talking to anyone. Just hurry back. Dave will be meeting us there, too."

When Dave was involved, it meant one thing—damage control. She was starting to get worried now. "I'll be there in thirty minutes."

After ending the call, she shook Parker awake. "I have to go. An emergency just came up."

Parker pushed himself up onto his elbows, attempting to follow her movements as she rushed to get dressed. "Is everything okay?"

"That's what I'm about to find out. I'm sorry for leaving like this, but I have to hurry home. I'll call you later." Kelly kissed him and was out the door before he could reply.

CHAPTER ELEVEN

Kelly maneuvered her SUV into the early Monday morning rush hour traffic, feeling skittish like a bat driven out of its cave. She drove the congested 405 Freeway in a dazed rush to get back to her Brentwood mansion, where Jessica and Dave, her publicist, would meet her.

When she turned on the small street that led to her property, she noticed an unusual number of cars parked in the available spaces. *This is not good,* she told herself while she negotiated the path leading to her cul-de-sac home, which was now filled with reporters and photographers. She groaned in protest, sliding on her sunglasses and plastering a stoic expression on her face.

When she slowed down to wait for the massive gate to open, hordes of people surged closer to ask questions and take pictures. She tapped her hand with impatience on the steering wheel. Urging the wrought iron gate to open faster, Kelly kept her gaze forward, refusing to be distracted by the muted inquiries coming at her from all directions.

"Who is the man with you?"

"Have you gotten over Matthew?"

"Is he in show business?"

The questions began to make sense, and her earlier nervousness gave way to extreme anxiety. Her biggest fear had now been realized. She gave the accelerator a gentle nudge, and the car moved forward, leaving the crowd and their questions behind.

As she rounded the driveway, Kelly saw that her resident housekeeper and all-around go-to girl, Lizzie, was already waiting for her at the door with a cup of coffee.

"Jessica and Dave are here. Go on in, and I'll park the Rover for you." Lizzie handed her the steaming mug and gave her an encouraging smile.

Kelly grabbed her purse and slid out of the car, feeling nauseous. She took a few quick sips of coffee before starting up the front steps, her muscles tightening with anxiety.

She entered the foyer and dropped her purse on the settee, hurrying toward the sound of voices in the kitchen. When she entered the room, Dave looked up from his seat at the counter, his expression grim. Jessica was standing across from him, about to take a bite of her bagel, but she stopped as soon as Kelly flopped down onto the bar stool next to Dave.

Dave Caldwell, a man in his late forties, had been her publicist ever since she'd made it big in Hollywood, having been introduced to her by a director she'd once worked with. He was trustworthy and direct, not one to soften the blow, but a true friend, nonetheless.

The *Natter Biz* sat staring back at her from the granite counter top. On the cover was a picture of her taken two days before, on her patio and straddling Parker. The headline read, "Kelly Storm—Hormones Raging? Has she found a new love of her life?"

Kelly winced at the sight of the snapshots, none of which showed Parker's face. They were all of hers—some licking his face, smiling, and seeming very happy. One thing to be thankful for, though—the camera angle was such that no one would be able to identify the man right away. She picked up the dreadful magazine and glared at the intrusion into her personal life.

"Kelly, this is not looking good," Dave said, after giving her a few moments to digest the enormity of the situation. "The intimate nature of these pictures is going to cause a firestorm, if they haven't already."

"Why don't you eat first before we start planning," Jessica offered before taking a bite of her bagel.

Kelly shook her head, not in the least bit hungry. This was going to stink. Despite her attempt to protect Parker from the prying eyes of the media, the incriminating pictures had thrust him into the middle of the storm anyway. She feared they might be zeroing in on Parker any moment now.

She turned to Dave, who was already jotting down notes. "What do you propose we do?"

Dave put down his expensive looking pen and sighed. "You know I'm not one to pry, but I need to know the nature of your relationship with the man in the photographs so I can come up with an acceptable statement." He watched her with his kind, gray eyes as she took a deep breath.

"He's my massage therapist. We've been seeing each other for weeks now." That much was true. She had no inclination to say more.

Dave pursed his lips, absorbing her explanation. "And you're planning to keep on seeing him?"

She nodded, taking a sip of her coffee. Jessica continued to eat but kept a steady eye on her. Her friend's body language told Kelly that she understood her disgust, as well as her frustration.

"Are you deeply involved with him?" Dave asked.

"We're getting there." It might have been overconfidence on her part to assume their relationship was going great, but she could feel they were meant to be together.

Dave stroked his chin, deep in thought. Kelly wondered what he could do to alleviate the interest of the media and the public in general.

"Do you think he'll be okay to come out and be seen with you? I mean, if the media and public see that you've found a man who cherishes you, it'll be great publicity, considering how everyone is so overprotective of you after what happened with Matthew."

Distressed, Kelly gritted her teeth in frustration at finding herself stuck in a tough situation. She had intended to tell Parker about her true identity this morning, but Jessica's call had come at the worst time. Telling him now would make matters worse.

Jessica came to her rescue. "The man is Parker Davis." Dave's expression registered recognition, but he said nothing as Jessica continued. "You may be familiar with his condition." Dave nodded. "Kelly went to him for a massage . . . in disguise. Well, one thing led to another, and she hasn't had the chance to tell him who she is. I'm sure you know why . . . ."

Dave nodded in understanding.

Then all of a sudden, Jessica turned to her and raised an eyebrow. "Weren't you supposed to tell him the truth last night?"

Kelly bit her lip and mentally kicked herself for not saying anything sooner. If she had gone ahead and told him, this situation wouldn't be as bad as it was now. "I was going to tell him this morning, but you called and I had to leave in a rush."

Jessica groaned. To Dave she said, "So as you can already tell, we *have* to protect his identity."

Dave rubbed his palm across his forehead and closed his eyes. When he opened them, he looked at Kelly with compassion. "Okay . . . I can tell you like this man. You don't want him dragged into the limelight, correct?"

Kelly gave a feeble smile, hating herself more and more with each passing minute.

"We'll refrain from commenting and won't issue any statements until you're ready. I'll screen the questions this afternoon at the press junket. Any inquiry not related to the film will be rejected." David thought for a moment. "*And* . . . I'll call for extra security tonight. I'm almost certain there will be pandemonium because of this."

The last time Dave had called for a bodyguard had been during the publicity firestorm following her breakup with Matthew. For months, photographers had camped outside of her house, taking pictures with their telephoto lenses and asking too many questions.

"There's a bunch of people outside already," Kelly said.

She pressed her fingers to her temples, feeling the start of a headache. Surreptitiously glancing at the tabloid again, she noted the happiness in her face. Kelly remembered the vivid scene, recalling how surprised Parker had been when she'd licked the ketchup off his face. Now that happiness had been marred by the fear of exposure. Her private life, once again, had been exploited.

"Yes . . . and there will be more. If I were you, I'd be careful. That particular pap . . . what's his name again?" Dave turned a questioning look at Jessica.

"Rigor 'Asshat' James," Jessica said with disgust.

"Yes, that one seems to be enamored with you. Be watchful. The man is relentless and might even be infatuated with you." Dave placed a sympathetic hand on her shoulder and squeezed before retrieving his cell phone and leaving the kitchen.

Jessica looked over her shoulder while she rinsed her plate. "Why don't you lie down and try to relax if you can? I'll stay with you until you and Dave have to leave."

Lizzie came in with her car key and placed it on the counter. "I started a warm bath for you. Jessica's right, Ms. Kelly. You should relax." Her housekeeper smiled and shooed Jessica away from the sink.

"Thanks, Lizzie. What would I do without you?" Kelly smiled, grateful for her housekeeper's thoughtfulness.

"You're welcome, Ms. Kelly. You're my lifesaver. What I'm doing here is nothing compared to what you've done for me." The woman returned her smile and began to load the dishwasher.

"If it weren't too early for a glass of wine, I would share one with you." Jessica laughed.

When they passed the morning room on their way to the stairs, Kelly heard Dave talking to the security company he'd used for her in the past.

The mansion, which had once brought her immense pleasure, felt like a prison to her now. With the media waiting outside, she had to stay out of sight. Bought and paid for by her acting earnings, the place had gotten a major overhaul. She'd hired an interior decorator to design a home that reflected her particular taste and style. Being a fan of minimalism, she'd opted for clean lines, subtle colors, and monochromatic artwork. Kelly held on tight to the black balustrade while she climbed the stairs, not to keep her balance but because of her pounding headache.

"I should've said something right away, but I just couldn't. He was too sweet, and I couldn't break his heart. I don't think I can afford to lose him." She stopped and faced Jessica. "I'm in love with him."

As soon as they entered her bedroom, Jessica opened the curtains, letting the early morning sunlight drift in. Kelly sank onto her bed, feeling rotten about the pictures in the tabloid.

"The right thing to do now is to tell the truth. If he finds out without you telling him, it's going to be a lot messier. You just might end up losing the guy."

Kelly shuddered at the thought of never seeing Parker again. How he'd managed to creep through her guarded walls still amazed her. But now that he was in, she wasn't going to let him go. She stared up at the cathedral ceiling and sighed. "I'll call him in a bit. I just need a little time to think. I can't just blurt it out now. I don't know how he'd react, and to be honest, I wouldn't blame him if he never wanted to see me again."

"Now, now. Stop being so melodramatic. Tell him and make him understand. I'm sure he will accept your explanation. Just don't wait too long." Jessica stood next to her bed. "Lizzie said she started a bath for you. Go in there and try to relax. The crew will be arriving in a few hours to get you ready. Stop worrying and let Dave handle the rest."

Kelly tried calling Parker several times during the next few hours, but every time she dialed his number, she ended up cancelling the call. She didn't have a clue as to how and where to start. Maybe it would be wiser to break it to him in person instead of telling him over the phone. Checking her schedule, she saw that she was due to leave that night for a whirlwind promotion of her latest film, along with a quick stop in Milan to attend the grand introduction of her new line of handbags. She wouldn't be back in LA until for another week. Kelly groaned at the timing, hating herself even more for being a coward.

The press junket went as well as could be expected, with Dave prescreening all questions as promised. Swarms of paparazzi were waiting for them at the hotel entrance, taking picture after picture. Kelly waved and tried to keep her composure. She kept a smile plastered on her face, even if it felt like she was about to crack. All she wanted to do was to see Parker and get her confession over and done with. How had everything gotten so out of control? It wasn't just herself she had to look out for now. She'd also dragged an unknowing Parker into the thick of it.

In between getting ready for her scheduled junket and packing, Kelly found the guts to call Parker. "Hey, I miss you. I'm so sorry for leaving in such a hurry."

"Hi, Ann. I miss you, too." He sounded wistful over the phone. "Is everything okay?"

"Yes. I'm calling to let you know that I'll be out of the country for a week. I was planning on telling you this morning when we woke up, but I didn't get a chance."

"That's all right. I'll be here when you get back."

"Um . . . Parker?"

"Yeah?"

"There's something I want to tell you, but I would rather say it when we're together."

He fell silent for a few moments before he spoke again. "Is it sensitive in nature?"

"Yes . . . it has something to do with me, but it will ultimately affect you *and* me."

"Then tell me when you get back. I'm not going anywhere."

Kelly hesitated. As relieved as she was with Parker's assertion that he'd rather wait until they were together, she wanted to give him a hint just to see how he'd react.

"But I want you to know before you find out from others."

"Ann, if it makes you uncomfortable discussing it over the phone, I understand. I'd rather we wait until we're together. That doesn't mean I won't be waiting for your call every day."

"Well, okay. If you think that's best. Don't worry. We'll be burning the phone lines." She breathed a sigh of relief. "Oh, I just wanted to tell you that I had a wonderful time with you, and I-I'm so glad I met you."

"Me, too, Ann. Me, too."

Her heart leapt with happiness. All she had to do was get back from Milan and just tell him. The prospect made all her qualms disappear.

"I'm glad to hear that. Gee, I have to go. I'll call you once I'm settled. Take care of yourself."

"You're the one who's traveling, so take good care of *you*. I'm looking forward to seeing you again."

Kelly smiled. "Bye, Parker."

"Bye, Ann."

Webster thought she'd lose it when she saw the headlines on the latest issue of *Natter Biz*. She bought a copy from the corner newsstand and hurried to her desk, where she gobbled up the entire article within minutes. Her anger was at the boiling point by the time Parker and Cork arrived for work.

She couldn't hide her disdain at her discovery but wasn't sure if she should meddle, or even what constituted acceptable meddling. When Parker left the room for his first appointment of the day, she went to see Cork down in his office and closed the door.

Cork glanced up, looking amused. Since getting together a week ago, she had refused to go public with their relationship. He rose and rounded his desk to where she stood, tabloid in hand. Cork pulled her close and kissed her. She returned the kiss but with much less passion. The information she'd discovered was too distracting.

"What's wrong?" he asked, searching her face.

Webster drew a deep breath. She had told Cork the nature of her relationship with his brother, and he seemed to have taken everything in stride, not that he could have done anything about the past anyway. He was well aware of her preferences and had been warming up to the idea, despite his earlier reservations.

"I drove Parker yesterday. He called to ask if I could take him shopping, and I did."

Cork raised an eyebrow but said nothing. Webster felt the need to explain further, even though he hadn't asked. "He feels more comfortable asking me for help in this matter. Well . . . you know why."

"You don't have to explain," Cork said, keeping his arms around the small of her back.

"As it so happened, I probed, and he told me about his mystery date."

"Oh, yeah. Mom grilled him about that woman the other night during dinner."

"I was harassing him about not knowing her well enough, so he gave me her name just to shut me up. It turned out that this woman said she was Ann Sutton. To make a long story short, as soon as I got home, I searched for whatever I can get my hands on about her. And guess what came up?"

"What came up?" Cork echoed her question while rubbing the back of her neck.

"Ann Sutton is Kelly Storm, the actress. You know . . . *Deep Ice*, *Hearts Afire*, and *Shattered Dreams* . . ."

Cork pulled back and stared at her in disbelief. "No way! Are you sure about this?"

"Positive. And now this." Webster held up a copy of the gossip magazine.

Cork read the headline first, and then gave her a questioning look. "So Kelly is seeing a new guy. Where does Parker come in?"

"Look at the man in the picture." True, the man had his back to the camera, but she'd bet her life savings it was Parker. The blond hair and the body build gave it away for her.

Cork studied the picture and cursed. "Oh shit! We saw her at Chateau Marmont Saturday night!"

"What?"

"Yeah, when we walked in, she was staring at Parker. I teased him about it and tried to get him to go over to her table to say hi, but he refused. Shortly after, she left in a hurry." Cork looked stumped.

Webster shook her head. "What the hell is going on? Parker has no idea Ann and Kelly are the same person. I'm sure of it. He wouldn't hide something like that from me." The deception was disgusting.

"I believe you. What should we do?" Cork let her go, and they both sank down on the chair.

"That's why I'm here. I don't think Parker is aware of this yet. But it won't take long before your brother finds out. God. Wait till I get my hands on that bitch. I'll wring her neck! How could she do this to him?" Angry tears pooled in her eyes.

"I want to tell him, but shouldn't we check the facts to be sure?" Cork laid a hand on her arm and rubbed soothing strokes.

"What else do we need to know other than she deceived him?" Webster shouted.

"I know you're upset. I am, too, but we can't go to Parker and just say it. Don't you think we ought to give this some thought first?"

"I don't know what to think anymore. For the longest time, I tried to protect him from women who would take advantage of his blindness, and now she comes along. Poor Parker."

Cork stood and pulled her to her feet, gathering her into an embrace. "I feel the same way. That's why I gave up my career to come and work for him. I hated the thought of that once proud man being reduced to asking other people for help. I don't mind it at all because we're brothers. Parker has always been there for me, protecting and watching my back ever since we were little. It was the least I could do. But we have to approach this situation with care. We can't barge in his office and tell him the woman he cares about is lying to him. There's a fine line between us getting involved and letting him figure this out for himself."

"You're going to let her hurt your brother?" Webster gaped at him in surprise.

Cork shook his head. "No, that's not what I meant. There are some things we have no control over, and one of those things is Parker getting his heart broken. This Ann, Kelly, whoever she is, has already done that. No amount of warning can undo her actions. Let's think about this a little more, okay?"

Webster nodded. If she ever got the chance to see Kelly in person, she'd make sure the woman would feel the shame and guilt of what she had done to Parker, or at least for what was coming at Parker thanks to her lies.

CHAPTER TWELVE

Parker waited all day Monday for Ann to call as she had promised and was still waiting the next day, but he refused to phone her like some insecure boyfriend. He wasn't her boyfriend, as least as far as he knew, so he kept himself occupied to avoid the temptation to call her. Instead, he spent long hours at the track with Andrew after work, but his friend's continued questions about his frame of mind were driving him crazy.

By the time Wednesday rolled around, he was going insane with worry. What if something had happened to her? Parker reminded himself several times to calm down and that she would call. People at work were beginning to ask questions about his foul mood. Even in his darkest hours, when he'd first gotten the news of his impending blindness, he'd managed to maintain an appearance of calm. This time, he couldn't help himself. He snapped at the slightest idiotic question, no doubt raising eyebrows and concerns among his employees.

As soon as he got to work on Thursday morning, Webster cornered him in his office. She handed him his coffee, and then sat down across from his desk.

"What's with the long face?" she asked.

He took a long sip before leveling his gaze in her direction. "What are you talking about?"

"Fine . . . play coy. But you're biting people's heads off for the littlest things. You jump whenever your phone rings—"

"I get it. Jeez, you're such a pain. So I'm a little worried because Ann hasn't called. Bite me." Parker scowled in her direction, hating the fact that Webster could read him like a book. "Have I been that bad?"

"Yes. You're like an ogre." She paused as if choosing her words carefully. "This Ann person . . . how well do you know her?"

He groaned. "Are we back on that subject again? I told you already, I know her well enough. What else do you want?"

"Well, maybe it's time for you to snoop a little and find out who this girl is. I mean, she hasn't called you when she said she would. She sounds a little suspicious to me."

"There must be a logical explanation for that. I'm just hoping nothing bad has happened to her." The thought sobered him. He'd give anything to know what was going on with Ann. Aside from her phone number, he had no way to get in touch with her. Although he'd been to her house, Parker had forgotten to ask for her address.

"I'm sure there's a good reason in there somewhere," Webster said, her tone filled with sarcasm.

Parker didn't quite understand what he was hearing in Webster's voice. He leaned forward and narrowed his eyes, trying his best to catch the expression in her face, to no avail. Everything remained hazy.

"Are you trying to tell me something?" he asked.

"I'm just saying you're losing your touch, Parker. You've never sat around and waited for a woman. If she wants you, let her come to you. Don't mope around as if the end of the world is upon you." Webster stood, reached for his hand, and gave it a soft squeeze. "I booked your flight to New York. You're leaving Sunday afternoon. Same hotel, and your transfers are all arranged. I'll e-mail the itinerary to you in a bit."

Parker wasn't certain what to say. Women seemed to have a knack for giving men whiplash. One moment they were talking about something important, and with a snap of a finger, they shifted to something frivolous.

"Thanks."

"Your first client should be here by now. I'll put Ms. Jones in room 104."

Parker nodded, still wondering about Webster's cryptic comment about Ann. He wished things were different, but he couldn't change the past. He'd met Ann, and now he intended to move forward with her.

He had a few minutes to spare before his first client of the day, so he typed a short text to Ann and hit the send button, leaning back in his chair and hating that he had no idea how to find her.

Normally he'd leave his cell phone in his office whenever he was with a client to avoid being interrupted while working. But this time, he silenced the ring tone and set the phone to vibrate.

He reached room 104 and tapped on the door before entering. The familiar scent of Flower Bomb perfume floated around him when he greeted Liz Jones, a local newscaster and one of his regular LA clients.

"Hello, Liz. I haven't seen you for quite some time."

"Parker, you won't believe what happened!" Liz jumped up and draped her arms around his neck, kissing him on the cheek.

Parker cupped her face and smiled. "Sounds like someone is very happy."

"Ecstatic, actually. Steve and I are having a baby!" she said, still clinging to him.

"Really? Congratulations!" Parker kissed her on the forehead before pulling away to get a good look at her face. "How far along are you?"

"Thank you. Steve's beside himself. Twelve weeks yesterday." She took his hand and placed it on her belly.

Parker felt the bump and grinned. He rubbed her stomach several times, eliciting a giggle from one of his most loyal customers. "I'm happy for you."

Strange as it seemed, the image of a pregnant Ann flashed through mind. The idea was a little far-fetched, but he couldn't deny the pride he felt at the thought of her carrying his child. *Whoa, Parker. You're really getting ahead of yourself!*

"Thanks to you. If not for our 'psychiatric' sessions, I would have left Steve already. I'm so glad you talked me out of it." Liz laughed.

That much was true. Liz had been close to hysterics during her scheduled massages. She'd often threatened to divorce her husband because of his passive nature, especially in the bedroom. One of their sessions had turned into a verbal therapy of sort, forgoing the massage in favor of talking.

Parker had met Steve at a gathering they'd attended together, and he'd somehow sensed Liz's husband needed a little spark in the bedroom. Quiet and reserved as he was, all Steve needed, in Parker's opinion, was a little nudge, a different approach on how to express himself. He'd ended up showing Liz a few tricks—in particular, how to find a person's erogenous zone. Of course, this was all based on his personal experience and what he'd learned from school, and there were no guarantees, as every single case was different. They'd spent several weeks practicing before Liz had felt confident enough to try his tips at home. He hadn't heard from her for over three months and had begun to think his suggestion hadn't produced the results they'd been hoping for.

"Well, you did all the dirty work." He laughed. "I didn't do anything except listen. You're the one who made it happen. So you're here for a pregnancy massage, then?"

Liz giggled again. "Yes, I want the whole shebang."

"You know the drill. Remove all your jewelry, except this time, lie on your side, and call me when you're ready."

Parker left to get ready, thinking of Ann the entire time. Why hadn't she returned his text or even called?

He had just finished strapping on his oil and lotion belt when he heard Liz's enthusiastic "woo-rah." He started the soft music, took a deep breath, and returned to the dimly lit massage room.

The hour went by so fast. Liz's chatter was a welcome distraction that kept him from thinking of Ann. Massaging a pregnant woman required specialized training, as well as a good amount of concentration. At the end of their session, Liz was near tears. Happiness and pride welled from her, and Parker could feel her emotions just by touching her. Pleased with the outcome, Liz thanked him before she left.

As soon as Parker emerged from his office to go to his next appointment, Cork intercepted him at the end of the hallway.

"Hey, bro, what's up?" Cork asked. He sounded a little too perky in Parker's opinion.

"Not much. You?"

He wasn't up for small talk at the moment. All he wanted was to finish his last appointment and have at it with the treadmill as soon as he got home. Cork walked alongside him while he made his way to the massage room.

"I got a call from a casting agent. They want you to do the next X-Pro commercial. Do you want details?"

Parker stopped and faced his brother. "Is that the new sports drink?"

"Yeah." Cork chuckled. "The one you said tasted like pee."

"I don't know. It sounds hypocritical to endorse a product I can't stand. What do you think?"

"I think it'll be good exposure for you and for Knead Me. Besides, it'll give you something to take your mind off whatever it is that's bugging you."

"Have you been talking to Webster? I swear you guys are acting like two mother hens. Lay off me, will you? I'm okay." Parker reached the room of his next client and not a moment too soon. "Fine . . . I'll meet with the agent. Give me the details later. Meet me at the bar after work."

"Dude, I'm sorry, but I can't. I have something planned after I drop you off later, but I'll give you a call tonight."

Cork was being evasive again, but he wasn't about to pry. Parker nodded. "Sounds good. I'll see you later."

The day passed at an excruciatingly slow pace. By the time five o'clock rolled around, Parker was not faring well at all. He needed to get rid of the tension building inside him. What he *really* needed was a massage, but he wasn't feeling up to talking or subjecting himself to Andy or Mark's scrutiny and inane chatter, so he decided to chill at home for the night and maybe run his treadmill into the ground.

As soon as Cork dropped him off, he changed into gym shorts and running shoes and got to work. Without bothering to warm up, he chose a full-out run and set the machine on a steep incline. Parker ran for over an hour, expending the same amount of energy he'd burn up if he was running outdoors. By the time he finished, sweat was rolling off him by the bucketful. Tired, cranky, and in need of a shower, he stayed under the spray until his nerves calmed down.

After dinner, he surfed through the channels until he found a familiar rerun of *ER*. He listened to the television program, hoping it would distract him. He needed something, *anything*, to keep his mind off Ann. Getting more agitated by the minute, he grabbed his cell and sent her another text message—the last one he was planning to send, since his other two had been ignored.

With several hours to kill before bedtime and with nothing better to do, he powered up his laptop and activated the screen reader program. He checked his e-mails first, none of which required an immediate response. Parker thought of what Webster had said earlier. How well *did* he know Ann? If Webbie had any serious doubts about Ann, why hadn't she mentioned anything? Regardless, he'd be dammed if he was going to ignore her subtle warnings.

Parker typed Ann's name into the Google search box, and after a few seconds, the mechanical voice announced several choices. He went down the list, but each one produced unfamiliar results. One Ann Sutton was an exhibit curator residing in Egypt, another was a real estate agent from Arizona, and another was a quilt maker from the South. He listened to a few more until he got to a blog written by a woman who claimed to have been a high school classmate of Kelly Ann Sutton—also known as Kelly Storm. The blog had more than four thousand hits. His interest piqued, he listened while the screen reader read the entry for him, not certain if he wanted to hear the blogger's entire post of her attempt to be famous.

The part where the woman claimed Kelly Ann had always been a great actress in their numerous high school plays intrigued him, so he listened for more. The woman mentioned the school where she and Kelly Ann had both graduated—Chicago High School, class of 2004. He recalled Ann telling him she was twenty-six years old. Was this a mere coincidence, or was the truth in there somewhere?

His stomach tightened at the improbable coincidence. He dug some more, opening another tab and then typing *Kelly Storm* into the search box. Parker couldn't see the images on the screen, no matter how hard he strained. All he could make out were blurry faces and figures.

Frustrated, he dialed Webster's number. When she answered, he didn't waste any words. "I want you to come over right away. Call Cork and tell him to swing by, too."

"What's going on?" Webster asked, sounding alarmed.

"Just come as soon as you can."

Parker threw the phone on the bed and paced the floor, feeling like a caged animal. He needed to confirm if the woman he was "seeing" was the famed actress. If it were true, then she was probably laughing her ass off at him. He got even angrier as he tried to walk off his growing resentment.

To help pass the time while waiting for Cork and Webster, he downed several shots of Everclear, one right after the other. He was nursing a good buzz by the time they arrived. Feeling a bit mellower than he had been an hour ago, he led them to his bedroom and his laptop.

Cork and Webster followed him. He sensed from their silence that they already knew what he wanted from them. He didn't say anything until he moved the touch pad and the screen reader announced the picture of Kelly Storm.

He heard them move closer to look. No one said a word, so he spoke first.

"Did either one of you suspect she might be the woman I'm seeing?" Parker laughed bitterly at his own words. Not seeing was the problem. He had no idea who he'd been *seeing* all this time.

Another silence stretched before them, and he assumed Cork and Webster were deciding who was going to answer him. Cork coughed and attempted to clear his throat.

"I'm not sure, bro. We saw her in the restaurant last week, remember?"

Parker nodded his head with impatience.

"I didn't know back then if there was a connection, but thinking about it now, there has to be. The way she was staring at you that night, the surprised expression on her face, and the way she left the restaurant might very well be signs that she's the same person. But I'm not one hundred percent sure because I haven't seen the *Ann* who came to see you at work." Cork's explanation made sense.

"I know you haven't seen her, but do you think they're the same people?" he asked, pointing to the monitor, his anger mounting.

"Could be, but don't you think you ought to ask her first before you get all upset?"

He ignored his brother's question and turned to Webster, who hadn't said a word since they'd arrived.

"Webbie, you've seen Madame Baba. Do you think she's Kelly Storm?"

She sighed and placed a calming hand on his arm. He shook it off and glared at her. "Tell me what you think!"

"It's hard to tell. Madame Baba had black hair. I can't remember her face that well. She walked fast and avoided eye contact even with her dark, oversized sunglasses. I wish I could be sure, although to tell you the truth, I suspected the connection when you gave me her name."

"Suspected? How could you not mention anything to me? You think because I'm blind that I wouldn't find out?"

"Hold on, Parker. I'm not the enemy here. No one is. If I haven't mentioned anything, it was because I wasn't sure if I should be the bearer of the bad news."

"Damn it, guys! I'm fucking blind, in case you haven't noticed! There's no way I'd find out about some things unless those closest to me point them out!"

"Park, I'm sorry," Cork said. "I should've listened to Webster when she came to me and asked if we should mention the connection to you. We've always minded our own business, right? I just didn't want you to think I was being overprotective *because* of your blindness."

As upset as he was by the possibility, Parker knew he was going at it all wrong. The only person who could answer his questions had gone missing. If he knew where to find her, he wouldn't be standing in front of his brother and his friend, blaming them for protecting him. He slumped down onto the edge of the bed.

"I'm sorry for yelling. I have no right to talk to either of you the way I did. It's just so frustrating. I thought I'd met someone worth pursuing, and now it turns out she's been lying all along."

"No harm done, bro."

Ann Sutton was Kelly Storm? Although he had no solid evidence, he had a sick feeling it was true, considering the way Ann . . . Kelly . . . whoever she was had been avoiding answering direct questions about herself.

"It's still early. Why don't you guys join me for drinks? We've got time to get ripped together."

"I'm game," Webster replied, sounding relieved.

The moment Kelly's plane landed at LAX, she turned on her cell and retrieved all her messages, including three texts from Parker. She checked each one as she waited for her luggage at the carousel. People around her were staring, pointing, and taking pictures while she tried her best to keep her composure. She kept her head low and tried to show very little emotion while she read all his incoming messages. He sounded worried and was urging her to contact him. A deluge of guilt rained down upon her.

The whole week had been hectic, and she'd been shuffled from one press junket to another to promote her upcoming movie. Afterward, she'd been whisked away to attend private and business parties hosted by Gucci bigwigs as part of promoting their new product line. As much as she'd just wanted to curl up in her hotel room, she had an obligation to fulfill her contract. The difference in time zones hadn't helped, either. The latter was more of an excuse, because she'd wanted to avoid hearing his anger and disappointment.

Feeling drained and in dire need of a bath, she couldn't wait to get home and soak in the tub, but she needed to visit someone first. When her luggage came, she met her ride and instructed the limousine driver to take her to Westwood Village Memorial Park.

Jessica was waiting for her at the entrance of the cemetery, where they switched her luggage from the limo to Jessica's Beemer. Jessica hugged her as soon as they stashed her stuff in the trunk.

"Welcome back."

"Thanks. I'm glad I made it in time." Her eyes brimmed with tears, and she wiped them away.

"No more tears, Kelly."

As they drove past the rows of headstones that lined the quiet and deserted cemetery, Kelly's heart began to break again. Even though it had been a year, she still hadn't gotten over her loss. That all too familiar feeling of guilt and heartbreak forced its way back into her soul, making her relive the past year.

Tears welled in her eyes, and she gave up on holding them back. There was no point in maintaining a pretense of courage in Jessica's presence. Her friend understood her pain and had suffered her loss, too.

The car climbed the sloping path until they reached the mausoleum, a white Romanesque-style building with several private plots surrounding it. Kelly had chosen one of the plots outside, liking the openness instead of being cooped up inside the building. Little angels needed to spread their wings, and she'd thought that fit her little girl well. A marble fence surrounded the white gravestone. A small angel stood watch over the marker, a silent sentinel in Kelly's absence.

The grass surrounding the immediate area was trimmed, and the ground was still moist from earlier watering. Kelly climbed out of the car and took one of the flower arrangements she had ordered from the passenger seat. The precious little wreath, made of lavender gladiolus, pink lilies, lilac chrysanthemums, and tiny blush carnations, was perfect for her tiny angel. Jessica brought the other arrangement, and they placed the flowers in front of the headstone.

Kelly read the inscription through the blur of tears, remembering her anguish as if it had happened yesterday.

Gypsy Sutton

A Pure Soul—Born and Died on October 13, 2011

Jessica wrapped an arm around her shoulder as waves of sadness engulfed her. Kelly had cried for her daughter every day, and the pain had never left her. She leaned on Jessica, who in turn began humming a tune. This was her secret pain, and the loss that had almost robbed her of her will to live.

"She would have turned one year old today."

"Gypsy is smiling down on you right now. Be happy for her, Kelly."

She nodded, not trusting herself to say more. When she found the strength to talk again, she said a little prayer before they sat down on the damp grass in comfortable silence.

An hour passed before they returned to the car. Kelly felt a little better after crying and took comfort in the knowledge that her baby was in the company of other angels who were watching over her.

"There's a blue car following us again." Jessica kept watch in the rearview mirror and made a sudden right turn. The tires squealed, and they almost hit a parked car on the street.

Kelly screamed in terror as she braced her hand on the dashboard. "Don't go killing us over some stupid paparazzi!" She turned to look behind them and was relieved they seemed to have lost their tail.

"I'll bet you it's that creep again. Gosh, the price you have to pay for fame." Jessica groaned and stepped on the accelerator.

Kelly tried to calm her nerves by taking deep breaths. "Don't remind me. I tried not to think of all the negatives while I was away. I thought the time away would give me a clearer perspective and a fresh outlook on things. But here I am again, back to where I started."

She had done a lot of thinking the entire week she'd been gone. The main occupant of her waking thoughts had been Parker. She planned on seeing him as soon as she got her schedule straightened out.

"I'm taking you straight home. Lizzie cleaned and locked up your cottage. She said the place is ready anytime you want to use it."

"Thanks. What would I do without you?"

"If you want to express your gratitude, just be around to help me celebrate Brett's birthday. It's going to be a surprise party at our place. Just you, your gorgeous masseur, and a few of our friends. Say you'll come."

"Of course I'll be there. I can't answer for Parker yet," she said, remembering what she had to do the moment she got home.

As soon as Jessica left and she was in the comfort of her pj's and her quiet bedroom, she pulled the phone from her purse and called Knead Me's LA branch. As soon as the receptionist answered, she disguised her voice.

"Hi, I would like to make an appointment with Mr. Davis, please."

"Sure. Are you a return customer?"

"I'm a new one."

"Great! Can I get your name please?"

"It's Kelly Storm."

There was a long pause on the other end. Kelly was expecting a squeal or something along the lines of hero-worship, which were the usual responses when people recognized her name.

"Kelly Storm, the actress?"

She was surprised to hear blatant disdain in the receptionist's voice.

"Yes."

"Ms. Storm, I'm sorry but Mr. Davis isn't taking new clients at the moment. And if I can give you a piece of advice, my boss doesn't need you or anyone else rubbing his blindness in his face. Be thankful you're not standing here in front of me, because I wouldn't hesitate to bitch-slap you into oblivion."

There was a click, and the line went dead. Kelly stared at the phone in shock, trying to grasp the meaning of the conversation. What had the woman said? Then the realization hit her—Parker knew who she was, and if she based his reaction on the woman's hostility, things didn't look promising for her.

With her heart slamming against her chest, she bit her lip to keep from crying. She dialed her personal florist's number and took the first step in what looked to be a long battle to win back Parker's trust.

"I want you to make the best arrangement of your most fragrant flowers and sprinkle them with white roses. Prepare twelve dozen arrangements and deliver them to all the Knead Me branches. I don't care how much they cost, just make them special, and make sure they're beautiful to touch, too. It's for Parker Davis. No need to put my name. Include this message with them—*No one can lie, no one can hide anything, when he looks directly into someone's soul. I apologize.*"

CHAPTER THIRTEEN

Instead of getting the rest she had been hoping for, Kelly spent the entire morning staring at the ceiling, cursing herself and crying for the lies she'd allowed to snowball out of control. Had she taken a moment to tell Parker her secret, things wouldn't have come to this. Now there was no telling if she'd get a chance to repair whatever damage had stemmed from her sin of omission. Would Parker even give her a chance to explain herself?

No matter how she looked at it now, she'd been wrong for keeping her identity from him, even if she'd considered it her right to privacy. The time away had given her some much-needed perspective. She'd come to the conclusion that Parker meant more to her than just a random sexual romp. Despite his blindness, Kelly would never see him as less than perfect. To her, his lack of sight just made him more in tune with her feelings and her needs, which was more than she could say for any man she'd known before.

As anxious and uncertain as she was of her future in acting and life in general, the only constant she saw was Parker's presence in her life. It didn't matter to her that he was different. His sexual quirk was something she could get used to. She'd be a fool if she let him go, unless he decided having her around wasn't worth the trouble. Parker was worth the risk. Too bad it had taken her several weeks to realize he was all she'd ever needed. Nothing mattered anymore, as long as she was happy in her own skin—and in the arms of the man who saw her as she wanted to be seen.

In spite of her earlier apprehension, she made up her mind to pursue a relationship with him, if there was anything left to salvage. With a deep sense of relief at knowing what she wanted and needed, she dialed his number. Her call went to his voice mail. She left a message and prayed for a return call. Afterward, she phoned his LA office, and the same hostile woman answered. Kelly breathed deep, telling herself not to lose her cool and just do what she needed to do.

"Hello. I'm going to pretend I didn't hear what you said earlier. I won't dignify your accusations with an explanation, because that's best given to the person I offended. I don't care what you think of me, nor do I expect you to believe that I never intended to hurt Parker. The only reason I'm calling is to get a chance to talk to him." Getting that off her chest gave her little satisfaction.

A long silence followed. Kelly thought the woman had hung up on her once again but was surprised when she spoke again.

"I was out of line earlier, but I won't apologize for my actions either. I love Parker like a brother, and I will do anything to keep him from getting hurt, even if it means cussing out a very popular actress."

"That's good to know. Parker is lucky to have you as a friend."

Another pause followed. "He isn't here. He flew to New York last night. I would advise you to give him some time to think things over."

"I understand."

Of course she understood, but that didn't mean she had to heed the woman's advice. The sooner she made him understand her reasons, the better she'd feel.

"By the way, the flowers are lovely. I'll make sure he gets the message you sent. I placed them all in his office."

"Thank you."

"Also, his brother and I didn't say anything about the article and photos in *Natter Biz*. We figured it would be best if you told him about it."

"I will. That's the reason why I wanted to talk to him. I want to see him personally and explain everything."

"Well, I wish you good luck."

Kelly needed all the luck she could get. "Thanks. I'm going to need that and more. What is your name?"

"I'm Webster, but just call me Webbie."

"It's nice to meet you Webbie."

After they hung up, Kelly went over her schedule for the rest of the week. After a quick phone call to Jessica, she was able to convince her friend to rearrange her schedule so that she could fly to New York and start the groveling process.

"I'm all for a happy ending, you know that, but I want you to be certain of your feelings before you fly across the country. Shit happened, even though it wasn't your intention to hurt him, and you have Rigor to thank for that."

"If there's anything I'm sure of in this life, it's that I want Parker in it, in whatever capacity he wants. At this point, I'd settle for him just accepting my explanation."

"I won't hassle you anymore. I think I've done enough. To be honest, I understand why you did what you did. There's no way of knowing who you can trust, especially in this business. I believe you're trying to protect him, too, but it's not going to work. You're a public figure, and everything you do is placed in a petri dish like you're a science project, to be watched and poked at, and every little movement is magnified. If you want Parker to share your life, you'd better warn him to develop a strong stomach."

"For now, let me just get over the biggest hurdle, and that is to get him to talk to me. I'm scared, Jess."

"Don't be. If he can't accept your explanation, there's nothing you can do about it. You'll just have to chalk it up as one love lost."

Love? That was the crux of the matter. She'd really fallen for him. How odd. She, of all the people, should've known better than to jump into the unknown. Kelly had been "in love" before, and it had taken her nowhere. Now she found herself in love with a man despite her efforts to deny the fact. She realized she was now ready to dive into new territory and gamble again.

"But it doesn't have to be. I'll do whatever it takes to get him to listen to me, even if I have to beg."

Jessica snorted. "Wow, I would love to see my best friend do just that. But all kidding aside, you made the wrong call. You wanted to protect yourself, and you didn't expect to fall head over heels with your massage therapist. There's still hope. I'm crossing my fingers for you."

After they hung up, Kelly made a flight reservation for Wednesday. Too bad she couldn't go any sooner.

۔ৣ

Parker's mood hadn't improved since he'd left LA. If anything, it seemed to be gathering momentum, leading him into a state where he needed to lash out, inflict harm, or just scream his frustrations until his voice gave out. Why had Ann—Kelly—chosen to hide her true identity from him? Did it have anything to do with his blindness? Was she so embarrassed to associate herself with him that she'd felt the need to keep her identity hidden?

Well, he had fallen in love with her, and what a joke he must have been for her. Mustering up a fake smile, he left for his meeting with the advertising agent. He'd scheduled it in his office, needing the familiarity of his surroundings to boost his eroding confidence.

As soon as the car stopped in front of the building that housed his newest office, he sensed something wasn't right. He looked in the driver's direction for guidance.

"What's going on out there?" he asked.

"Sir, there's a bunch of people in front of your building with those professional cameras. There's about a dozen or so. Do you want me to walk you into the building?"

Parker pressed his lips together. What had he gotten himself into? He shook his head. "I'll be fine. Just keep your phone handy for my call."

"Will do."

He stepped out of the car and into the chilly morning air. As soon as the throng spotted him, footsteps rushed in his direction. Parker saw the blurry figures and recognized the flashing lights snapping around him. He faked yet another smile and trudged forward, counting his steps, hoping he would make it to the door without trampling anyone or making a fool of himself.

"Mr. Davis, are you Kelly Storm's new boyfriend?"

"Are you going to attend the premier of her new movie?"

"How does it feel to be dating a beautiful actress?"

With forward movement becoming impossible, it occurred to him that he might not make it to the door of the building. He reached forward, trying to get his balance while ignoring questions and the snapping flashes.

"People, will you please let my boss pass?" A high-pitched voice rose above every other noise around them while Arianne made her way to him, surrounded by two of his biggest masseuses. She took his hand and squeezed.

The group parted grudgingly, but the sound of cameras clicking continued. Parker gave Arianne a relieved smile as they walked through the door that was being held open by another employee.

"Thanks for coming to my rescue." Parker gritted his teeth to keep from muttering a curse in front of his office crew. He plastered on a smile and swept his gaze across the room. "It's all good, guys. I'm glad to be back."

Someone from his left started clapping, and before he could say anything, the entire room erupted in encouraging hoots and applause. Disgusted at himself, he waved them off and walked in the direction of his office. An arm slipped under his and guided him forward.

"I'm sorry. I should've come sooner. I didn't realize the paps were after you until I got a call from Webbie," Arianne said, sounding contrite while she closed the door behind him.

He flopped on the chair, shaken. "Does everyone know but me?" Parker fumbled for his cell but stopped when he caught a whiff of fragrance all around him. "What's that scent? Flowers?"

"Yes . . . I had to accept all of them. The delivery guy wouldn't take no for an answer. He didn't say who sent them—"

Parker cut her off with impatience. "Ari, how many flowers are we talking about?" He followed his nose until he reached the row of file cabinets at the right side of the room.

"There are three dozen arrangements in here. There are different flowers in each arrangement, but all of them have these tiny white roses sprinkled in each display. They're stunning."

Tentative, Parker touched the arrangement closest to him. He felt the unusual textures, soft, velvety and silky, as he ran his fingers along each bouquet.

"Does it say who sent them?"

"There's a note, but the envelope is sealed. Do you want me to read it to you?"

He nodded, resenting the fact that he needed help to read the note. Another downside to his blindness was his inability to keep some level of privacy in his life.

" 'No one can lie, no one can hide anything, when he looks directly into someone's soul. I apologize.' " He didn't miss the awe in Ari's voice.

"Thank you."

"Do you need a moment alone?" Arianne was already moving toward the door.

"Yes." His voice sounded strangled, even to his own ears. "I have a ten thirty appointment with an agent. Please direct him to the conference room and tell him I'm running a few minutes late."

When Arianne closed the door behind her, Parker sank back into his chair and rubbed his face, trying his best to stay calm. Ann . . . Kelly, whoever she was, had steamrolled her way into his life, rattled his orderly existence, and shaken him to the core. The sad part was that he had no idea how to handle the situation.

Why had she sent him flowers? Was she trying to massage his bruised ego? If she thought that would get him to call her, she was mistaken. Nothing would change the fact that she'd lied. Then a sudden thought came back to him. Before Kelly left, she wanted to talk about something. Could this be it? Regardless, she had deceived him, and a bunch of silly flowers wouldn't flatter him.

He went to the filing cabinet with the intention of destroying every single arrangement. His anger flared. He lifted his hand to swipe the vases on the floor but found that he couldn't do it. Parker slumped back in the chair and cradled his head in frustration.

When he was certain he'd gotten his emotions under control, he called Ari. "Can you and all the girls get these flowers out of here?"

"Where do you want us to take them?"

"I don't care. Take them home, donate them to the hospital, do whatever you like. Just get them out of here." Parker turned away, not wanting Ari to see how upset he was.

Cork had been right, a distraction helped. As his meeting with the advertising rep stretched on past lunch, he found his troubles pushed to the back of his mind while he discussed the offer in earnest. At the end of the meeting, Parker felt a slight shift in his mood. Even though he was still seething about the photographers, the flowers, and Ann, at least something productive had come out of his day. The agent had made an offer, and all they needed was Parker's signature. With the photographers still waiting outside, he was forced to order from the Thai restaurant around the corner, forgoing the pleasure of dining out in the city he'd grown to love.

His phone vibrated and announced a voice mail from Ann. Instead of listening to her message, he deleted it. Parker had no idea what he was going to do yet, but talking wasn't an option until he sorted out his scattered thoughts.

Arianne peeked in the door. "Do you want me to clear your schedule for the rest of the afternoon?"

"Yeah, reschedule them for next week if they don't mind being serviced by the other staff. I need a drink."

"If you give me fifteen minutes to make the calls, I'll be happy to join you. Just don't forget, Mrs. Crawford is coming tomorrow. She's your first appointment."

"All right. She'd never forgive me if I cancelled on her."

"Better not cancel on your favorite client." Arianne laughed. "Oh, let's go to the pub close to Greenwich village. I recommend the place."

"That'll be great."

After his meeting with the advertising agent, which had gone well, Parker sent a quick text to Cork, asking him to fly in right away. Hearing the details about the contract was one thing, but reading the fine print was another. He needed his brother's help with the whole process. Cork promised to catch the red-eye and arrive in the morning. The agent wanted to get the deal done before Parker left the city.

Although his spirits remained low, the alcohol and Ari's company enabled him to get through the rest of the evening. Ari hadn't mentioned anything about Kelly, the photographers, or even the flowers, much to his surprise. Instead, she provided nonstop chatter about their customers. She helped him catch up with the office gossip, giving him the latest trends in the city and keeping all thoughts of Ann from creeping back in.

By the time he made it back in his hotel room, he was too drunk to care about anything except going straight to bed. Sleep would give him the reprieve he needed from all the haunting thoughts about Ann.

Parker woke up the next day with a mean hangover. He dragged himself out of bed and into the bathroom, dreading another brush with the photographers like the day before. He took three painkillers for his headache and settled for a quick shower. Parker added sunglasses to his usual outfit of dark jeans and black cotton T-shirt. Although he hated the thought of hiding behind the dark glasses and what they stood for, they were his best defense against feeling naked in front of everyone.

His car was waiting for him at the front entrance of the hotel. He slid into the back passenger seat and pulled out his cell to check his messages. One was from Ann. He deleted it. Another one was from Cork. He was at the airport and would be arriving in the next hour or so.

Parker knew the minute he got out of the car that a horde of people were waiting for him again, just like the day before. However, thanks to Ari, he now had two massage therapists-slash-bodyguards to escort him inside the building, but not before he heard a question that got under his skin.

"Does your blindness bother Kelly at all?"

He glared in the direction of the speaker but said nothing. *Get in line, dude. That's the million-dollar question.*

Parker walked to his office, hoping to get a few minutes respite before having to face Mrs. Crawford. Ari delivered his steaming cup of coffee a few moments later and then left. He slowly took a sip, scalding or not, and thought about the photographer's question. It still bothered him, because the truth was, he'd wondered the same thing all along.

Callous as it sounded, he'd known the question would come up. A disability seemed to make many people uncomfortable. They often hid behind their ignorance and fear of someone different from them. Little did they know that many disabled people functioned independently and were productive citizens just like everyone else. There was nothing he could do to change people's opinions, but he'd be damned if he would let their negativity pull him down.

It was too bad he'd gotten involved with Kelly Storm, a woman who epitomized beauty and perfection. Wouldn't that dampen her popularity a bit? If she had been thinking straight, she would have realized the last thing she needed was to get involved with a man who would never be able to see her beauty as the world saw it. He would never fit the idea of a perfect man, someone she could ever be proud of.

How in the hell had he managed to get involved with a woman whose main selling point was her flawless good looks? The answer had been there all along—he was blind, literally and figuratively. He'd let Ann—Kelly—walk into his life and take the one thing he'd not been ready to give but somehow had ended up giving anyway. Parker wasn't ready to fall in love, and certainly not with someone who'd made a fool of him.

He shook his head in disgust. Somehow, he needed to get over this stumbling block and move on with his life before this inadvertent mess affected everyone around him.

"Parker?" Ari's voice piped in from the speaker. "Mrs. Crawford just arrived. She's one hell of a lady, I'm telling you. She cursed out all those people outside just a minute ago. Gotta love the woman."

"Take her to room 101, and I'll be there in five." He took a deep breath and then muttered to himself, "Show must go on, Parker. There's no pity party allowed."

Mrs. Crawford took his hand the moment he walked in the room. "Parker, you have to do something about those vultures out there. Don't let them run you out of our lovely city." Her voice, though authoritative, lacked its usual spunk.

"I'm working on it." He laughed and led her to the chair. "You know the drill. Get comfortable, and I'll be right back."

As he walked to the adjoining room to wait and get ready, he heard Mrs. Crawford snort. "I'm not surprised you landed yourself a beautiful woman."

He stopped and stared in the direction of the older lady's voice. Since when had she been interested in his personal affairs? There was no answer to give, so he stayed quiet.

"I hope she's good to you."

Again, he had nothing to say about that subject. "Are you ready?"

"Did you hear me say woo-rah?" she snapped, and Parker had to smile at the old woman's candor.

"Sorry. What would you like today?"

"Just a light massage. I'm very tired, and I just want to talk." She coughed. "Woo-rah!"

He started the music and entered the dark room. Mrs. Crawford was already lying on her stomach, her hands tucked up against her body.

"Are you okay?" he asked, laying a soothing hand on her head before massaging her pressure points.

"I've had better days."

She sounded tired. Parker started with a light pressure on her neck, rubbing and kneading. He heard her sigh. Sensing her need to talk, he pushed his own troubled thoughts aside and concentrated on asking questions.

"If someone was to ask for your advice about a relationship based on lies, what would you tell that person? Run or stay and listen?"

She twisted around as if to look at him and stayed in that position for some time. He was almost certain she was scrutinizing him.

"I believe in second chances. There are always two sides to every story."

Parker fell silent, wanting to believe there was hope for him. Shaking his head, he tried to push Ann—Kelly—out of his mind. He closed his eyes and concentrated on each gentle stroke while he worked his way down to her shoulders.

"You're like a son to me, Parker, the son I never had. And I'm going to give you some lasting advice. To love is to risk not being loved in return. If you dare hope, you're opening yourself up to pain. You have to try and risk failure. Think of risk as a necessary evil in order to achieve what you want out of life. Not risking anything is the greatest folly, in my opinion. You have to give more than a hundred percent in everything you do, and not expect anything in return. If you can follow that, then you will find contentment in life, no matter if you end up with the person you love or not.

The key is trying, hoping, and giving."

They both fell silent while he pondered Mrs. Crawford's advice.

"Parker, don't press too much. I just want a light massage this time."

"I'm barely touching you." Then he heard a strange wheezing sound. He inclined his head in curiosity. He laid his palm on her back just as a shudder racked her body. "Mrs. Crawford, are you all right?"

There was no answer. Even before he trailed his hand along her shoulder toward her neck, he knew something was wrong. Parker pressed his fingers against her jugular, searching for a pulse. When he felt nothing, he leaned down and rested his ear against her back. He listened for breathing, but there was nothing. Turning and running toward the door, he caught his foot on the chair leg in the process. Parker stumbled forward but was able to brace his body against the wall to keep from falling. He felt for the knob and wrenched the door open.

"Call 911! I need someone who knows CPR! We have a possible heart attack victim here!" Parker was moving forward in a daze, blindly reaching for something familiar to ground himself. He'd lost count of his steps and had no idea where he was.

"I'm calling," he heard someone yell. Then footsteps came rushing toward him.

"Parker, hold on to me. Tell me what happened."

"I'm going to do CPR," Joe, a part-time massage therapist, said as he squeezed past them in the hallway.

Ari took his hand and looped it around her arm. They pivoted and headed in what he guessed was the direction of room 101.

"She requested a light massage, and that's what I gave her." He stopped to catch his breath. "Then she complained that I was applying too much pressure, and then there was a wheezing sound and she went still."

They reached the room, and Parker started feeling his way around. "Tell me how she looks. Is she alive, Ari?"

He heard her gasp before she answered. "I don't know . . . she's not moving, but Joe is working on her right now." She choked back a sob.

After what seemed like eternity, they heard the distant sound of sirens.

Cork walked in the door just as Parker pulled Ari against him to comfort her.

"What's going on?"

He looked in the direction of Cork's voice. "I think Mrs. Crawford had a heart attack."

Parker heard more footsteps, and several people began speaking at the same time. Cork pulled him to the small adjoining room, with Ari sobbing against his chest. Orders were shouted from outside the room, and more people ran inside. Someone had turned the lights on, because he saw the blurred figures of several people huddled around the massage table.

"What happened to her?" a male voice asked.

"I was giving her a massage, and then she made a wheezing sound and stopped moving."

"Couldn't you tell she was having a heart attack?" another one yelled.

"No . . . he couldn't," Ari answered.

"Why not?" the first man asked.

"Because he can't see, damn it!" Cork bellowed.

A hush fell over the room. Parker gritted his teeth, hating his blindness for the very first time in his life.

"Is she going to be okay?" Parker tried to move toward the people, but Cork held him back.

"We don't know yet. We're not getting any response. Not even a pulse."

Then someone shouted, "Clear!"

Medical terms were thrown about in hurried exchanges by the paramedics as they worked to revive Mrs. Crawford. The noise made his head ache and added to his confusion, which was something he'd never felt before. He wanted to turn off the sounds around him, even if it meant shutting himself off from the rest of the world.

Parker closed his eyes and tightened his arms around Ari. "It's going to be okay," he whispered.

"I'm worried about you." She continued to sob against his shirt while she clung to him.

"Don't worry about me."

"Parker, are you okay, bro?" Cork asked from his left.

"Yeah, just tell me what's going on."

"They're taking her out right now. A cop is standing outside. I'm sure he wants to get all the details of what happened. I'll go and talk to him right now. Stay here. I'll be back."

Parker heard the scraping of footsteps when the group moved toward the front entrance. The sharp wailing of the siren began, and in a matter of seconds, the sound faded away. He stayed where he was, afraid to move, not knowing where to go or what to do next. An inexplicable wave of sadness engulfed him while he waited for Cork to return. Ari stayed close, making sure she was touching him—a sign that he wasn't alone.

He endured an hour of questioning from the cop and another investigator who came to let them know Mrs. Crawford had been pronounced dead at the hospital. Parker shook at the announcement but fought to keep his calm.

It was well after closing by the time he and Cork found themselves alone in his office. Ari and several other therapists had opted to stay since there was still a big group of photographers and curious onlookers waiting outside.

"Are you okay?" Cork handed him a bottle of water.

Parker took big gulps and realized he hadn't eaten anything since he'd gotten up that morning. "I'm cool, but I need you to take me home. Call the agent tomorrow and apologize for our missed appointment."

"No problem."

While Cork was booking their flight back to LA, Parker went to the men's room to get some time alone. He walked straight to the sink and splashed water on his face, trying to calm his nerves and conceal his weakness. He was perilously close to reaching his breaking point. Taking slow breaths, he fought the urge to bawl like a frightened child. All he wanted to do at that moment was to go home and hide, maybe for a long time.

CHAPTER FOURTEEN

Kelly was having a bad day. Her meeting with the producer had been extended longer than she had hoped, and she'd almost missed her flight. She was hauling ass on the freeway and veering in and out of traffic. Jessica was a nervous wreck by the time they reached the airport. Dragging her wheeled carry-on behind her, Kelly snaked through the pockets of people who seemed to be in no hurry to get anywhere.

With her dark glasses and baseball cap providing enough coverage to keep her from being recognized, she whispered hurried excuses while she negotiated the long walkway to get to the exit. When she passed by one sports bar, she glanced at the television hanging overhead and saw a familiar face on the evening news. Her heart took a nosedive. Parker was trying to get into his New York office, and the hounding photographers were blocking his way.

Kelly froze, her heart aching for what she had put him through. She got a glimpse of his face, but his expression gave no indication of his emotions. God, if there was anything she could do to rewind the past weeks, she'd do what was right.

Not only had she screwed up big-time, but she'd also pushed him right into the middle of the storm that was her life. The urge to protect him from her lifestyle had been overwhelming, but looking back at what had transpired over the last few weeks, it seemed like she'd just made things worse by not telling him the truth. Had she kept her identity a secret just to shelter him from her invasive life, or had she done it for her own selfish reasons?

Kelly instructed the limo driver to take her straight to Parker's New York office and found the place looking like a ghost town. During her first visit, it had been buzzing with energy, but today it almost seemed like someone had died. The usually perky receptionist appeared subdued when she walked in. When she glanced up from her desk, the woman didn't seem surprised to see her.

"Is Parker available?" She removed her sunglasses and rested her arms on the counter.

"I'm sorry, but Mr. Davis flew out last night." There was an intense sadness in the woman's eyes.

Kelly's face fell. Surely, she hadn't flown thousands of miles just to miss him. "He left? But he usually stays for a week, doesn't he?"

The woman nodded. "Something came up, and he had to leave."

Kelly had a sinking feeling it might have something to do with her and the paparazzi she'd seen harassing him on television.

"Is Parker okay?"

"He's fine, but he's a little shaken. I'm sorry, I am not comfortable talking about him." The woman sounded like she was done answering questions.

"Thanks for your help." Kelly turned to leave.

"Ms. Storm?"

"Yes?"

"I'm rooting for a happy ending." The woman offered a small smile before picking up an incoming call.

The words touched her deeply. "So am I."

Kelly left with an insurmountable feeling of disappointment, which was directed at herself. She rummaged inside her purse for her cell phone and dialed Jessica's number. Some passersby stopped to gawk at her, but at that point, she was beyond caring and hiding behind her sunglasses. There were more important things besides worrying about people watching her every move.

"Hey, I need your help. Can you book a flight for me? I need the first flight going out of JFK to LA"

"What do you mean first flight? Where's Parker?"

Kelly heard her already thumping on the keyboard. "I missed him. According to his secretary, he left last night. I don't know why, but I have a hunch it might have something to do with the paps." She waved to the driver who was parked just up the street watching for her signal.

"They found out about him?" Jessica sounded incredulous. "The pictures didn't show his face at all."

"That's what it seems like from the news. You know how they can find anything if they set their minds to it. And it's obvious Parker is the flavor of the week now. I'm afraid he'll end up hating me even more because of this."

"Okay, give me a few minutes to find you a flight."

The limo parked at the curb. Kelly didn't even bother to wait for the driver to open the car door for her. "We're going back to the airport. Drive as fast as humanly possible."

Feeling a headache building, she closed her eyes and leaned back against the leather seat. Jessica came on the phone a few minutes later.

"Okay, you're booked to fly out in . . . let me see . . . two hours. Just head to the kiosk of United Airlines and print your boarding pass. Call me if you need anything else."

Kelly sighed. "Thanks."

"Kelly? Don't worry about anything. Just take care of yourself."

A tear slipped through her lashes. "Why is this so much harder than I thought?"

"Because, my dear, love isn't easy. Go and win that man's heart."

"I hope I'm not too late."

"Don't be too pessimistic. I'm rooting for you, babe."

Kelly wished she had the same confidence. There were some things even fervent prayers couldn't answer. Maybe she was too late.

"Thanks, Jess."

For the duration of the ride to the airport, she tried to forget all the worries that had been gnawing at her but was unable to rid her mind of Parker's haunting image. She was too tired to fight the memories of the last time they'd been together.

During the flight back to Los Angeles, Kelly powered up her laptop and secured a satellite Internet connection. She skimmed through the pages, something she'd thought she would never do in her life. When stardom struck, most of her friends in the business had advised her not to read articles about herself. For the most part, she had stayed away. But this time, she was curious to see what garbage they'd concocted about her.

Once she typed her name in the browser, an astounding number of articles appeared, some dating back three years. Pictures upon pictures of her graced the monitor, thousands if she kept looking. Most were taken during events, with her in a gown, walking the red carpet, attending a gala opening at the MET, or posing with countless costars in films. She felt very empty as she kept scrolling down the innumerable images of her basking in the glory of fame and fortune.

More pictures showed up of her and Matthew attending the Academy Awards together. Some were taken during happier times, and a few were of her alone, after their relationship had ended up in the dumpster. Then there was the picture of her crying aboard a friend's yacht, taken by Rigor James using a telephoto lens.

Memories surged back in torrents, as if they'd just happened yesterday. She closed her eyes to stop the torment, but once the memories started, it was a futile effort. It all came back with a vengeance.

She thought of Matthew, who had used her celebrity status to get ahead in the business, and his eventual unfaithfulness. There was also the short-lived happiness after finding out she was pregnant, only to lose the baby. And now Parker had learned of her lies. There would be no way to bring back her daughter, but there was still hope for her and Parker—granted he listened to her and accepted her apology.

"Ms. Storm, would you like a glass of champagne?"

The flight attendant's question brought her back to the present. Kelly had no idea she had been staring out the window the whole time.

She looked up and shook her head. "But I could use a glass of water and a couple of Aleve if you have them."

The woman left to do her bidding. Kelly glanced out the window again while the merciless pounding in her head continued. A lump formed in her throat, and errant tears trickled down her cheeks. She brushed them away.

"Here you are, Ms. Storm." The flight attendant took one good look at her and panicked. "Is everything all right? Can I get you something else?"

"It's just a monster headache. Thank you." Kelly accepted the glass of water and the pills, and then looked away, not wanting to explain herself any further.

"Call me if you need anything." The attendant left as soon as Kelly nodded.

After taking the medicine, she continued her search for the latest gossip about her. Parker's pictures came up, captioned as the new love of her life. "A blind, self-made man has calmed the storm," another article said. At least they'd gotten their facts right for a change. She had indeed fallen for Parker.

Why do people have to refer to him as a blind man? Kelly didn't understand the tag being affixed to his name. When she'd first seen him, she had to admit, he hadn't seemed blind at all. What she'd seen was an attractive man, so sure of himself and quite capable of stringing hearts along. She'd had no idea it was hers he would catch.

True, she'd immersed herself in researching everything she could about his condition, even read a few articles about him and how he'd dealt with the disease with grace and courage. The more she'd learned about him, the more her fascination had grown. For Kelly, the single threat his blindness posed was his uncanny ability to probe her deepest emotions just with a touch of his hands on her body.

Kelly didn't realize that she had fallen asleep. She woke up in a daze and found that they had landed. After gathering her things, she deplaned, rushed to her car, and noted that several reporters and photographers were trailing behind her. She hated to be rude, but there were times when she just wanted to be left alone—something she knew would never happen. The public owned her, and the media would do whatever it took to get pictures of her.

The first thing she did when she got into her Rover was dial Parker's number. She backed out of the reserved parking space as soon as the valet gave her the go-ahead. She noticed with annoyance that several cars were already geared to follow her.

After several rings, her call went to his voicemail. "Parker, I need to speak to you. Can you please call me?"

Her plea sounded desperate, but she was beyond caring. Kelly waited a few minutes, unable to decide where to go. When she decided to take Sepulveda Boulevard to get to the freeway, she noticed two cars trailing her. She recognized them as the same cars that had been waiting for her in the parking lot.

"Damn it!" She slammed on the accelerator.

Her SUV responded with enough power to create a big gap between them. Snaking in and out of cars, she tried her best to lose them. With her heart pounding hard, she kept up the pace, but one of the two cars was gaining on her.

She was approaching eighty miles per hour, and yet the pap was closing the distance between them. With a furious dose of adrenaline pumping within her, Kelly floored the gas just as a car veered into her lane. Instinct pushed her to react, and she stepped on the brakes. She swerved to avoid hitting the car, sending hers spinning out of control. Although she tried to counter by hanging on to the steering wheel, the car continued to turn. Her screams drowned out the screeching brakes around her while other cars swerved to miss her. At one point, all she could think of was that she was going to die because of her own stupidity, and without even getting a chance to talk to Parker.

"No, no, no!"

Reining in her fear, she allowed her car to spin a few more times while it seemed to be losing its momentum. It rammed into the center divider with enough force to send shards of broken glass and metal flying around her. The airbags deployed, whipping her head back at the impact. Kelly heard a sickening crunch. Her scream rose to a fevered pitch as her left arm was pinned against the door by the airbag.

When the car halted, steam sizzled from under the hood. When the airbag deflated, she had a chance to survey the damage. She hoped her recklessness hadn't caused anyone else to get into an accident. With trembling hands, she tried to remove her seat belt, but it wouldn't budge. Stifling an urge to cry, she fumbled with it, punching the release button several times, but it still wouldn't release. She tried to open her door, but she was trapped by the concrete divider. Stuck, she buried her face against the steering wheel and began to cry. Kelly heard voices around her while cars slowed and others came over to check on her.

"Miss, are you okay?" one gentleman asked.

"I already called for help. Just stay where you are," another one said.

She continued sobbing at the realization that her choice to outrun the paps could have gotten herself and others killed. In a matter of minutes, she heard sirens. Orders were shouted, and then someone wrenched the door open from the front passenger side.

Someone tapped her on the shoulder. "Miss, can you move?"

Kelly looked up, trying to see through the blur of tears, and gave a weak nod. "I'm okay. Is anyone else hurt?" Her voice shook, and for the first time, she tasted blood in her mouth.

"I need a gurney here, stat!"

Kelly had no idea what happened next. All she remembered was the sympathetic face of one of the fire crew before her vision blurred and everything went dark. When she woke up, she was lying on a hospital bed surrounded by Jessica, Dave, and Lizzie, their faces marred with worry.

Jessica moved closer to the bed. "Oh, Kelly, I'm glad you're okay."

She looked around and winced at the sudden pain in her arm. "How did I get here?"

"Reports said you passed out," Dave said as he moved to the other side of her bed.

"Can I get you anything? Water perhaps?" Lizzie asked.

"If you don't mind." Kelly turned to Dave. "I made a big mess. What am I looking at?"

"According to police reports, several motorists said that they noticed another car chasing yours, and then that car veered in front of you, which was why you swerved and lost control. Regardless, you'll be getting a speeding ticket and maybe a fine for damaging public property. I'm not sure yet. I contacted your lawyer and asked the investigator to speak to him directly."

"No one else got hurt, right?" She held her breath while she waited for Dave's answer. He shook his head. Relieved, she closed her eyes. "I'm glad."

"As for your pursuers, they got the bastards' license plates. One of them was Rigor James, your favorite pap. Your lawyer is building a strong case to get him off your back once and for all. I can't believe the lengths people will go to get that perfect shot. He could've killed you." Dave shook his head in disgust.

Jessica snorted. "I don't understand his fixation on you. I guess your picture is worth so much he just doesn't care about the outcome."

"I'm here, and I'm alive." Kelly forced a smile. "Let's just hope he's nailed this time. He can't be doing this to others."

"Believe me, the bastard won't be able to get near you again," Dave said and moved toward the door. "I'm going to make some phone calls. I can't believe how news can travel so fast."

She looked at Jessica. "What is he talking about?"

"You made the news again. You're all over the Internet—Twitter and wherever else you can think of." Jessica threw up her hands in disgust. "I had Lizzie bring an overnight bag for you."

Lizzie handed Kelly the water and helped her into a sitting position. Her head throbbed when she moved, but she drank in greedy gulps, and then sank back against the mattress.

"I have to get out of here. I need to see Parker."

Jessica sat down on the bed next to her. "Sorry. The doctor said you'll have to stay overnight for observation."

"But I've wasted so much time—"

"Look, you have a nasty cut on your forehead." Jessica pointed to her head. "And your arm is banged up, in case you haven't noticed."

Kelly felt the bandage on her forehead and flinched when she caught sight of her left arm, which resembled an eggplant. The bruising had started, and she guessed it would look a whole lot worse in the days to come.

"I can't wait any longer." She pushed the sheets down and tried to get up.

"Oh, no, you don't." Jessica held her arm, preventing her from getting out of bed. "Lizzie, call the nurse."

Kelly tried to shake off her friend's hand, but the throbbing in her head was much too painful to ignore. She was forced to remain motionless to get the pounding to stop. Tears threatened to spill again, and she hated them for making her feel weak.

"Have you seen what they've been doing to him? Following him wherever he goes? And he had no idea what was happening because I was too damned selfish, thinking only of myself." She felt raw, tired, and hopeless.

"I know what's going on, Kells, but there's nothing we can do about that. You need to rest tonight if you want to be discharged tomorrow. I called Debbie and told her what happened. She's planning on taking the first flight out of Chicago in the morning."

Not her sister. The woman would be fussing nonstop, and that was the last thing Kelly wanted. What she *really* needed at the moment was to get out and find Parker. Her hopes of escaping were dashed when the nurse entered the room holding a medicine cup.

"Ms. Storm, Dr. Keller said you could use some of this." The cup contained one white pill.

Kelly recoiled. "What is it?"

"You need to calm down, and this will help you sleep." Jessica took the pill from the nurse and the glass of water from Lizzie.

"When you wake up in the morning and after a consultation with the doctor, then you can go home and do whatever you want."

"Ms. Storm, you need to take the pill and rest. You've been through a lot today." The nurse nodded.

Without any other choice, she took the pill and popped it into her mouth.

"Parker, what the hell? Will you answer your damned calls?"

He listened to Cork's message, one of the many his brother had left, and then deleted it. It had been two days since he'd come back from New York and relegated himself to staying indoors, opting to hide until he was ready to face the world.

The image of Mrs. Crawford flashed in his mind, creating havoc and confusion. He took a swig from the bottle of vodka, enjoying the momentary respite the alcohol offered. How could he have missed the signs she was in distress? What kind of man wouldn't see if a person was dying right there on his table? Parker knew the answer to that question—*only a blind man.*

Of course, people around him offered the customary platitudes to ease his guilt—it wasn't his fault that Mrs. Crawford died of a heart attack, and there wasn't anything he could have done about it. That was all bullshit. Nothing they said changed the bitter reality. He could have done something if he'd been able to see, if he'd been able to identify the symptoms. But it was too late. Parker's hands had failed him. His touch hadn't been enough.

His phone rang again. This time it was Webster. He listened to the voicemail before getting rid of it. His mood had spiraled out of control. Even running for hours on the treadmill couldn't lift him from the rut he'd been dwelling in the past few days.

Parker paced the room, rage engulfing him. He hadn't turned on his computer, nor had he listened to the news since Mrs. Crawford's death. As it turned out, she owned one of the largest media outfit in the nation. A detail Mrs. Crawford conveniently left out during their conversations. The reports about the incident had escalated to the point that his lawyer had to get involved to do damage control. To top it all off, the news about his relationship with Kelly Storm, the famous actress, was being replayed over and over.

Then along came another incoming call. He pressed voice-over, and it announced Ann's name. His jaw tightened. Unable to control his emotions, he flung the cell across the room, hitting the wall. A loud bang followed by shattering ended the annoying ringing. He hated the patronizing phone calls, the concern . . . all because he was blind.

"Damn it!" he yelled and pulled another long one from the bottle. Parker sank down on the sofa and closed his eyes, trying his best to get Ann out of his mind, without success. He had no idea what to think anymore. One thing was for sure—she'd deceived him.

Kelly signed the release papers confirming she was going against medical advice by discharging herself prematurely from the hospital. Jessica continued to bristle on their drive home. Dave had taken off to sort out the media frenzy following the news of her accident.

"Let's swing by Parker's office. I want to talk to him."

She reclined in the seat and closed her eyes. Her body ached from her head down to her toes. Kelly knew it was stupid of her not to listen to her doctor and stay another night in the hospital.

"You're not going home to rest like you told the doctor?"

"I can't wait any longer. He's been ignoring my calls, and that's a bad thing. I don't care if I rest or not, but I have to give him an explanation, once and for all."

"I'm not going to argue with you anymore, but if you end up in the hospital again, I swear you're never going to hear the end of it."

"I'm going to be okay once I get a chance to see him." Kelly exhaled. "It doesn't matter if he turns me away. I just need a chance to talk to him." That wasn't at all true. She wanted him to forgive her, too.

"Whatever, but I'm not going to leave you there. I'll drive you home after."

Jessica pulled up in front of Parker's business and parked the car next to a meter. Kelly pulled her baseball cap down and adjusted her sunglasses. She allowed Jessica to steady her while they approached the reception desk. Once there Webster looked up, her expression showing a range of emotion —surprise, pity, and helplessness.

"Ms. Storm, what are you doing here? I just saw you in the news yesterday. You were in an accident." Webster ushered them to the lounge where there seemed to be more privacy.

"Please, call me Kelly. This is Jessica, my friend and assistant." As the girls exchanged pleasantries, Kelly looked around, appreciating the break from prying eyes.

Webster nodded and gestured for them to sit. "Can I offer you anything to drink?"

"I'll have a glass of water, please," Jessica answered.

Kelly declined. "I want to speak with Parker, if he's around."

"Hold on, let me get the water." Webster hurried out of the room.

"I'll wait in the car while you and Parker talk. I don't think I want to hear the names he's going to call you." Jessica took a magazine resting on the table and flipped through the pages with disinterest.

"You're so funny. I wouldn't dream of having you around when he blasts my head off." It wasn't a joke. Kelly knew Parker's reason for avoiding her was because he was angry, and she couldn't blame him.

Then a guy walked into the room, and she felt like she'd seen him somewhere before.

"Hello, Ms. Storm. I don't think we've met—"

Kelly rose from her seat, recalling the memory. "You're the man from the restaurant with Parker, right?"

"Yes, I'm Cork, his brother."

"Call me Kelly. This is Jessica, my best friend and assistant."

"Have a seat."

Cork took the chair opposite them. "Webster told me you're looking for Parker."

His eyes left her face and traveled down to her bruised arm. He winced and must have been wondering what she was doing out of the hospital.

"Look, Cork, I'm sure you know why I'm here. I have to speak with him. Is he here?"

It took him some time to answer. "I'm not sure if you heard, but one of his clients died while he was giving her a massage."

"What?" Jessica interrupted.

"Yes, it was a heart attack, but the media seems to be painting a different picture."

Kelly's heart jumped into her throat. "Is he okay? Where is he?" She could imagine his frustration and the stress he must have been under with all he was going through.

"He hasn't come to work for the last two days or answered any of our calls."

Her heart ached for the man. "I've been calling him, too. He hasn't answered any of my calls or texts." Kelly frowned, not knowing what else to say.

"I think it's better if we leave him alone for now and let him sort things out on his own."

Cork watched her with sympathetic eyes when the tears started trickling down her face. Kelly shook her head just as Webster walked in with Jessica's glass of water.

"No, I can't wait any longer. I flew to New York to talk to him, and I'm not waiting a minute longer." She turned to Jessica. "Drop me off at his place and I'll call when I need a ride home."

Jessica started to protest, but Kelly shook her head.

"Just take me, Jess. I can't take this anymore."

"Kelly, I don't know if this is a good idea, but I'm not going to tell you what to do," Cork said.

As soon as they were back in the car and en route to Parker's place, Jessica glanced over and gave her a worried smile. "Call me if you need anything."

Kelly nodded, afraid to say anything more. Her nerves were raw. She was worried for Parker while she tried to imagine what he had gone through. They drove in silence for the rest of the way. Once they were parked in front of his townhouse, Jessica gave her a concerned look.

"There are no lights on. What if he's not home?"

"Then I'll call you."

"Maybe I should wait out here," Jessica said.

"Just go. Don't worry about me. I'll be fine." Kelly placed a reassuring hand on Jessica's arm.

Once Jessica drove off, Kelly took a deep breath and knocked on Parker's door. The whole house was dark, and she began to suspect that Jessica was right after all—he might not be home. She waited half a minute, then knocked again. She kept pounding at the door until it opened, and she stumbled forward.

"What the hell?" Parker caught her by the waist and recoiled once he recognized her. He let go of her right away, as if he'd touched hot coals.

"Parker, I'm sorry for coming here like this, but I don't know how else to talk to you." Despite the darkness, she could see the disarray inside his house—a chair was lying in the middle of the room, throw pillows were strewn everywhere, and he reeked of alcohol.

He glared at her, pushing her to the door. She winced at his tight grip on her bruised arm. "This is not a good time," Parker said, his voice filled with anger.

Instead of backing down, she pushed her way past him. "This is the *only* time. You've ignored all my calls and refused to talk to me."

"Get out now, while I can still control myself," he rasped, trying to follow the sound of her footsteps.

"No. I won't leave until you listen to me."

"I'm telling you to leave, *now!*"

Parker moved in the direction of her voice, his body rigid with fury. In a harsh tone devoid of the tenderness she had grown to love, he said, "I'm not in the mood to listen to your lies, *Kelly*."

CHAPTER FIFTEEN

Panic shook Kelly when he stalked in her direction. She had expected anger from Parker, but this man was beyond livid. His eyes burned with rage, unlike the Parker she knew. She felt his radiating fury even with the distance between them. Kelly moved away to avoid him, but he grabbed her arm as if he could see her and yanked her closer.

"You think you can just waltz here and make demands?" His warm breath brushed her face, and the strong odor of alcohol suggested he'd had more than enough.

"I wanted to explain—"

"No, your time is up. You had all kinds of chances to come clean. Now get the hell out!" he spat.

Her heart thumped and sweat beaded on her skin. Kelly struggled to pry her arm out of his grip, but he tightened it even more. She stifled a cry as pain shot through her bruised arm.

"No—you can't throw me out."

Parker stopped and faced her, his mouth thinning into a cruel line. "I can't? Watch me!"

He dragged her toward the door while she wrestled against him. Twisting her arm and breathing through the pain, she managed to break free.

"Ann, come back here!" Parker groped for her in the darkness.

Kelly clamped her mouth shut and tried to control her breathing. Her heart pounded against her chest, and her body burned with fear. She didn't answer him and made sure she put enough space between them, far enough away so he couldn't throw her out. As upsetting as it was to her, she used his blindness to her benefit and inched away as quietly as she could.

Her mind raced while she dashed toward his bedroom, ignoring the throbbing in her arm. Her intention was to stay until he listened to her, and then she'd leave just as he wished. Without much light to guide her, she tripped on something in the hallway. She reached out and tried to brace her fall, but her injured arm couldn't handle the weight. It gave way, and her body slammed against the wall. Kelly let out a yelp and closed her eyes, blocking the pain and quieting her cry down to a whimper. She heard his approaching footsteps.

"Is this your idea of a sick joke? Playing hide and seek with the blind man?"

"No . . . no . . . I want to apologize for not telling you—"

"Save your lies, *Kelly*. I'm not buying it." Parker towered over her, pinning her against the wall to prevent an escape. A slow and deliberate smile appeared on his face, but it never reached his eyes.

Anguish tore through her at his denial. Parker's face was devoid of the tenderness she had come to love. There was no hint of pardon in his expression. Instead, she saw anger in its ugliest form.

She reached up to touch his face. "I'm so sorry. It was never my intention to hurt you in any way."

Parker tilted his head and brushed her hand away. "You're an actress, Kelly. The public might applaud your effort, but I won't." He grazed her cheek with his fingers in a slow caress, his gaze trained on her, anticipating her every move.

She shuddered at the contact. His words stabbed her like a knife to the heart, but she deserved this. She'd known that her actions could come back to bite her, and now that they had, she had no idea how to make him listen.

"I'm not acting," she said. "Please believe me."

"The hell you're not. So you wanted to see the circus up close?" He burrowed his fingers into her cheeks. "Now that you have, are you satisfied?"

Kelly tried to break free, but he held her face captive. "You're getting it all wrong, Parker!"

"Oh, so I'm not only blind, but I'm also an idiot?" The fury that flashed in his eyes made her recoil.

"Don't twist my words. That's not what I meant." Kelly touched his face again, trying to get him focused on her. "I-I wanted to protect you . . . from *them*, from the hurtful things they might say about you." Words tumbled out of her mouth, mirroring her fear and confusion. There were so many things that needed to be said, and yet nothing was coming out right. He had closed his mind to any explanation, and it looked like nothing she could say would change what he thought of her.

Parker gripped her chin and pulled her face closer. The disgust in his eyes and the stench of the alcohol added to her building terror. His jaw clenched, and every muscle twitched with anger.

"Protect me? Like the good little girl that you are?" His words were cold and hard. "Did you ever stop to think that what I needed was protection from your lies? Get out, Kelly! Get out and take your lies with you!"

A paralyzing dread settled over her, and the words tumbled out in broken rush. "I-I did it because . . . I-I was falling in love with you."

Those reverent words she'd planned to say to him didn't sound right now. What she'd intended to be a tender profession of affection had come out in a rush. Her life depended on this moment, and yet she couldn't seem to save herself. Parker's expression grew more menacing, as if her declaration had made the situation much worse. He laughed without mirth and released her.

"Love me? What the hell do you know about love, *Kelly Storm*?" As if a light bulb had turned on in his head, his mouth twitched into a wicked grin. "I think I know what you want from me. You're here for a fuck job, aren't you? Then by all means, I'll give you one good fuck!"

"Parker . . . I—"

"You don't want it? I can practically feel your body buzzing with want, my dear Kelly. Tell me you don't want it!"

"I want you, but not this way. You have to believe—"

Parker grabbed her arm and pulled her into his spare bedroom. She flinched from the pain but gritted her teeth to keep from crying out. *I deserve this*, she reminded herself.

"Safeword!" he demanded, dragging her to the massage table. The room was dark, the blinds drawn tight. "Get on the table!"

Kelly stumbled backward, inching toward the table, not taking her eyes off him. She scrambled up, feeling her way in the darkness.

"Parker . . . I—"

"Safeword!"

He turned on the lights. Kelly blinked, adjusting to the sudden glare. His lips twitched into a harsh smile. She wanted to say something, anything to diffuse his anger, but nothing came out. Hunger burned in his eyes when he gazed in her direction. Her breath hitched as he removed his shirt to reveal his muscular torso. Then he shed his pants, revealing powerful thighs that rippled with each movement.

She reached out, aching to run her fingers over every taut muscle and commit each hard line to memory. He licked his lips. As if he'd read her mind, he stopped short of pulling his boxers down. Parker was deliberate, forcing her to watch his every movement. She couldn't peel her eyes away, because the thought of not seeing him anymore was unbearable. Despite the crippling fear, her body responded to him, her stomach tightening with arousal. Kelly gasped when he pulled down his underwear and taunted her with his proud erection. Her gaze traveled up and down his magnificent body.

"Can't come up with a safeword? Let me give you one." Parker moved toward her like a predator after its prey, his eyes flashing with the same fury she'd seen out in the hallway. He circled the table, his muscles flexing. "Fraud. Repeat it, Kelly. Say it."

His accusation bit into her as tears of guilt slid down her cheeks. "No . . . I won't use it. I'm not a fraud. I left some things out because I wanted to protect you, even if you don't believe me. But all the time we were together, everything was real. Every act was me, and every single word was true." She paused to catch her breath. "Forgive. Forgive is my safeword."

He smirked. "So it is," he said with enough sarcasm to make her flinch.

After snatching a condom from the drawer, he made a big production of sheathing himself in front of her, taking his time and showing her every bit of the process. She wrapped her arms around her body in a useless attempt to hold herself together. Feeling terrified, yet aroused in a sick way, Kelly realized the right thing to do would be to get out of the room, but all this had been her doing. There was a steep price for her intentional omissions, and this was it. Parker flicked off the lights and turned to her, his eyes narrowing. He tugged on her blouse.

"I'm going to fuck you more than once because I know you like it. You have the option of leaving now if you think you can't take it. Do it while I still have some control left. Once I begin, I expect nothing from you. I don't want to hear any explanations or apologies. You're only allowed to utter your safeword. After this night, we're going our separate ways and forget we ever met."

Parker worked at yanking her blouse open, one button after the other. She shivered, not from the draft in the room but from the coldness of his words.

Kelly bit her lip, trying to stifle her cries. *How can someone so beautiful turn so ugly?* The whole night was morphing into a nightmare.

When the last button was undone, he pulled her blouse free and threw it on the floor. She covered her breasts with her hands, feeling vulnerable and outright exposed.

"Lie down, spread your arms and legs," he commanded while mounting the table.

She followed his orders, stretching her legs apart and raising her arms over her head. Parker pulled a strap from each corner.

"I'm going to tie you up while I show you what I really am in the bedroom." He hesitated. "Now is the time to leave."

"No . . . I'm staying." She tried to keep the nervousness from her voice.

He started restraining her wrists and sneered. "You're gonna love this."

Parker fitted and checked the straps on her ankles, cinching each one tight, making it impossible to touch him or to wrap her legs around his body. Each click of a buckle added to her unspoken terror. He moved away for a moment, and then produced a mask. Kelly shrank back and suppressed the urge to cry out, fighting the hysteria coursing through her.

"This is for you." Parker taunted her, dangling the mask over her face.

She understood his pain, his loss, and the sting of her betrayal. He'd trusted her, and she had lied to him. It was her doing that he'd turned into this unfeeling man before her—vengeful and on the verge of blind rage. Parker had let her behind his guarded walls, and she'd crumbled them to pieces, breaking him apart.

How ironic could it be? Kelly had hid beneath disguises while seeking obscurity. Now that she was baring herself to him, he shoved a mask on her, as if to tell himself she'd been a different person all along. She shivered, and another wave of panic shot through her when he fitted the mask on her face.

"You're getting excited. I can feel it," he whispered.

Kelly began taking shallow breaths as soon as the mask was in place. It felt cold, isolating, and impersonal. She kept her emotions in check, not wanting to fuel his rage by her cries of weakness.

With the small eyeholes restricting her view, she couldn't see what Parker was about to do next. Cold air brushed her bare skin when he shoved her skirt up around her waist. She trembled, chills racing across her body. His rough and demanding touch traced every contour, so different from his usual light caresses. A ripple of anxiety mixed with a strange sense of anticipation wreaked havoc with her emotions as he hovered over her center.

"You're already hot for me," he said beneath his breath.

With one powerful stroke, Parker yanked her lacy thong and ripped it away from her body, shredding her heart and hope into a million pieces. Then he stopped.

Kelly smothered a moan when Parker's mouth grazed her center and teased her folds. The velvet touch of his tongue licking, flicking her clit, made her scream with pleasure. Even with the harsh words he'd said earlier, flames of lust still flickered inside her, igniting her. Shivering with want despite her fear, she arched her body upward to allow his tongue to drift further inside, but he shifted his position and appeared in her line of vision.

She focused on his mouth and yearned for his soft kisses, his tongue sucking and nibbling hers. Kelly wanted the damned mask off. If she could kiss him, she'd be able to redeem herself in some small way and show him just how much he meant to her. Of course, he'd never kiss her, not now, not ever. Instead, he reached around her back and unsnapped her bra. Her breasts spilled out of its confines like hot lava, burning and ready. Parker yanked the bra down across her chest, low enough to leave her exposed. He braced his body and moved down to her chest. She shuddered when his tongue toyed with one nipple, brushing the other tip once before sucking it hard enough to send a delicious thrill mixed with discomfort through her. She quivered as he applied more pressure by drawing in the apex with his teeth. She cried out as he bit each tip, climbing to the peak of delicious arousal as he played with each one.

Parker grunted with satisfaction at her response and sheathed his dick inside her. Kelly jerked forward, and her walls felt like they were ready to tear while accommodating his sheer size. Moaning with the mix of pleasure and pain, her body adjusted to his invasion. She suppressed the urge to scream at the confusing thoughts searing inside her. He paused yet again and brought his face closer to her.

"I'm going to fuck you real hard. I'm going to make you scream with pleasure and pain." It wasn't a threat. It sounded more like a promise.

Parker began pounding into her, imposing his will upon her. If he was rubbing her faults in her face, then he was getting his explicit message across. If he wanted to humiliate her as payback, he was succeeding.

His promise became reality—she screamed at the painful friction of his dick against her walls while he slashed in and out of her with punishing determination. With his body pinning her down, he didn't let up until all emotions but humiliation drained out of her.

Kelly couldn't help but think of what Parker had gone through in the past few days. He had always been gentle, reassuring, and careful. She couldn't even begin to fathom the hurt and embarrassment she'd caused him with her dishonesty, making him more conscious of his disability. The woman dying on his table had added to his misery and vulnerability. What man would want his weakness shoved in his face?

The small table shook with each hard thrust, grinding and punishing until their bodies were drenched in sweat. Parker bellowed as his first release came. Seeming pleased with himself, he jumped off the table and walked around. His footsteps, aside from her thudding heart, were the only sound she could hear.

"That's your first fuck for the night."

Breathing hard, Kelly tried to follow his movement, but the mask restricted her vision. After a few minutes, he was back on top of her.

"Remember your safeword," he whispered before spearing his engorged dick inside her again. True to his words, Parker fucked her one more time. Rough, hurried, and filled with unconcealed loathing, he ground his body against hers, plunging himself deep into her with each thrust. "I trusted you, Ann. I loved you. How could you not tell me? Is it because I'm blind? I thought you were different. I expected more from you." His voice was low but reproachful.

Loved? The weight of each accusation he hurled at her was like knife to her heart. With crystal clarity, a realization hit her with full force. Her betrayal had triggered something he'd been concealing from everyone. Somewhere in his past, he had been hurt, rejected. Her lies had magnified his deepest fears and uncertainties.

"Parker, I love you—"

"Not a word. No more lies, Ann. No more." He called her by the name he'd known her by, and it wasn't the first time. Was it an indication there could still be hope for them?

Parker continued his rough thrusting. The unspoken answer was clear. *No.* There was no hope for them. His formidable jaw clenched, and his eyes closed, effective in shutting her out. Kelly ached for him and felt useless to help heal his hurt. She wished she could wipe away the deep-seated inadequacies her lies had awakened in him. He groaned as he pummeled into her, mindless of her distress. Parker didn't ease up. He kept hammering away at a steady pace. She was ashamed and angry at herself. It was too late.

"I had wicked dreams of you, Ann. Now all I see is your deceit and how you used me to quench your appetite for sex. Are you happy now?" He panted, trying to catch his breath. "This is the fucking you wanted, right?"

In the glow from the corner nightlight, she saw the hard lines and the dreadful expression on his face. *I deserve to hear this,* she thought, miserable and unable to control the flood of tears.

"No . . . I wanted to tell you, but you told me it could wait. I know it's a bit late now. Can't you give me a chance?"

Parker muttered an oath before thrusting harder and deeper into her. She gasped at his violent response, but in spite of it all, every inch of him left her breathless, making her ache for more.

"You're wasting your breath," he said, and his ragged breathing rang in her ear. "There is no *us*." His fingers dug into her shoulders, his pounding turning more intense. "If that one night managed to produce a child, I *will* stand as its father, but there is no us."

She cried out at the cruelty of his words. The world as she knew it crumbled around her, killing even the tiniest of hope.

His words slashed deep, puncturing her already wounded soul. Oblivious to her misery, he kept his pace. Parker was relentless, rough, and furious, and all she could hear was the angered thumping of their bodies coming together. The rasping of her back scraping the leather table burned her skin. She was a mere ragdoll, and her body was his playground. He pummeled her until he screamed his release, and hers shattered soon after. Kelly's muffled cries echoed beneath the stifling mask as a he appeared in her line of vision. If vengeance had a face, it was looking down on her now.

Kelly raised her head and spoke as clearly as she could from the confines of the mask. Not seeing him anymore would be unbearable, but there was no telling how deep his issues were and if he could ever get over them. This was about more than just her lies, she realized. Parker had been harboring insecurities and anger long before her deceit.

"Forgive, Parker. Forgive. I love you, whether you want to believe me or not, but I'm not going to sit around and let you use me to deal with your issues. I made a mistake, a big one, which cost me this relationship, but don't lay all the blame on me. If your wish is to forget I ever existed, you have it. I'll walk out of your life and forget *we* ever happened."

Those were the most difficult words she'd ever spoken. Losing Matthew was nothing compared to the gut-wrenching reality of not seeing Parker anymore.

For a fleeting moment, Parker looked at her with remorse, but then he rebuffed her. "We will walk away and pretend we never met." His voice was flat, cementing the inevitable end.

When he pulled out, it almost felt as if life was being sucked out of her. Kelly knew this was the last time she'd ever feel him inside her. The moment his body was gone, she felt barren, wilted, and empty. Torment descended upon her at the sudden absence of his warmth. Like air, she needed him to survive. She'd been the one to trigger his issues, but she'd have to accept that she couldn't heal him.

He removed the mask from her face and loosened the restraints, his expression tight. Sweat and tears trickled down her cheeks when she pushed herself up. Another realization hit her. Yes, she had been dishonest, but he had no right to treat her the way he just had. His anger had pushed him to react on an impulse, inflicting emotional wounds that rivaled the roughest physical punishment he could ever give her. She made a last ditch effort to make him understand.

"I made a mistake by hiding who I am. It was wrong, and I apologize. I should've said something, but I was scared of losing you if you found out my real identity."

He ignored her apology and instead turned away. "Call *that* my last gift to you. Now it's time for you to get out of my life."

Parker slipped into his jeans without sparing a glance in her direction and stormed out of the room just as the doorbell rang. As soon as the door slammed behind him, Kelly wept. She cried for her stupidity, for the pain she'd inflicted on Parker, and for the love that would no longer be. He had asked her to forget they'd ever met. *How can you forget the person who made you feel it is imperative to love again?*

Kelly climbed down from the massage table, weary but resolute about the hell she'd be facing in the days, months, and maybe years to come. She ignored the various aches and pains all over her body stemming from the accident and the sting he'd left between her legs. With mechanical movement, she put on her clothes, intent on pushing back her tears.

No, I won't fall apart here. I have to get out now.

She was determined to hold her head up and walk out of his house, and his life, with dignity. Trembling and feeling as if the world were closing in on her, she fastened each button on her blouse as the numbing truth sank in. Parker was out of her life.

"Parker, open the damn door!"

His brother continued to press the buzzer. The annoying sound grated on his already raw nerves. Parker gripped the knob and muttered a curse. He wrenched the door open and seethed at the intrusion.

"What the hell do you want?"

Cork didn't bother with pleasantries and pushed his way in, followed by Webster. Parker could feel a fight brewing, and his nerves twitched in anticipation.

"I called you several times, and you ignored—What the hell is going on here?"

He closed his eyes as light bathed the room, trying to smother the explosive rage that was simmering inside him.

"What are you doing here? I thought I made it clear that I don't want company." He heard the rustling of footsteps and stuff being picked up from the floor.

"No wonder you're not picking up your calls. You fuckin' busted your phone. What's wrong with you, man?"

"Parker, c'mon. You're scaring me. You need to calm down." Webster placed a tentative hand on his arm.

"Will you two mind your own goddamn business and stay out of mine?" he shouted, not knowing in which direction to fling his anger. He shook Webster's arm away and stalked over to the kitchen to grab another bottle of vodka.

"Jesus Christ. Haven't you had enough to drink?" Cork asked, snatching the bottle away from him.

This fueled his rage even more. "No." He gritted his teeth. "I'm going to make it easy for both of you. I'm going to go to my bedroom and give you five minutes. I want you both gone by then."

"The hell I'm going to let you kick us out," Cork said. "You're not going to like what I'm about to say, but I'm going to say it anyway. Stop being a dick—"

Parker turned around when he sensed Kelly's presence. Everyone froze while she made a beeline for the door. He heard her muffled sobs when she passed him, as well as Webster's surprised gasps. Then he heard the door shut.

"You're a bastard," Cork said, grabbing his collar and shoving him against the wall.

He fought against his brother, pushing and shoving back. Because Parker was much bigger and stronger, Cork couldn't hold him for very long. They struggled with each other until Webster stepped in and tried to pull them apart.

"Will you two stop it? You're acting like idiots!"

"This moron needs to know the fuckin' thing he couldn't see." Cork let go but stayed close to Parker's face.

"Maybe coming here wasn't such a good idea. Cork, honey, let's go. Let's leave him alone," Webster chastised.

"Do you think your insults could make things worse for me? Well, think again! The woman I love just made a complete fool out of me. Then a woman that I admired and respected died on my table. And it's all because I'm blind and can't see what is happening around me. So, ease off a bit, brother!"

Cork slapped him on the shoulder before moving away. "Spare me the bullshit, will you? So Kelly made a big mistake. I'm not letting her off easy, but you're acting like a fool for placing all the blame on her. So Mrs. Crawford died. Everyone knows it wasn't your fault. You seem to be the only one who doesn't believe it. If you want to keep beating yourself up, then go right ahead and throw a fit. But I'm not going to sit around and watch you hurt someone."

"Bullshit?" Parker repeated. "You think being fucking blind is bullshit?" He followed Cork's voice, itching for an outlet for his rage.

"So you're blind. Boo-fuckin'-hoo. It's not the end of the world. Have you stopped to think how lucky you are? Some people would die to be as successful as you are."

Parker flinched at the patronizing words. "Lucky? You call me lucky? I can't even piss without touching the damn toilet to know if my aim is right. I have to feel my food to know what it looks like. I can't even fuckin' go anywhere without asking you or someone else to give me a ride. You call being dependent and at the mercy of other people lucky? Maybe you ought to get your head examined, because you're just as blind as I am. You can't see how screwed up my life has become." Parker laughed. "You have no idea what I'm going through, so don't try to talk like you could survive one day in my shoes."

"So you've had some bad cards dealt to you, but I never thought I'd see you cry in the corner like a pussy and have a pity party. That's not the Parker I know. Sure, you've asked for help, but who hasn't? We're a family. That's what we do."

"Shut the fuck up!" He shoved Cork, not wanting to hear his sentimental bullshit.

"Hey, hey . . . stop it. I think it's time for us to go. Parker's under a lot of stress. We need to give him some time alone," Webster said.

"Not until I tell this idiot that he has a whole life ahead of him, and he's wasting his time dwelling on the things he can't do!" Cork shouted.

"Idiot? You're a bigger idiot for taking your brother's hand-me-downs!" The moment the words left his mouth, he knew he had crossed the line.

"Son of a bitch!" Cork cursed just before his fist connected with Parker's face.

Parker staggered backward and landed on the floor. Cork loomed over him as he struggled to get up. Pain shot through his nose, and blood trickled from his nostrils.

"You're a lousy drunk," Cork said.

Before he had a chance to react, Cork yanked him to his feet. Webster put an arm around his waist when he staggered and led him to the sofa.

"Parker, are you all right?" She turned to Cork. "Enough, Cork. Let's just get out of here."

Parker wiped at the blood dripping down into his mouth. He looked up, not sure where to focus. "Guys, listen. That was uncalled for. I'm sorry."

"Save your regret, brother. I think Kelly deserves your apology more than we do. In case you didn't know, she was in a car accident the other day. She's pretty banged up, but she still came here because she wanted to explain herself. It looks like you didn't even give her a chance." Cork shook his head. "I don't know why I'm even bothering with you. If you want to dwell in your misery, go right ahead. We're leaving."

Parker heard the rustling of footsteps and the door opening and closing.

Once he was all alone, he rubbed the tears from his useless eyes.

"Fuck, *fuck*!" He hoped for once that the earth would open up and swallow him.

CHAPTER SIXTEEN

Kelly burst into tears the moment Parker's front door shut behind her. The sound cemented the grim reality. She was out of his life, and there was nothing she could do about it. Parker had made it clear he intended to forget about their relationship and she should do the same. She stumbled across the lawn and ended up sitting on the curb with her face buried in her hands.

She felt wretched, confused, and empty, furious at herself for not doing the right thing sooner and angry at Parker for taking his frustrations out on her. If she'd listened to Cork's warning, she would still have had a chance to explain herself. She wouldn't have been sitting on the cold pavement without a car and no place to go to unload her burden.

Had the warning signs been there all along and she had been just too dumb to see them? Parker had been gracious and had even downplayed his disability. Had it all been just a front he'd put up to show that he was dealing? He'd seemed well-adjusted to her, but how could she have known his innermost feelings? In hindsight, Kelly should have asked more questions, but she wasn't comfortable prying into people's lives and wasn't going to start with Parker's. He obviously had enough suffering in his life without her making it worse.

Kelly rubbed her eyes, hating every minute of what had happened between them. Her body still ached from the accident, and her heart was aching even more. She should have fought for her right to voice her feelings. Instead, she'd taken everything he'd given her, like the submissive he wanted her to be.

Footsteps approached. She buried her head between her knees to keep from retching, hoping whoever it was would walk on by. To her dismay, the footfalls stopped beside her.

"Kelly?" a female voice asked.

She'd heard that voice before. Kelly raised her head, and through blurred vision, she recognized Webster and Cork. Webster knelt in front of her.

"Are you okay?"

Webster's worried expression made her cry even more. She nodded, but then decided to tell the truth for once.

She shook her head. "It's my fault. I should have told him sooner."

"Why are you sitting here in the dark?" Cork asked, squatting down next to Webster.

"Jessica dropped me off here . . . I was supposed to call her, but I think I left my purse in her car."

Cork sighed and sat down next to her. "Listen, it's none of my business, so I'll stay out of it, but this is not the place you want people to see you. If you want, Webbie and I can drive you home."

"Oh, thank you," she replied, grateful for the offer. "I don't even have anything with me to pay for a cab."

"An address is all we need." Webster helped her to her feet.

They spent most of the drive back to her mansion in silence. Kelly gazed out the window, rewinding the evening's nightmare. Had it been so bad to want him to be happy with her without the added weight of her celebrity? The sweetness of their time together would forever haunt her dreams. She held back the tears once again. It was bad enough that his brother and friend had already seen her at her worst.

When Cork made the turn down her street, Webbie gasped at the scene before them. Paparazzi were hovering by the gate like vultures searching for their next meal, those juicy tidbits to whet the public's appetite.

Webster turned to her in shocked surprise. "Is this what you have to deal with every day?"

"Every waking hour," she answered.

Webster clucked in sympathy. "No wonder you hide behind disguises."

"They are the reason I lied to Parker. To protect him."

"Oh, Kelly. I understand now."

She struggled to keep her voice calm. "I wish he saw it the way you did." If he'd only given her a chance and listened.

Kelly slid down in her seat, hoping they wouldn't spot her. But as always, they converged close to the car and started snapping pictures. Cork bristled while he inched closer to the gate. He glanced over his shoulder at her.

"How do we get in?"

"There's a buzzer by the side of the gate. It's a speaker. When Lizzie answers, say 'Parker' and she'll let you in."

Cork raised an eyebrow but didn't say anything. He managed to get out of the car and push his way through the crowd that surrounded it. He returned after a few minutes, just as the gate started opening. Kelly shielded her face with her hands. She'd be damned if she was going to let them get a picture of her with her eyes all puffy from crying again.

"I have a newfound respect for your restraint," Webster said as they wound their way up the circular driveway.

Kelly snorted despite her throat closing up. "You have no idea how many times I've wanted to tell a few of them to go to hell. I just couldn't do it. You know what they say—if you can't take the heat, get the hell out of the kitchen. This is the life I've chosen . . . but sometimes I feel ready to walk away from it all."

Lizzie was waiting by the front door when they drove up. Her smile was gracious and welcoming as always, but her eyes were glued to Kelly with worry.

"Good evening, Ms. Kelly."

"Hi, Lizzie. Everything okay?" she asked as they made their way to the formal living room.

"I've been worried about you. Ms. Jessica told me to give her a call if you didn't show up before midnight . . ." Lizzie's mouth gaped open in silence when she got a clear look at her face. "Oh my, are you okay? You need to rest. A concussion is not a joke. You shouldn't even be walking around—"

"Lizzie, I'm fine. I'm just a little banged up and shaken. Why don't you make some coffee for us?" She turned to Cork and Webster. "Would you like to stay for a cup?"

Webster had been checking the place out and turned in embarrassment. "Oh, sure. Coffee would be nice. I have to agree with Lizzie, though. You need to go to bed. You don't look well."

Cork shifted in his spot, looking uncomfortable. "Webster's right. You need to rest."

Kelly waved away their advice. "Let's talk in the solarium," she said and preceded them down the hallway. The walls were lined with fine art pieces she had accumulated over the last few years. She heard soft murmurs of appreciation behind her.

When they were seated in the sunroom, Cork glanced Webster's way. They seemed to be giving each other silent cues.

"Kelly, can I ask you a personal question? You don't have to answer. You can just tell me to go to hell and—"

"Just say it." Kelly leaned back against the rattan chairs and fought the urge to throw up. She was thankful she hadn't had anything to eat for a while.

"How do you feel about Parker?" Cork looked embarrassed while he waited for Kelly's answer.

She closed her eyes, thinking of Parker's kisses, his touch, and the sound of his voice. How could she say how she felt in one breath? The man evoked too many emotions within her. He'd demolished her resolve with his charm, his easygoing nature, and his attention to everything about her. Tears trickled down her cheeks, and she brushed them away.

"I'm in love with him."

Webster nodded and turned to Cork with a smug grin, looking like she'd already known what the answer would be. "See? I told you. My guess was right."

Cork's jaw clenched. He sighed in frustration. "I suspected the same thing, too, but I didn't want to assume anything." He met Kelly's gaze straight on. "I apologize for asking such a personal question, but I'm trying to see if there's any way we can talk some sense into my brother and get it through that thick skull of his."

Kelly shook her head. She was already resigned to the fact that Parker had slammed shut the doors of reconciliation. It was over.

"No . . . I think it's all for the best. I don't want Parker to have to deal with the life I lead. It's not fair to put him under the same microscope when he has so much to deal with as it is."

"Oh c'mon. You can't mean that. If you love the man, you have to fight for what is yours." Webster threw her a challenging stare.

Kelly stared back, incredulous. "You have no idea how bad it could get. They wouldn't stop until he was torn apart. They'd use his blindness or anything else to twist things around and make him regret he was ever with me. They'd say hurtful things because they think Parker is not the ideal man for me."

Cork snorted. "My brother is an ideal man, inside and out. His blindness isn't a burden at all."

Kelly admired Parker's brother. At least they were both on the same page. "That's how I feel about him, too," she whispered.

Webster sipped her coffee. "Give him time. He'll soon realize what is more important. You have to remember the man took a big hit to his professional ego, and then he found out you weren't who you said you were. Parker tries too hard to make everything look seamless, but I often wonder if he's just doing it for everyone else's benefit."

"I don't know what to think anymore. He made it clear that I'm out of his life. I understand his anger, though not all of it. Regardless, I'm going to take his advice and move on." Although the process of forgetting and moving on would be impossible. "I'm leaving in a few days to start filming in Africa. That'll be a good time to think things over."

After Cork and Webster left, Kelly cried even more, hiding in her bedroom until she fell into an exhausted sleep. Putting everything behind her would be a painful and difficult ordeal, but she'd done it before. She hoped she could do it again.

❧

Parker awoke and realized he had fallen asleep in the living room. He knew he'd hit bottom. The moment he'd lashed out at his brother, the meticulous walls he'd built around himself had crumbled, leaving him exposed and fragile, a position he'd been avoiding from the very beginning.

All this time, he'd thought he was coping well. The fear and uncertainties about his blindness were tucked away behind the happy front he put up for everyone to see. He believed he'd conquered his doubts about himself until Ann . . . Kelly . . . had shown up in his life.

Now he was back to where he'd started—and in worse shape. Good thing he couldn't see himself in the mirror, because he knew he wouldn't like the man staring back at him. Somehow, while he'd been busy trying to hide all his insecurities, he'd managed to forget that dealing and total acceptance were two entirely different things. Both needed to be addressed, and shoving one or the other aside had only bought him some time. There was no running away from reality.

Parker walked back into his room, not caring if he stumbled along the way. He had a pounding headache, his face throbbed, and his nose was clogged. He hated that he'd cried. Weakness was unacceptable, and he despised himself even more for succumbing to its pull.

He leaned against the bathroom sink and listened to the running water. His nose felt wrong; he was almost sure it was broken, but he didn't care. It was well-deserved. He struggled to control himself, to stop the tears so he could think.

Visions of Ann invaded his mind. For the first time, he wished he could see her face, to see the damage he'd done so he could torment himself even more. Though he'd accepted—or so he'd thought—his blindness years ago, there were days he regretted not being able to see. This had been one of those days. He'd wanted to see her face when she'd said she loved him.

Parker thought back over what had happened. He'd been wrong and had gone too far, losing the very control he'd always tried so hard to maintain. He'd subjected her to his own insecurities, taken everything that was wrong in his life out on her. But the worst of it all was that he'd hurt her with his misplaced anger.

He cried at his own stupidity for refusing to let her speak. Kelly had claimed she was protecting him, and he wanted to hate her for that. He was a man, and his ego screamed in protest. Men were supposed to protect their women, not the other way around, but as much as he wanted to hate her, he found it impossible.

"I only did it because I was falling in love with you."

Parker leaned over the sink and squeezed the bridge of his nose to clear his nostrils of dried blood. He washed his face, scrubbing away the tears and gore until his face felt raw. Then he stumbled back to his room and sank onto the mattress, feeling lost and empty. Sleep and fatigue soon took over, but Kelly's face haunted him. What had he done?

Parker was awakened by the shrill ringing of his house phone. Disoriented, he climbed out of bed and headed for the kitchen, feeling nauseated. Instead of answering it, he yanked the cord from the outlet and was instantly gratified when the ringing stopped. He wished everyone would just leave him alone. He wobbled from the effort. Bracing himself against the counter, he knocked something off. Parker waited until the spinning stopped and felt around for the item on the floor. He groaned once he realized what it was.

Ann's CD.

How could he have forgotten about it? She gave it to him the night they had unprotected sex. He stumbled back to his room and popped the disc into the player. Rigid, he sat on a chair to listen.

"Hello Parker! As I mentioned earlier, I wanted to write you a card filled with all the frills and gooey sweetness I'm feeling right now, but since reading it would be a challenge, I decided to record everything I wanted to say. I don't want to be around when you listen to this, because I'm afraid you'll laugh and find it sappy.

"I have to admit, I'm using some rather well-worn quotes here, just because they say what I mean. Try not to laugh too hard. In the end, you'll find out why I went this route."

He leaned closer to the speakers, not wanting to miss a single word.

"Okay, this one is by Amanda Peet."

He had to smile at the sound of her bubbly laughter.

"Yes, the actress.

" 'Beauty is only skin deep. If you go after someone just because she's beautiful, but don't have anything to talk about, it's going to get boring fast. You want to look beyond the surface and see if you can have fun or if you have anything in common with this person.'

"I particularly adore this quote because it was a sentiment by someone who is judged because of her appearance and not how she is as a person. Cool, huh? Well, you'll find out soon enough why this holds a special place in my heart.

"Moving on, listen to this. This one is by John Burrows.

" 'I still find each day too short for all the thoughts I want to think, all the walks I want to take, all the books I want to read, and all the friends I want to see.'

"Let me add to this. I find myself wanting to be with you every second of the day because I want to feel your touch, hear your voice, and see your smile. The day is not long enough to show you how much you mean to me, even with the short time we've known each other. I never thought instant attraction was even possible until I met you. And I believe that I have a good man holding me and keeping me close."

She laughed, and it felt like she was in the room with him.

"This next one is another of my favorites. All I ask is for you to consider this.

" 'Faith is taking the first step even when you don't see the whole staircase.'

"Martin Luther King, Jr. said that. What I'm getting at here is the fact that even if you have doubts and all you see are dead ends, your faith will lead you through all the humps and tumbles. I'm asking you to extend that faith to me. I'm not saying this to waste your time. On the contrary, I see a beginning of a relationship between us so unique that our names are already drawn into the sand.

"And this one is by good old Albert 'kickass' Einstein."

Her laugh was electric, and he couldn't help but laugh with her, despite the mounting sadness in his chest, making it impossible to breathe.

" 'Few are those who see with their own eyes and feel with their own hearts.'

"I'm sure you've heard the saying that love is blind, right? Well, I think you can see better than the rest of us. And I'm sure you know by now that I have fallen in love with you. I've been hurt before, Parker, and that's what's kept me from fully giving myself to anyone. But with you, I feel there is still

hope for me. You see, a man broke my heart. I trudged along because he gave me a gift, a life. That life was the reason that kept me going—a precious little girl who brought me unbridled joy. But she was taken from me, too.

"Then you came along, giving everything you've got and asking very little in return. You have no fear. You give love like it's the most natural thing to do. You've taught me how to love again, and I'm risking a lot here to let you know that I want to give this relationship everything I have.

"And this one is from me. I'm here, telling you how I feel, naked and afraid, uncertain if you will have the heart to believe me after you find out who I am, which is the secret that I've kept from you. I want you to call me after you've listened to this. I'm hoping you will as soon as possible, because I'm aching to tell you that I love you and I want to feel your touch as I say the words.

"There is no love greater than the one coming from the heart. And this, my Parker, is coming from deep within my soul."

Jesus Christ. A beautiful, caring woman had fallen in love with him, and he'd driven her away. Parker squeezed his eyes shut to keep the tears from falling. He really was blind after all. He'd blinded himself with rage and his stupid belief that she couldn't love him because he had nothing much to offer. She had opened up to him despite her fear, and all he'd done was turn her away without even giving her a chance to explain. With everything she had said, he now realized he'd been wrong about her, and he was nothing but a giant ass.

After conferring with her doctor, Kelly was given the thumbs-up to set her plans in motion. She began by packing two months' worth of paraphernalia. Production and filming was set to begin for *Cradle of Life*, a story based on a novel about a freelance photographer caught in a moral dilemma of whether she should expose ape poachers in Africa. The story was interesting, but what appealed to her most was the location. The out-of-town filming provided her with an opportunity to mend her broken heart. The timing couldn't have been more perfect. Two months away from LA was just what she needed.

The bruises had already faded, and her accident had been forgotten. With the apprehension of Rigor James a few days ago and the possibility he'd serve some jail time, her mind was finally at ease. Thank God, the court had recognized the danger posed against celebrities by overzealous paparazzi. They'd issued a restraining order that would keep him at a distance. That was a triumph for her. A small victory, but still, nothing could ease the gaping hole Parker had left in her.

The stinging behind her eyelids meant her resolve was on the verge of crumbling again. Kelly breathed in and out, just as her hypnotherapist had instructed. She'd had two sessions so far. In time, she'd begun to address her low self-esteem issues. Despite the fame, her self-image had plummeted with each failed relationship. According to her therapist, the subconscious mind had the ability to achieve emotional and physical wellbeing, with a little help. She'd had the answers all along, and all she had to do was dig deeper to find them within her.

They'd practiced a drill together that helped her relax her mind and channel all her critical thoughts to give way to reframing the immediate problems and to promote self-awareness. It wasn't easy. She was a work in progress, but she'd taken the first step just by addressing the issue.

Kelly was looking around her bedroom, taking stock of whatever else she needed to pack, when her phone rang.

"Hi, Dave."

"I just got a call from your lawyer. Rigor James is getting slapped with community service for pleading guilty. The restraining order is in place, so you can stop worrying for now."

He sounded pleased with the outcome. Dave had been working nonstop to downplay her relationship with Parker at her request. Since he hadn't been available for comments, she'd seen his brother and employees being harassed to make statements. Cork had declined to comment and had hired a spokesman on behalf of Parker and Knead Me.

"That's good. What time should I be ready?" she asked, zipping her suitcase closed.

"Are you sure you want to do this?" Dave asked. He knew her fragile state of mind and was still wary about her decision to address her relationship with Parker in public.

"It's going to give me some closure and put the rumors of a romantic affair to rest once and for all. It's over. I'm moving on." Just saying the words was enough to make her panic and want to cry. "Don't worry about me, Dave."

He didn't sound convinced, but he relented. "If you say so. I just want you to be happy, Kelly. You know that."

"Yes, I do. Once I'm out of here, it'll be a different atmosphere, and I can begin to forget. A couple of months away will do wonders, I'm sure." She tried to feign lightness but failed as a sob hitched in her throat.

"Son, you're a grown man, and your mom and I should be minding our own business, but your brother called us. He thought you might need us to come and talk to you." His father laid a firm hand on his shoulder.

Parker had given them a key to his townhouse, in case of an emergency. He guessed this constituted an emergency. His parents had let themselves in and found him slumped next to the CD player, where he'd been listening to Kelly's recording over and over.

His mother sat next to him, wrapping a comforting arm around him, but he was beyond comforting. Everything he'd done pointed toward his idiocy, the madness he'd brought upon himself, and his cruel treatment of Kelly. Parker's emotions were too raw, and he couldn't wrap his head around everything that had happened to land him where he was now.

"Mom, I-I think . . ." He swallowed the lump in his throat and tried to keep his voice even. "I pushed Kelly away . . . the only woman who ever thought I had something to offer."

"Oh, Parker. You have so much to offer. Never doubt that. Your blindness does not mean you have to stop looking for someone to love. Think of it as a challenge instead of a hindrance."

"I think it's too late . . ."

"Why, son? Why do you do you think it's too late?" His father's voice sounded distant. He seemed to be on the other side of the room, tinkering with something.

Parker breathed long and hard and fought the tears. He had no idea where or how to begin. It was hard enough to admit to himself that he'd made a big mistake. "I-I was too rough with her. I crossed the line. There's no taking back the words I've said." No matter how hard he tried to hold them back, the tears fell.

His parents were silent, as if they were weighing the information he'd shared with them. After some time, his father spoke. "It's true that there's no taking back whatever was said between the two of you. But . . . realizing your mistake is the first step toward righting the wrong you've done. There is no guarantee you'll ever get her back. The right thing to do is to address your problems first. You might need to see an expert to talk about your feelings and your fears. That is the best advice I can give you."

"Listen to your father. We all make mistakes. Some last us a lifetime, but what's important is doing something about them. You'll have to forgive yourself at some point. You've got to try to move on, and after you're comfortable with who you are, *then* seek her out. If she's a good woman, and we can tell she is, at the very least, she'll listen to what you have to say."

Pursing his lips, Parker nodded, letting their advice sink in. It wouldn't be easy, but then, *nothing* had been easy since he'd lost his eyesight.

"I don't mean to add to your misery, but I have something I want you to listen to, just to reiterate what a good woman she is." He heard his father flick the button of the television remote. "I connected your laptop to the TV, and we're on YouTube right now."

Parker had no idea what was going on until Kelly's voice drifted around him.

"We were friends," Kelly was telling someone.

"Just how close were you? The pictures showed you in a very friendly position. Were you lovers at one point?"

He held up his hand. "What is this? Where is Kelly? What's going on?" Words tumbled out of his mouth, and he gripped his mother's hand tighter. The recording stopped.

"That's a segment that aired on *Entertainment Tonight*. I wanted you to *see* it as soon as Cork told us what happened. Kelly was sitting in front of reporters, with a guy next to her. Don't ask me how she looked, because it'll break your heart. She was answering questions about your relationship at a press conference." His father sounded as defeated as he was feeling.

"Oh God, what have I done?" Parker tried to breathe, but every attempt just produced more tears he couldn't seem to stop. "Go on."

"We were quite friendly. But we're over each other. It didn't work out."

Parker heard the sadness in her voice, and his heart wrenched. He could imagine her torment, facing countless people whose goal was to capitalize on her pain, just to get the perfect story—a headline.

"Right here, Ms. Storm. Is it because he's blind? You lost interest because he doesn't fit in your perfect world?"

He waited, feeling helpless. Half of him wanted to hear her response, the other was not sure if it would solve anything. He leaned closer.

"First of all, Mr. Davis is perfect. The relationship didn't work because I let other considerations dictate my actions. He doesn't fit in because our world is too judgmental for people with disabilities. Second, he is the one who let me go. I want to make that clear. Now all I'm asking for is for you to respect his privacy."

Parker lost concentration when his landline rang. Cursing, he stumbled to get to the phone. He wondered who it could be, since only his parents, Cork, and a few close friends had the number.

"Parker speaking," he said into the mouthpiece.

"This is Jessica Renoir, Kelly's assistant. I'm—"

He couldn't even wait for her to finish. His heart was pounding hard. "Yes, she's mentioned you in the past. Is Ann . . . is Kelly all right?"

"She's fine . . . recovering well from the accident . . . um, but she wanted me to call and tell you that . . . gee, this is a bit awkward for me." She paused.

"Did you say she was in an accident?" Parker gritted his teeth. Sweat trickled down his forehead while he gripped the phone tight in his clammy hand. "Where is she?"

"I can't tell you that. I'm sorry."

His face fell. Jessica had something she wanted to say, and he was going to explode if he had to wait a moment longer.

"She wanted me to tell you that she's not pregnant."

Parker went rigid at the news. Sadness gripped him, and it took him several moments to regain his composure.

"It's probably better that way."

It was the wrong thing to say, when all he wanted was a reason to bind him to Kelly. He was certain now that he wanted her back, wanted a baby with her, and most of all, he wanted a life with her.

CHAPTER SEVENTEEN

It took Parker a week to pull himself together—and it had been hell. Talk about the getting hit from all sides. But the clincher had been the news that Kelly wasn't pregnant. He'd thought it was for the best, but now he wanted it more than anything. Of course he'd been lying when he said he wanted her out of his life, because in reality, she was the very air he yearned to breathe. Only Kelly could complete him. Then again, like all broken things, he needed to fix himself first.

It had taken tremendous effort to leave the house when all he wanted to do was wallow in self-loathing. He'd downed an immeasurable amount of vodka over several days, drinking himself into sleep—often sick and dehydrated. But after hours of reflection, Parker had decided that, instead of self-destruction, the better course of action would be to get out there and win Kelly back.

It wasn't going to be easy, but with his parents' steadfast support, he took the first step and made an appointment with a psychologist.

At first, he was vehement about denying he had a problem. But after some time, he was compelled to admit they were right. In his efforts to show the people around him that he was coping well, he'd neglected the most basic aspect of dealing with his blindness—how he *felt* about it. He'd failed to address the crux of his fears and insecurities. Instead, he'd swept them aside, showed a cheerful demeanor, and pretended they would go away in time.

There was much to be done before he considered himself worthy to ask Kelly for forgiveness. Besides, even if he wanted to call, the problem remained that he had no way of contacting her.

Parker grimaced at the thought before pulling on his sunglasses. He was on the way out to wait for Cork to take him to his first psych appointment when he heard the honking outside. He hadn't spoken with Cork since that night. Webster had dropped in a few times, bringing paperwork from the office that needed his attention. She'd kept their conversation on a professional level, and judging from her silence, he knew she was still upset about his outburst. He had attempted to apologize several times, but she'd scoffed at him and left.

Parker slid into the passenger seat and felt for the seat belt. "Hey, how's it going?" He faked a smile, hoping Cork wouldn't see right through him.

Cork grunted and started the engine.

Okay, I deserve that.

"Cork, listen. I acted crudely. I'm not making excuses. I was wrong, so wrong about everything. I'm not sure how to make it up to you and Webbie, but I'm sure as hell not going to stop trying."

"You're an asshole," Cork muttered.

"Yes, I am."

"And a dumb, blind, stinky bastard, too," his brother added. "You haven't shaved."

Parker grinned, feeling a sliver of hope. "That, too. You can keep going."

"You're not forgiven yet," he said. "What you said that night hurt, Park. I was just trying to help."

There was unmistakable pain in his brother's voice. Parker took a deep breath, knowing if there was anyone he could bare his deeper fears to, his brother was the one who would understand.

"I know . . ." He jammed his fingers through his unkempt hair.

Cork didn't answer right away, and he could guess his brother was choosing his words.

"Webster and I can forgive you because you're family and you're her friend."

"Somehow I managed to push away everyone who meant well. You don't know how bad I feel about what I said to you . . ." *And Kelly*, he added.

"We're willing to overlook what you said, but I don't know about Kelly. She looked messed up when she left. You know she was in an accident the day before. She went to New York to see you, but you'd already left. When she landed at LAX, the paps followed her, and the whole thing escalated to an all-out chase. Poor girl. It wasn't a pretty picture."

Parker's chest tightened. He knew he'd done irreparable damage. Nothing could undo his stupidity. "Yeah, Jessica told me."

"She'll be ok." Cork put a reassuring hand on Parker's shoulder.

"Thanks, Cork. I promise . . . man, I don't know what to say. I guess I'll just have to make it up to you and Webbie in time. If this trip to the head doctor means anything . . ." He took a deep breath. "I know I lost my credibility with Ann. Heck, I don't even know what to call her. She'll never want to see or hear from me again, and I can't blame her."

"Getting your shit together is a big step, bro." Cork patted him on the shoulder.

Parker clenched his fists, wishing he could do something, anything, besides being helpless. Kelly had gone through so much to get a chance to explain, and all he'd done was shut her out and hurt her.

"We took her home that night after she left your place. We found her outside on your sidewalk, crying. She was a mess—"

His heart turned somersaults. "You know where she lives?"

"Yeah, but—"

"I want to see her. I feel like an ass for the way I treated her. It wasn't right. I didn't even let her talk—"

"As I was saying, we dropped her off at her house. Gee . . . it's not just a house. It's a goddamn football field."

Cork seemed impressed, and Parker was annoyed by that. "What the hell? I don't care what kind of house she lives in! Where in the hell does she live? Take me there!"

"Calm down, Park! She's in Africa, filming. She won't be back for some time. I think that's what she said."

Parker groaned, feeling his tiny bubble of hope burst. "Damn it."

"I have some brotherly advice. Take it if you have even the faintest hope to win her back. Get your shit together first and see what you can do to improve yourself. You know . . . you've fucked it up." Cork chuckled.

"I don't see what's so funny. I'm hooked. I can't get her out of my mind. Some days I think I'm going insane."

Parker closed his eyes. His temper had gotten him nowhere, but self-flagellation wasn't the best route either. Cork was right. There were so many issues he needed to address first. His knee-jerk reaction after discovering Kelly's lies, along with Mrs. Crawford's death, had sent him down a disastrous road. He should have given himself some time to think before he reacted.

"I only did it because I was falling in love with you." Kelly's heartfelt words played on constant loop in his mind. His heart broke into a million pieces each time.

"Are you okay?" Cork asked, worried.

It took Parker a moment to answer when he realized the cause for his brother's concern: he was crying. He wiped away the tears and swallowed the lump in his throat.

"Yeah."

They didn't talk the rest of the way to the doctor's office. When he emerged after the one-hour session, he felt lighter, as if a weight had finally been lifted off his shoulders. Baby steps, the psychologist had told him. They had discussed some simple things he needed to do to get his life and confidence back, one of which was to accept his visual impairment and embrace the consequences that came with it. Parker had no other choice, and the sooner he welcomed his reality and faced it head on, the better off he'd be.

Another appointment had been scheduled, and he couldn't wait. It felt like he'd seen life in perspective for the first time since he'd gone blind. He strode out of the office feeling relieved and thankful for the opportunity to start his life over again.

Cork met him at the entrance of the building. "Where to now?"

"I need a cell phone," he said.

Cork chuckled. "That's right. You annihilated the last one."

On their way to the store, Cork started talking business, filling him in on the financials as well as employee gossip. Parker hadn't been to any of his three offices in the last two weeks. Although dying to get back to work, he felt he needed the time away to heal.

"Larry called yesterday."

"What's up?" He sat straighter. Larry was his lawyer and represented him and all of Knead Me's interests.

"He said he got a call from NYPD and the coroner's office about the autopsy results." Cork paused, and he was sure his brother was waiting for him to say something.

"Go on."

"She died of a heart attack just like the initial reports said. As it turned out, she was in the advanced stages of lung cancer. There wasn't anything you or anyone else could have done for her. If you're thinking that by seeing her distress you could have saved her, think again. She was going to go. So if you're still blaming yourself over her death, you can start fixating on something else because it wasn't your fault."

Parker exhaled, relieved, in part, and also sad. It was difficult to think that his adored client was gone.

"It doesn't change anything, though. I still feel bad. She had no family." He recalled their conversation and couldn't help but think of the lonely ending to her life.

"And that's another thing. She had no heirs, right?"

"As far as I know, no."

"She willed her Manhattan penthouse to you and donated the rest of her huge fortune to research on retinitis pigmentosa. Can you believe it?"

Parker was dumbfounded. "What? Why?"

"I don't know. There's an envelope in the office waiting for you. I think the old lady was expecting it and prepared everything beforehand."

The car stopped, and Cork turned off the engine. Parker heard the door open and close, but he remained in his seat, unable to grasp the news. Why would a wealthy woman bequeath a fortune to her masseuse?

When he got his bearings, he slid out of the car, still thinking of Mrs. Crawford and her death. Once more, his chest tightened as the final moments with the old woman hit him like a punch to the face.

One of the production people poked her head inside the trailer door. "Ms. Storm, they're ready for you."

Kelly put down the book she was reading and checked herself in the mirror, scrutinizing her hair and makeup. "Not bad," she said before smoothing her khaki pants.

She'd been in Africa for over a month, spending her first Christmas away from home. She was mending, thanks to the daily mental exercises her therapist had suggested. It helped when the memories came flooding back. Every day she thought of Parker. Forgetting him was proving to be an impossible feat, but she was determined not to repeat the past, even if it meant hiding in order to cope.

Closing her eyes, she willed the bittersweet memories away. There was no point in getting lost in the past. Moving forward was the best thing to do. Kelly grabbed the fedora resting on the table and proceeded to the set.

Nerissa Bryant, the director, looked up and smiled when she arrived on the set. Kelly switched into acting mode. The production had been moving along as planned. She had immersed herself in the project, pushing her inner struggles to the back of her mind until she was alone in her room at night, where she spent most of her time berating herself for her stupidity. Soon after, she'd cry herself to sleep.

After strapping the camera around her neck and reviewing her script, Kelly signaled to Nerissa that she was ready.

She lost herself in the role, reciting her lines with complete abandon, happy to be working and not having time to think of anything else for the next seven hours. The day of filming was a success—no multiple retakes, which was always a nightmare for the cast. She was heading for her trailer when she heard Nerissa calling after her.

"I'm going into town today. I need a decent meal and maybe a couple of drinks. Want to tag along?" she asked when she finally caught up with Kelly.

Kelly thought it over. Their meals, although gourmet, had been too predictable. She wouldn't mind a change in her daily routine. It wasn't as if she had anything better planned.

She smiled and bobbed her head, grateful for the distraction. "I'd love to."

Nerissa looked relieved. "I'll meet you by the car in thirty minutes," she said before turning in the direction of her own trailer.

Thirty minutes later, Kelly found herself seated next to Nerissa in a Suburban packed full of other production people. They were cramped, but it didn't matter. Everyone was in high spirits and talking about the film.

Once they were all seated in an antiquated restaurant in the small town of Mbandaka, Kelly began to relax. Despite the oppressive heat, she enjoyed the easy banter. It felt good to be seen as "one of the guys," a regular person who fit in with everyone else.

The food was delicious, and the beer flowed like water. After the meal was over, her phone started buzzing. Kelly was surprised to be getting a call at this time of the evening. Most of the US would be in a dead slumber by now. She checked the caller ID and was even more surprised.

"Dave?"

"Kelly! Boy, am I glad you picked up."

"What's going on? Shouldn't you be sleeping?"

"I was, but then I got the call from the Academy. You've been nominated for *Hearts Afire*. Jesus, Kelly! Can you believe it?" he exclaimed through the phone line.

Kelly heard him but was too stunned to say anything. She gripped the phone and noticed the group had quieted down and was staring at her.

"Kelly, are you still there?"

"Y-yes."

"I'm sure you have something better to say than *that*."

"Dave . . . oh my God, this is great news. I'm . . . I don't know what to say." She blinked, feeling overwhelmed.

"Well you have to prepare a surprise speech. They're sending a crew for you to get your comment about the nomination."

"Really?"

"Really. So I expect to see that Kelly Storm spunk again. Congratulations, and I'll be in touch."

After they disconnected, Kelly stared back at the sea of faces around her, still in shock. She took a deep breath, and despite the big lump in her throat, she made the announcement.

"I've been nominated for best actress for *Hearts Afire*."

The room erupted in joyous hurrahs and good wishes. More beer was ordered. They toasted, drank, and toasted again. When the boisterous congratulations were over, Nerissa took her hand and squeezed.

"Darling, I never doubted your ability. Congratulations! I'm so happy for you and, at the same time, proud to have the chance to be working with you."

Kelly squeezed back. "Thank you."

Good news and momentous events were always sweeter when shared with the ones she loved. A bittersweet feeling swept over her while she dialed her sister's number. After a rapid-fire conversation filled with questions and tears, they said their good-byes with a promise to see each other soon.

Kelly was in bed in her tiny hotel room when a flashback hit her. Her mind rewound back to when she'd realized she wasn't pregnant, the day before she'd left for Africa. She had just finished the press conference that evening when she'd started her period. She'd known it was too much to hope for, and then it had slipped away.

It was stupid to feel so sad about it. Had she been pregnant, she'd be in an even worse situation now. But at the oddest moments during the past month, she'd smiled at the idea of having Parker's baby. Kelly sighed and tried to think logically. She was better off without a child. What kind of life could she give a baby, anyway? She would have ended up hating herself for binding Parker in a relationship just because she was having his baby—not the kind of life she wanted for anyone involved.

That evening, despite the exciting news of her nomination, a big gaping hole still sat in the center of her chest where Parker had once been. Kelly buried her face in her pillow and cried herself to sleep . . . again.

Parker had just gotten home from his hour-long run at the track when his cell started ringing. He released Sasha's harness and heard the clack of her paws while she headed to her water bowl. Sasha was a Labrador retriever and his new companion. He'd accepted that he needed help and that a guide dog would make him less dependent on others. Cork had put him on the list almost a year ago, and Parker had spent several weeks at a training facility to familiarize himself with his new friend. Last week, Sasha had been sent home with him, and the pairing had been wonderful. Although they were still in the "getting to know you" stage, they were warming up to one another.

He pressed the voice-over, and it announced a call from an unfamiliar number. Parker hesitated for a moment on whether to answer but decided to pick up the call.

"Hello?"

"It's Jessica."

"Hey, how have you been? How is Kelly?" Just saying her name brought on the longing he'd been trying to stifle over the past weeks.

"I'm good, and she's fine—"

He didn't even let her finish. "Is she back yet?"

"She's still in Africa."

Africa. So far away.

He heard Jessica sigh. "I don't want to pry, but I can't help it. I love my best friend, and I'm sure she's miserable. What went wrong, Parker?"

Parker had to tell her the truth. That was the only way he could live with himself and be able to keep moving forward.

"I treated her unfairly. I didn't even give her a chance to explain. I know about her baby girl . . . oh, god. I hate that she's so far away and dealing with everything alone."

"It's not too late. I think if you had a chance to tell her how you feel, she might listen. I don't know. I can't promise."

He felt a small flicker of hope. "Jessica, I will do whatever I have to do to get a chance to talk to her."

"As I said, no promises. But I would love to get the chance to play cupid." Her soft laughter was somehow reassuring. Parker would follow any glimmer of hope he could find, no matter how faint—anything to win Kelly back.

Monday morning was his first day back to work after more than a month on hiatus, and it was also Sasha's first day on the job. Parker was anxious to introduce her to everyone. As soon as they emerged from the car together, he knew he had company. He held onto Sasha's harness tighter than he intended, and she yelped in protest.

"Sorry, girl," he murmured, loosening his grip just a fraction. "I'm still getting the hang of this."

"Parker, the vultures are waiting for you," Cork whispered on his left, sliding a protective arm around Parker's shoulder.

Parker laughed. "Don't worry, I'll be fine. I was expecting this to happen. It's something I have to deal with," he said, trying to reassure his brother.

"If you say so." Cork didn't sound convinced but stepped back nonetheless.

Parker was on his own now. He took a deep breath and continued walking.

"Mr. Davis, you've been gone for some time. Does that have anything to do with Ms. Storm?" one reporter asked.

He stopped and turned in the direction of the voice. "Yes and no," he replied.

The man persisted. "C'mon! There are reports that you had broken up with her. She admitted in an interview that it was her fault. Can you confirm this?"

"I made a big mistake when I let a very special woman go. I was stubborn and . . . well, blind." That got everyone laughing. It was time that he acknowledged the elephant in the room. Parker continued. "I took some time off to think and repackage myself, so to speak. I'm back now and eager to start the groveling."

"Aren't you worried she'll grow tired of you . . . well . . . because of your condition?" a female voice asked.

He shook his head and smiled at the absurdity of the question. "If there's anyone who'll get tired of me, it's me. Kelly was just protecting me all along. She kept our relationship a secret, not because she was ashamed of me, but to keep *me* away from the prying eyes of the . . . well . . . you guys, actually."

That brought on another round of laughter. He nudged Sasha to move forward. They were now just a few feet away from Knead Me's entrance.

"From *us*? What did she think we'd do to you?" another reporter asked.

Parker continued to inch forward. "Exactly what you're doing right now. But there was no need to protect me. I'm a big boy, and I have nothing to hide. You can ask me whatever you want, and I'll answer you to the best of my ability." He smirked and waved them off.

He was about to close the door behind him when another woman asked, "Are you in love with Kelly Storm?"

Parker nodded and turned away. *Without a doubt.*

While he made his way toward the reception area, he caught sight of Webster's hazy but familiar figure standing in his path.

"Make way for the boss!"

He heard sounds of people moving his way, followed by ear-splitting hoots, clapping, and other assorted well-wishes. It took him several minutes to make it to his office. Sasha felt tense but stayed close to his side.

"Good girl." Parker patted her head and released the harness. She sniffed around her immediate environment before settling down next to his chair.

"Here's your steaming coffee. It's at two o'clock, and there are papers that need your signature at six. Some New York lawyer sent you a huge brown envelope. Do you want me to read it to you, or would you rather have your reader do it?"

Webster was back to her old self and as efficient as ever. He heard her sit down in the chair across from him.

"Read it for me, please. I'm sick of that robot voice." Parker laughed, hoping the tension between them had eased.

"Sure thing." She opened the envelope. "Okay, there's some legal mumbo-jumbo crap I don't understand." Webster continued mumbling while she read. "Ah, well . . . the Manhattan penthouse has been willed to you. There's a note attached. It looks like it's her handwriting."

"Go on and read it, please."

There was the sound of papers shuffling and Webbie getting comfortable in her chair.

"This letter is dated the day before she died."

Parker closed his eyes and nodded.

" 'Dear Parker, if you're reading this, I've most likely croaked already. I'm leaving you my house here in New York because I don't want you running around in this big city alone and without any place to stay. I have one request. Please retain Albert's services. He is our butler and a very loyal employee. He would make an excellent companion to you. Enjoy and love the house as Edison and I loved it. You're the son I never had, and this is such a little thing to give in return for the hours you spent listening to an old lady ramble on and on. Take care of yourself and don't let that beautiful actress get away. I sense she's everything you're looking for. Good luck, my son. Thank you for the wonderful memories.' "

Webster sniffed. "You're one lucky son of a bitch," she muttered while she refolded the papers.

Parker closed his eyes and sighed. "Yes, I am. She was quite a woman, wasn't she?"

"I'll say."

He sipped his coffee and worked on signing the papers. "Who's my ten o'clock?"

Webster snickered. "It's Madame Butterfly."

Parker's head shot up. "What the hell? Are you joshing me again?"

"Nope. That's the name the lady gave me." She turned to leave. "Room 101, boss."

Madame Butterfly? What the hell is going on here?

He gave the customary knock before he entered the room. The first thing he did was inhale the air, praying he'd get a whiff of the familiar fragrance he loved. "Madame Butterfly?"

"Hi, Parker."

His face dropped. The voice was all wrong.

"Jessica, what are you doing here?"

"Sorry. I know you were expecting someone else." She laughed. "I don't want a Monday Delight, but I'm here to share some things with you."

He laughed at her playful tone. "Sure. Where's Kelly?"

"I'm expecting her at the end of the week. So do you want to hear my idea?"

"I'm listening."

⁂

"Here's your coffee, Ms. Storm. Can I get you something else?" The flight attendant waited for her answer.

Kelly pulled her eyes away from the magazine she'd been flipping through for the last hour and shook her head. The trip had been long, and all she wanted was to get into the tub and soak.

Sipping her coffee, she let her mind drift back over the last two months. So much had happened in her life, which had helped her reach a decision. Her choices had been dictated by her failed relationships, especially with Parker, but she felt it was for the better. Kelly needed a change. It was important for her to stay away from him and anything that reminded her of him. He only came to New York once a month, which helped. The logical thing to do would be to buy a place there. They'd be living in different cities. She hated leaving LA, but it would make moving forward much easier. Marcy, her broker, had some good prospects, and the whole week would be devoted to finding the new perfect beginning for her.

Kelly glanced out the window. The sky was turning a subdued orange, and the sun was dipping below the horizon. Without a reason to hide anymore, she planned to shift her focus to her career, the one part of her life that seemed to be working. The Academy nomination had inspired her to devote all her time and energy to her acting.

The pilot's voice came over the speaker, announcing their landing. Kelly finished off the coffee. Africa had been a welcome refuge and had served to give her a clearer outlook. She'd cleansed her soul, gained some much-needed peace, and for the most part, was well on the road to feeling better about herself. Kelly was moving forward and ready to face whatever the future held for her.

Jessica was waiting for her outside the terminal.

"Why can't I have my regular ride?" Kelly asked as soon as they maneuvered out of the busy airport.

"I'm taking you to look at a house that's for sale. Marcy's going to meet us there."

Kelly glanced at her friend in surprise. "It's seven o'clock at night, just in case you haven't noticed. I'm sure Marcy is already off the clock, and the owners won't appreciate the intrusion either."

"She's the one who tipped me off about this place, and she's already made arrangements with the owner. What could be more beautiful than seeing the city at night? Besides, it's not on the market yet, but it will be in a day or two. Marcy wanted you to get first dibs before the property is listed. She also mentioned the owner is very anxious to sell."

"Sure, I'm looking to buy, but I'm not desperate enough to look at a property at night," she protested. "All I want is to get into the tub."

"You're going to love this place! I checked it out myself this morning, and the neighborhood is quiet. I think all the neighbors are in their AARP years—old money and they mind their own business."

Kelly shot Jessica a curious look, not sure where her friend's enthusiasm was coming from, but then again, Jessica had always been enthusiastic with just about anything. She lay back against the comfortable leather seat and tried to relax.

"I cleared up your schedule for the whole week, by the way. You have seven days straight to relax and look for a place. Don't you just love the way I work miracles?" Jessica laughed.

"Yes, you're fantastic," Kelly said.

Time away had done so many positive things for her, but it hadn't decreased Kelly's longing for Parker. As soon as she set stepped out of the car, memories of them making love in this city flooded her mind and seduced her body. She hugged her coat closer and groaned, hating each minute he resurfaced in her mind when she was trying so hard to forget him.

"Is everything okay?" Jessica asked, glancing over her shoulder before they climbed the steps.

Even in the faint glow of the moonlight, Kelly could tell that the house was spectacular. She couldn't make out the exact color of the exterior, but she knew it had to be a pastel with white trim.

Jessica rang the bell, and the door was answered by a uniformed gentleman.

"Ms. Renoir, good evening. It's a pleasure to see you again." The man had an impeccable English accent and bent low at the waist. Kelly couldn't help but grin at his formal greeting. He smiled when their gaze met. "Good evening, Ms. Storm. I see that your flight has delivered you to us safely."

Kelly smiled, baffled at the man's comment. "Yes, thank you," she answered before raising an eyebrow at Jessica, who in turn shrugged at her.

"Oh crap! I forgot my cell phone in the car. Kelly, why don't you go ahead, and I'll be back in a jiffy."

Jessica excused herself and was out of the door before Kelly even had the chance to respond. She hesitated. It would be impolite to keep the man waiting, but she would rather wait for her friend. As if sensing her reluctance, the man smiled, revealing a set of crooked teeth.

"You're safe here, Ms. Storm."

The butler led the way, ushering her along a tastefully decorated foyer. Everything in the room screamed wealth and elegance. The magnificent artwork adorning the walls absorbed her attention until they reached a small elevator shaft that looked straight out of an old movie. With reluctance, she stepped in.

While the elevator rose, Kelly thought about what she'd seen so far. The house was structured to her liking. When they stopped, she was surprised at what the doors slid open to reveal. She gasped at the uniqueness of the walls, which were stenciled with hands, feathers, and hearts. Her curiosity was piqued. She wanted to see the rest of the house right away. If the price was right, she'd be looking at an impulse buy, not that a house in the city would ever be a dead investment.

"This way, please." The butler preceded her to dimly lit room.

Kelly adjusted her eyes to the darkness, hoping for more light so she could further appreciate the house.

"There's a cabernet in the decanter for you." He proceeded to pour her a glass without even asking if she wanted it.

"Where's Marcy, and what's taking Jessica so long?" she asked, taking a seat on the sofa. She started to wonder why she was being served wine, and not just any wine, but her favorite red at that.

"Oh, forgive my manners. Ms. Marcy phoned earlier and said she wouldn't be able to make it tonight—a family emergency. She sent her assistant on her behalf. I will call on him now."

"Wait. Marcy's not coming?"

"No, Ms. Storm, but she wanted me to reassure you that her assistant is very competent." With a warm smile, he strode out of the room.

Soon after, she heard the whir of the elevator, followed by soft murmurs. Since she was now alone, she decided it wouldn't hurt to look around. Kelly took a sip of wine and crossed the room to switch on the lights.

The first thing that caught her attention was the sound of her own laughter coming from a hidden speaker system.

What the hell? Kelly went on instant alert as goose bumps rose on her neck. When she looked around, all she saw were hundreds of pictures of herself hung on the wall in a neat collage. Every space held an image of her.

Was this some sick joke? She was poised to flee when her own voice came over the speaker.

"I find myself wanting to be with you every second of the day because I want to feel your touch, hear your voice, and see your smile. The day is not long enough to show you how much you mean to me, even with the short time we've known each other. I never thought instant attraction was even possible until I met you. And I believe that I have a good man holding me and keeping me close."

Kelly stopped, unable to believe what she was hearing. She'd said those words to Parker. *The CD!* Her eyes welled with tears. She couldn't fathom how or why she was being subjected to such torture. Nobody knew about the disc except her and . . .

Running to the sofa, she snatched up her purse and set the glass on the table, spilling the red wine all over it. She groaned, hoping it wouldn't leave a stain.

"Damn it!" She fumbled inside her bag for a tissue. Kelly was attempting to wipe it up when she heard footsteps outside the door, and another noise she couldn't quite place. She turned around just as Parker walked in the room, and in his hand was a harness connected to a dog.

He pointed at the table. "I'm sorry if I can't help you with that."

Tongue-tied, she stared at him. She slung her purse on her shoulder and was making a run for the door when he reached out for her. Parker caught her arm and pulled her closer.

"No."

"Please, Ann . . ." He hesitated. "Kelly, I want to explain."

Just like that, her body responded to his voice, his touch, betraying her resolve. Still, she hadn't forgotten what he'd said to her the last time they were together. Kelly braced her palms on his chest and pushed him away.

"If this is your idea of a sick joke, no one's laughing but you." She took a step back, hating the burning protest from her hands the moment they left his chest.

Parker released his hold on the harness. "Stay, Sasha." Kelly couldn't take her eyes off his face. He seemed calmer, a far cry from the last time she'd seen him.

"Kelly, please. I beg you to give me a moment to explain." He paused. "Please give me the chance I refused to give you."

Just as she was about to respond, another one of her quotes drifted from the speakers.

"What I'm getting at here is the fact that even if you have doubts and all you see are dead ends, your faith will lead you through all the humps and tumbles. I'm asking you to extend that faith to me. I'm not saying this to waste your time. On the contrary, I see a beginning of a relationship between us so unique that our names are already drawn into the sand."

She faltered, and then remembered what her hypnotherapist had told her —self-preservation is the first law of nature.

"I'm through hiding my feelings. I refuse to be that unfortunate person you vent your anger on." Kelly's voice grew stronger with her conviction.

"I'm not going to let you or anybody hurt me again!"

Parker's face dropped, but he persisted. "What I did to you was unforgivable, but I'm owning up to my mistakes. I'm ashamed of what I've said and done. I crossed the line and broke a very important principle of the lifestyle. I was drunk as hell and unfair. I can't change what happened, but I hope you'll find it in your heart to give me another chance."

He took a step in her direction, and Kelly froze, remembering the night when he'd stalked her like she was his prey. She braced herself.

"I wasn't expecting this . . . you . . . I can't do this, Parker."

She turned toward the door, and he followed her movements, turning exactly where she was headed. Then he stopped, his expression defeated.

"I can't blame you. I've been an ass. I just want you to know, despite everything I said before, I never stopped loving you."

"I'm sorry, but I don't have anything left in me. I have to go. This was a lousy idea, and I don't like being manipulated."

Kelly stalked out, her heart thumping hard in her chest, and her eyes stinging from unshed tears. She ran to the elevator. The butler took one good look at her and pressed the doors open without comment. She fought the tears, wishing she could just disappear. Just when she thought she'd put everything behind her, Parker came storming into her life once more, creating havoc with her heart and making her ache for him all over again.

She found Jessica sitting inside the car, drumming her fingers on the steering wheel, immersed in a phone conversation. Kelly tapped on the window and glared at her friend, who got that deer-in-a-headlights look. She ended the call and unlocked the door.

"I don't appreciate your participation in Parker's stupid attempt to win me back. If there's anything you should know about me, it's that once I've made up my mind, it's damned near impossible to change it."

Jessica placed a comforting hand on hers. "I know what you're going to say. I'm sorry. I was just trying to help. You're miserable, and Parker is the same way. Please forgive me."

Kelly shook her head in halfhearted frustration. "You are *not* forgiven, but I need a drink right now, so I'll try to endure your company. Just don't talk about Parker . . . ever again."

Jessica grinned, looking relieved, and she started the engine. "Let's hang out at the bar in your hotel. I promise, no more mention of—um, of him."

"Good!"

Kelly folded her arms across her chest and stared out the windshield into the dark. Despite her stubborn desire to forget, she was certain that even if his name didn't come up, she'd still be thinking of him all night and for the foreseeable future.

CHAPTER EIGHTEEN

Parker brushed his fingers across her nipple, stirring the longing she'd been trying so hard to repress. Her body responded, as if it was thinking for her. Kelly ached for him to touch her in other places. He smiled before crushing his lips against hers, hot and hungry. Goose bumps rose on her skin everywhere he touched her, from her chest to the juncture of her thighs. She felt his erection straining against his jeans Parker was as ready as she was. She gave in to her body's heated desire and pressed closer.

"Tell me you love me," he commanded when their mouths parted.

"I love you."

Kelly squirmed, ready to explode when he vigorously rubbed her nub. She couldn't wait any longer. Dying to welcome him and get a taste of heaven, she moaned with absolute pleasure the moment he eased his dick inside her. She trembled beneath him, spreading her legs to accommodate his hard length.

"Do you love a good fuck, Kelly Storm?"

"Yes! I love a good fuck."

And before she could get that good fuck, she woke up. Drenched in sweat and her body still tingling, she pushed herself up out of bed in frustration and ran to the bathroom. She'd been having these nightly sex dreams ever since she'd seen him in that house. She splashed cold water on her face, hoping it would be a distraction.

"Damn you!" She glared at herself in the mirror. "This has got to stop!"

After winning her first best actress award, she immediately immersed herself in work. Yet, the months following Parker's attempt to explain had been difficult for her. All she wanted was to be with him, but how could she? She was not going to allow anyone to hurt her again, not after the time it had taken her to heal and get some normalcy back in her life. To her chagrin, every attempt to forget him had so far been unsuccessful.

The dreams had been her connection to Parker since she'd flat out refused to talk to him. The flowers he'd been sending her every day were sweet, and she hated to admit it, but her steadfast resolve was starting to crumble. Despite the fact that she'd been avoiding his calls and resisting the daily urge to go running back into his arms, she knew it would be a matter of time before she gave in.

"If this is another mistake, I am swearing off men for good!" Kelly glared at her reflection in the mirror.

Parker had just arrived in his San Francisco office when his receptionist informed him that his ten thirty appointment had already arrived and was asking if she could go early.

"Sure," he said. "Just give me five minutes to make a phone call."

"She'll be in room 104, and her name is Shelby Davis."

Parker listened for her fading footsteps before he made the call. He wasn't expecting an answer, so he wasn't surprised when it went to her voice mail.

"Kelly, it's me again. I know you're getting sick of hearing my voice, but I just have to hear yours. Please give me a chance to explain myself. One meeting is all I'm asking for. Please, darling."

He wasn't a quitter, and he'd keep trying until she agreed to meet with him. If their relationship was beyond salvaging, at least he'd get to *see* her one last time and explain things.

"Sasha, stay and be a good girl, okay?" He rubbed the dog's head before proceeding to his appointment.

Parker tapped the door and then stepped into the room. "Good Morning,

Ms. Davis." One whiff of the air and he froze.

"Woo-rah!"

That voice!

"Kelly?"

For once, he didn't trust his hearing. He had to touch her. It didn't matter if he looked like a fool. One touch was all it would take.

"Yes, it's me."

Kelly stood in front of him, took his hands, and placed them on her cheeks. He ran his fingers over her face, trying to gauge her emotions through his fingertips.

"I-I'm glad you came. Who's Shelby Davis?"

It took her a moment to answer. He began to panic, afraid that he'd asked the wrong question.

"If you don't want to answer, it's okay."

"If I would have been pregnant, I hoped that would have been the name of our baby boy or girl."

He felt her smile beneath his fingers and wished he could see her face.

"I'm sorry. I wish you were, Kelly. There's so much I want to say to—"

She placed a finger on his lips to silence him.

"You've said enough in your daily phone calls." She sounded nervous. "Those long messages and explanations . . . you've given me enough reason to come here and tell you why I think this relationship still has a chance."

Parker tried to speak, but she kept her fingers on his lips.

"Let me do the talking first. This is not the bedroom where you can dictate everything that happens. If we're going to be together, we have to trust each other. I'm not the poster child for honesty, and I want to change that."

"Lie down." Parker dropped his hands to her waist and discovered that she had nothing on. He grinned, and then lifted her onto the massage table.

Kelly turned and lay on her stomach while he strapped on his oil and lotion belt. Applying soothing pressure to her back, he began the rhythmic massage, waiting for her to speak.

"I love you, Parker—love you like I've never loved another man before. I don't care if you're blind. My love for you is stronger than that. The past months have been hell for me. I didn't think I'd survive. There were so many fears I had to overcome, memories that I had to let go in order to move on. We've both made mistakes, but we've both moved forward."

"I made these changes in my life because I wanted to be the kind of man who deserved your love. From everything you've said, it sounds like there's still hope for us."

"There is. But I want you to promise that you'll talk to me if you have doubts. And I promise to always give you an honest answer. No more lying."

Parker ran feather light touches across her back, gliding toward her neck, and easing the tightness in her muscles. He couldn't resist the urge to touch her face again, trailing his fingers along her lips and feeling them quiver.

"God, I love you so much," he said after he eased away.

"Give me your word that you won't take your frustrations out on me ever again. I don't think I could handle another outburst like that from you."

"You have my word. I broke the rules, and not a day goes by that I don't regret subjecting you to such cruelty. I've gotten some help, and now I have a firm grasp on who I am and what my limitations are. Just give me a chance to prove to you that I'm a changed man. I need you in my life, Kelly. I want to be the father of your children. I want to hold you in my arms every day for the rest of our lives. I want—"

Kelly turned and sat up. "I want all those things, too. But most of all, I want to be your partner in everything." She traced his lips with her fingers, and all his anxiety began to fade away. "I meant every word I said in that CD. Faith in each other will guide us through."

"Ann . . . Kelly, I don't know what to say. I just wish I could take back every stupid thing that came out of my mouth."

She threaded her fingers through his hair. "Kiss me, Parker Davis, and wipe away the past."

He smiled and touched his lips to hers. Parker tasted heaven, and that was where he wanted to be. He lightly brushed his hand down her back, loving the silky feel of her skin. She shivered beneath his touch, and he knew everything was going to be all right.

"Oh, and I've done a lot of thinking about your lifestyle. I'm willing to embrace it because it's important to you," she said after their long kiss.

"So . . . are you trying to tell me that you don't enjoy it? You're just doing it to please me?"

Kelly laughed. "I'm not going to lie. It's intriguing, and I'm enjoying it. So just show me what you want, and you've got yourself a willing partner."

"What made you change your mind, darling?"

"It's simple. I can't live without you. It's either be miserable or try to work it out. And since I want you with me every day, I'm here to work it out."

"Are you sure this is what you want? I mean, I'm not complaining, but are you sure?"

"Yes, I'm absolutely sure. Now, here's my question. Are you okay with my career and everything that goes along with it?"

"I wouldn't have you any other way."

He climbed on the table and invited her to sit on his lap. When she did, Parker wrapped his arms around her. He wasn't going to let her go ever again.

"I want us to get away for a while," he said. "There's this special place I want to take you. Would your schedule allow for a week of vacation?"

"Of course! I'll make time for you. When and where are we going?" she asked, excited at the prospect of spending time with him.

"Next week, and I'm not telling you anything more."

He skimmed mouth along Kelly's neck and felt her body slackened.

"Oh . . . don't tease. I've missed you so much."

"I'll stop, not because I want to, but because I want our reunion to be special." He waggled his eyebrows and grinned. "Be ready for me, sweetheart, because Parker Davis is back!"

"How much longer before you let me in on the surprise?" Kelly gripped his hand inside the limousine that was taking them to the rental house outside San Francisco.

"Just a few more minutes, love. And I'm sure it's worth the wait." He ran his hand along her blindfold to make sure it was still in place.

With the help of Cork, Webbie, and Jessica, he'd been lucky enough to secure this secret gem overlooking the ocean in the tiny coastal town of Mendocino. Parker had visited the town many years ago and couldn't wait to share it with Kelly. The private beachfront property would be theirs for a whole week.

After another ten minutes, the driver spoke. "Mr. Davis, we're here." The purr of the engine stopped, and the door was whisked open.

"Love, this is going to be a little tricky. The blind leading the blind." Parker laughed as he helped her out of the car.

"I trust you." Kelly's grip tightened, and he smiled down at her, even though she couldn't see it. Hearing her say she trusted him eased his worries. They were making strides.

"Mr. Davis, I'll place all your things in the bedroom for you. I'm just a phone call away if you need anything," the driver said.

"Thank you." Parker nudged the dog forward. "Go, Sasha. Take us to the front door." They proceeded along the graveled path. "What do you hear?"

"I can hear waves in the distance." Kelly sniffed. "And I smell saltwater. Are we close to the beach?"

"You'll find out soon enough."

They reached the front of the house. He held on to her elbow and helped her up the steps and through the front door. Once they were inside, the hardwood floor creaked beneath their feet.

"We're inside a house?" Kelly asked, turning to him.

"You're very perceptive." Parker took her hand and counted his steps while he led her to the spiral staircase. He placed her hand on the banister.

"Hold onto the rail and keep going. I'll be right behind you."

Kelly climbed while he and Sasha followed. As soon as they made it to the top, he released the dog's harness. "Go on, baby." When he was sure Sasha was gone, he turned to Kelly. Praying that all his instructions had been followed, he brushed his lips across hers and removed the blindfold. "Tell me what you see."

It took a moment for her to answer. Then he heard her gasp before she threw her arms around his neck.

"Parker! This is wonderful! We have a house, and there are flowers everywhere!"

Her excitement told him that he'd done well. "I requested white baby roses. I know you love them."

Kelly buried her face against his chest, her tears dampening his shirt. "Thank you. They remind me of Gypsy."

"You're welcome. Making you happy is going to be my life's mission."

"I'm terribly happy," she said before raining grateful kisses on his face.

Parker wanted the moment to last, but if they kept going, there was a big possibility he wouldn't be able to set his plans in motion. He pushed her away.

"Tell me what you see beyond the doors."

Kelly groaned before moving to what he guessed was the door leading to the patio. He followed the sound of her footsteps until he felt the cool ocean breeze on his face.

"Nothing but blue water, and not a neighbor in sight. Oh, honey, I could live here forever."

He grinned, satisfied. "I intend to run naked with you along that path that leads to the beach, and I plan to taste you in every corner of the house. I'm going to show you what forever means."

"Then what are we waiting for?" The naughty tone of Kelly's voice was enough to make his cock jerk to attention.

Parker pivoted her around and slapped her on the butt. "You're such a cave woman. Now, go to the bathroom across the hallway, and you'll find what I want you to wear. Take no longer than fifteen minutes to get ready. I'll be waiting in the bedroom next to it." He winked. "Knock before you come in."

Kelly skittered to the bathroom like a bunny on crack, eager to see what Parker had planned. She opened the box and marveled once again at his attention to detail. Pulling away the tissue paper, she giggled when she found the clothing he wanted her to wear. Kelly held the garment up to her body and checked herself out in the mirror. The woman staring back at her looked happy and content.

"You see? If you hadn't given him a chance, you'd still be having those wet dreams." She stuck her tongue out at herself and stripped off her clothes, replacing them with Parker's choices.

She tapped the bedroom door. "Parker?"

"Jane, is that you?"

"Yes," she answered.

She eased the door open. Strategically placed candles cast a sublime, erotic glow across the room that made her heart race. Then she spotted him standing in the shadows.

"Let me take you back to the beginning of time," he murmured just before he stepped into the glow of the moonlight streaming through the windows.

His magnificent body was covered by a loincloth. Kelly devoured every inch of him, each contour, and every tight muscle. The anticipation was killing her. She took a hesitant step forward, unsure what to do next.

"Safeword, woman!"

Kelly grew wet just from hearing his command. She closed her eyes and searched for a suitable word.

"Banana!"

Parker laughed, and then drew her close. "I'm going to make love to you until you scream." He led her to the end of the room and braced her against the wall. "This is going to be a little rough, but I promise not to hurt you. You know what to do. Utter your safeword, and I'll stop right away."

"Okay."

As soon as she consented, he fitted the leather restraints on her wrists, strapped a cuff on each of her thighs, and bound them together, keeping her arms pinned to her sides. Then he knelt on the floor before her and pulled out another contraption she'd never seen before.

"This is a leg spreader. It'll give me full access to lick and suck your cute kitty."

As impossible as it seemed, lust consumed her just from listening to Parker explain what he was going to do. His lifestyle was different, but Kelly was finding his brand of kink pretty damn exciting. She ached to rub her legs together, to get some relief from the intense throbbing his words evoked, but the spreader kept her legs open and in place. Still kneeling at her feet, he trailed his fingers up her legs, caressing them and sending chills up her spine. Kelly moaned in anticipation, dying to see what he'd do next.

Parker caressed his way up her thighs with his lips. She longed to close her eyes and just take pleasure in the fire raging inside her, but she couldn't deny herself the joy of watching him devour her, until he lifted her skirt and blocked her view. When he kissed his way to her center, Kelly almost forgot to breathe. The warmth of his mouth fueled her need even more, and she cried out. Parker slid his tongue between her folds, exploring, touching every crevice, and leaving a tingling behind that left her panting with need.

"Honey, you're going to kill me," she protested in weak voice. The pleasure was driving her insane.

He grunted and moved into position. "I make love to Jane."

Kelly whimpered when he began toying with her clit, spiraling, moving slowly, and cried out with impatience while the fist of need grew tight in her belly. He cupped her butt with his strong hands, kneading until her body swayed in rhythm with his movements.

"Soft."

His one-word guttural comment made her realize that Parker had gone into full role-play mode, and she had to play along, now that the throbbing between her legs had become unbearable.

"Please, don't tease me. I'm—ready!"

She'd tangle her fingers in his wild hair if she could and lick his mouth at the same time, but all she could do was clench her teeth to keep from prematurely combusting. Kelly writhed beneath his slick tongue as he slid it inside her, and she strained against the wrist cuffs holding her immobile. She screamed out in ecstasy as his tongue drifted in and out of her, rubbing her ultrasensitive walls, making her clamor for more.

Parker stood up and rubbed his hard-on against her stomach. "Woman, make baby tonight?"

"You decide."

She was beyond rational thinking. All she wanted was his dick inside her instead of against her stomach.

Parker grunted and skimmed velvety kisses down her neck and along her collarbone until he reached her breasts. He unsnapped her bra and let her tits cascade into his hands.

"Suede good for woman. Boobs ready." He groaned and threaded his fingers through her hair. "Hair beautiful. Like flames."

"I'm dying here!" Kelly panted. She was so ready for him and didn't know if she could bear to wait any longer.

Her knees weakened when he sucked on one tight nipple, his tongue twirling in circles and flicking her perky tip. Each time he stroked her coral peak, her kitty clenched tight. Kelly was aching for release, and she could feel the moisture drenching her inner thighs. Nothing could ease her pain except his thick length inside of her. She arched closer, delirious, grinding her belly against his pulsing erection. She shrieked in frustration when Parker stopped sucking and bent down to release the leg bind.

There was one breathless moment when he poised his hard tip against her opening, and she wanted to rip off the restraint and engulf him in the fire boiling inside her. Then his swollen shaft stormed its way into her, rough and stretching her to the delirious limit, but she yearned for more, wishing he'd go deeper, harder. A low hiss of satisfaction escaped his lips when he filled her. Then he was holding her waist and hoisting her up.

"Wrap legs," he commanded.

She did as he ordered with fevered enthusiasm, circling her legs around his waist and clasping them behind him. He shoved her against the wall and began pounding, her back scraping against the cold surface with each thrust. Her heart raced, and explosive desire raged through her veins. Parker was in the zone. He pumped harder, rougher, as if he was branding her for life. Their moans and primitive grunts echoed in the darkness. He tongued his way into her mouth, thrusting in rhythm with his penetration.

He ground into her hard and dug his fingers into her ass, pummeling her, lodging himself deeper inside, the friction pushing her to the edge. For one mind-numbing moment, she wanted to scream because she didn't know if she could take it any longer.

"I'm coming!"

Parker thrust harder just as she exploded in a quaking release. He roared as he came and didn't stop pumping until he'd emptied his seed into her.

Out of breath, but blissful and contented, he rested his head at the juncture of her breasts. "I'll die a happy man if I can make love to you like that every damn day."

"I'll take you any damn day." Kelly batted her lashes. "Can you release me so I can touch you? I want you in my arms."

Parker smiled apologetically and lowered her until her feet touched the floor. He removed the restraints and kissed her wrists. Her eyes filled up with tears. Her wonderful and tender man was back. She wrapped her arms around his neck and kissed him with everything she had in her.

He pounded his chest and let out a primitive cry. Kelly laughed and tugged at his arm. "You and your crazy role-play!"

Parker grinned and took her hand, kissing it. "I'm crazy about *you*. Can't you tell?"

She answered him with another kiss.

"There's something I want to give you." Parker carried her to the bed and laid her down. From the mysterious smile on his face, she wondered what he was up to now. He turned on the lamp and rummaged around in his suitcase. "Close your eyes, please."

"Why?"

"Because I asked you to," he answered, staring into her eyes.

Kelly saw the same happiness mirrored in his face that was in hers. She smiled before shutting her eyes. "Okay. They're closed."

She felt him reach around her and a clasp sounded. Something cold and heavy dangled on her chest. "You can open them now."

Kelly looked up to see him beaming with pride, and then she looked down and saw a platinum key pendant surrounded by large glittering diamonds lying on her chest.

"You hold the key to my heart," he murmured. "When you're ready, I want to marry you."

"Is that a promise?" She squealed with joy when he nodded. "I love you, Parker!"

"I love you more." Parker smiled in contentment. "Now let me show you what paradise looks like." He scooped her up into his strong arms. "Direct me to the patio."

"But we're naked," she protested, snickering and wrapping her arms around his neck.

"Even better. We don't have to worry about undressing each other anymore." He grinned. "Directions?"

"Six big steps, and the loungers are to the right."

Parker followed her directions and placed her into the lounge chair. She couldn't stop the shiver when her body made contact with the cold fabric.

"Here, let me warm you up."

He slid next to her and cradled her against him, blanketing her body with his masculine warmth. Kelly snuggled closer, taking in his familiar fragrance. Words were unnecessary as they held each other and gazed up into the blue sky.

"You have no idea how happy you've made me," Parker whispered.

"I think I do . . . because I feel the same way."

She sighed in contentment. Kelly Storm had arrived, and she'd conquered a good man—a man who made her feel like the luckiest woman on Earth.

Feeling her lids growing heavier, she mumbled, "Remind me to give Jessica a lifetime gift certificate for a massage next time I see her. It was her idea to come and try your Monday Delight. "

Parker smiled. "I can have Webbie arrange that right away."

He gathered her closer, tightening his arms, staking a claim of ownership, and giving her a glimpse of their future.

EPILOGUE

"You're beautiful," Parker whispered, kissing her cheek.

Kelly laughed as cameras flashed around them. "How would you know?" she teased.

"I feel your skin, and it's oh so soft." He ran his fingers along her back and smiled. "You smell delightful, like a rose in full bloom. I know, even without seeing, that you're stunning in that red gown. And most of all, you fit right in *here*." He dropped his gaze down to his crotch.

"Parker! People are watching!"

He laughed and snake his arms around her waist. "Let them. They live for this."

Kelly shifted in his arms, and he followed the cue to look up and smile. The flashes came from all directions as fans clamored for her attention, calling out her name.

"I have to tell you something."

The sudden shift in her tone worried him. "Is there anything wrong?"

"How is married life, Mr. Storm?" a reporter asked. Kelly gave him the silent signal to face in the same direction as her. A few hours of rehearsing had paid off. He smoothly turned to the sound of the voice and grinned.

"I'm loving every minute of it."

"How does it feel to be walking the red carpet?"

Parker shrugged, smirking. "Didn't notice it was red."

The reporter laughed. "Do you think Kelly will win again this year?"

"I've already cleared a place on the mantel for the li'l man."

Kelly squeezed his hand, and he gazed down at her. "Parker, I'm pregnant," she murmured.

He'd heard her, but he couldn't believe it. The crowd forgotten, Parker cupped her cheeks and searched her face.

"Kelly, please tell me you're not joking."

"Shelby's six weeks old." She stood on tiptoe and brushed a feather light kiss on his lips.

"I'm going to be a father?"

When he felt her nod, his smile widened. Parker wrapped his arms around her waist and spun her in a circle. Kelly's giggles rose above the noise around them. Then he turned to the crowd, still holding Kelly, and blurted out with joy.

"A *storm* is on the way!"

Amid the thunderous applause, he felt like he would explode with happiness. Parker smiled down at his wife with total adoration, because life really couldn't get any better than this.

Acknowledgments

My immense gratitude to the ladies at Free Writers and Readers for all your support and encouragement when I took the plunge into an unknown territory known as Erotic Romance. And to all my friends, relatives and supporters who voted for the story every week.

Donna Rogers- This story is as much yours as it is mine. I can never thank you enough for your time, patience, pep talks, and most especially, the invaluable lessons during the course of the contest. I couldn't have done it without you.

Kristen Giles- This has been a wild ride. I'm glad to have you by my side.

Wendy Depperschmidt- Sisters don't have to be related by blood. I'm glad we found each other.

Judith Somera- You wear countless hats, my friend; among my favorites are, therapist and cheerleader.

Claudia Trapp- 'Fantastic' should be your middle name.

Trenda Lundin- You brought out the best in Kelly and me.

To Mavvy Vasquez- Believe it or not, you've kept me sane. Brownie points for you, toots!

And lastly, to my wonderful and supportive family- Thanks for picking up my slack, for keeping me well-fed and hydrated, and for the constant reminder to step out of my cave once in awhile.

About the Author

A professional daydreamer, Lorenz Font discovered her love of writing after reading a celebrated novel that inspired one idea after another. Since being published in 2013, she has been conspiring, butting heads, and enjoying her spare time with vampires, angels, samurais, and other creatures she has created in her head.

Her perfect day consists of writing and lounging on her garage couch (a.k.a. the office) with a glass of her favorite cabernet while listening to her ever-growing music collection. She finds writing urban fantasy exhilarating and places an intense focus on angst and the redemption of flawed characters. Her fascination with romantic twists is a mainstay in all her stories.

Lorenz lives in Southern California with her supportive family and three demanding dogs.